A show like *The Twilight Zone* allows a writer to find what moves him to passion and write about it. There are suddenly no confines of character, no stories that can't be told, no limits except that of the thirty-minute format, no expectations except a tale well told about something that matters.

It was, without question, an affair of the heart, born of passion and long-frustrated need, exhausting and exhilarating, a rush of days and weeks and vibrant passions.

And *that* is what working on *The Twilight Zone* was like.

—J. MICHAEL STRACZYNSKI,
from his preface

Books by J. Michael Straczynski

THE COMPLETE BOOK OF SCRIPTWRITING
DEMON NIGHT
TALES FROM THE NEW TWILIGHT ZONE
THE OTHERSYDE

Also from Bantam Spectra Books:

THE TWILIGHT ZONE COMPANION,
  Second Edition by Marc Scott Zicree

TALES
FROM THE NEW
TWILIGHT ZONE

J. Michael Straczynski

BANTAM BOOKS

NEW YORK · TORONTO · LONDON · SYDNEY · AUCKLAND

for Rod Serling
in whose garden I was
privileged to play

TALES FROM THE NEW TWILIGHT ZONE
A Bantam Spectra Book / December 1989

ISBN 0-553-28286-7

Published simultaneously in the United States and Canada

Bantam Books are published by Bantam Books, a division of
Bantam Doubleday Dell Publishing Group, Inc. Its trademark,
consisting of the words "Bantam Books" and the portrayal of a
rooster, is Registered in U.S. Patent and Trademark Office and in
other countries. Marca Registrada. Bantam Books, 666 Fifth
Avenue, New York, New York 10103.

PRINTED IN THE UNITED STATES OF AMERICA

KR   0 9 8 7 6 5 4 3 2 1

Acknowledgments

Thanks are never enough, but they're a good place to start. Endless appreciation is rendered to those in whose absence this collection would never have come into existence: Kathryn Drennan, Tom and Phyllis Drennan (for additional inspiration), Harlan Ellison, Alan Brennert, Lou Aronica, Henry Morrison, Mark Shelmerdine, Carol Serling, George R. R. Martin, Marc Scott Zicree, Doug Heyes, George Clayton Johnson, Ed Bryant, Robert Simpson, and all of the other writers, directors, and performers who gave of their talents to create a doorway into the Twilight Zone.

Contents

Preface

For me, working on *The Twilight Zone* was more than just another assignment. It was an affair of the heart.

Like a lover, hopeful and innocent, hardly suspecting how much would shortly be expected of me, I came to that series, that job, that affair of the heart, with the standard freightload of despair, mishaps, and a history of previous liaisons that had each started out looking like the Grail, but had turned out to be a used Dixie cup.

On April Fools' Day 1981, after years of planning and a multitude of false starts, my wife Kathryn Drennan and I arrived in Los Angeles, fresh from San Diego, eyes wide as a raccoon caught in the headlights of a 1967 Camaro doing seventy down a back road.

We had pooled our resources—an offer to Kathryn of a research job with Carl Sagan, and my first book contract—and had conned a friend into driving the rented truck filled with our stuff the one hundred twenty-five miles to the Big Time, undeterred by our lack of money after having paid for the move.

It was the Leap of Faith everyone insists you have to make if you're going to Break Through. *I* was going to write full time, working in books and television, perhaps even in film, and *she* was going to do the same.

A Leap of Faith.

What no one ever seems to tell you is that the Leap of Faith is often better described as a Leap Off a Rocky Cliff.

The years 1981 through 1984 were a saunter through a smoggy landscape of promises that evaporated like so much smoke, job offers that never quite materialized, and brief gigs on magazines that folded with remarkable speed (including the infamous *TV Cable Week,* a publication of Time, Inc., which seemed a sure bet to last forever, only to fold after six months and twenty-four million dollars).

We quickly went through the advance on the book. Then Carl Sagan Productions closed up shop . . . and for the first time we felt the terrible and narrow ledge on which we were standing begin to crumble. Suddenly the possibility of crashing and burning was no longer an abstract thought. It had form and substance and a frightening weight.

There comes a moment, in your life, in Kathryn's, in mine, when you are presented with the knife or the rope: you can stay in an unstable, dangerous situation, pursuing something that looks like The Dream . . . or you can cut and run, write the whole nightmare off to experience and go crawling back to safety.

We stayed.

And Mojo, great god of the poolroom, looked the other way, a two-headed calf was born on the steppes of Outer Mongolia, somebody who was supposed to get a royal flush got only a pair of deuces—and our bet paid off.

Without warning, I was offered a staff job on a television series, writing my own scripts and rewriting others. It was the first of many such jobs, most in the area of science fiction, fantasy, or horror (or as dark as TV horror is allowed to get, which is "dark but not grim," a phrase best left to linguistic scholars to unravel).

I became something of a nomad, moving from studio to studio, show to show, enjoying the work but always feeling, somehow, that Something Wasn't Right. I was telling stories. I loved that part of it. But they weren't *my* stories. I was making characters talk, but they weren't *my* characters. I was merchandising dreams, but I didn't have a percentage of the gross.

Unless you are lucky enough to create your own show, you're always sticking your words into the mouths of other people's characters. You can never sit down and just tell a story to please yourself, to let it run. Unless you've known the freedom of creating little pocket universes where strange and wonderful things happen to people you find fascinating, you cannot understand why people like me become writers. Denying a writer that basic creation makes the writer a poet-for-hire in a beanfield.

Then, on 1 October 1987, two remarkable things happened. An earthquake measuring 5.9 on the Richter scale knocked greater Los Angeles out of its collective bed at eight in the morning, sending Hollywood types and civilians alike scurrying into doorways and wondering if this was The Big One.

And . . .

Two hours later, a phone call came from Mark Shelmerdine, producer of the BBC's *I, Claudius,* and president of London Films (founded by Alex Korda, and the studio responsible for, among others, *The Thief of Bagdad).* His current project: to produce, for first-run syndication, a new revival of *The Twilight Zone.* "Are you still alive out there?" he asked. I allowed as how I was.

"Good. Then how would you like to come work as story editor on *The Twilight Zone?"*

Six and a half years.

It had been six and a half years since fleeing San Diego to Los Angeles, and finally the opportunity to Just Tell Stories had come.

The book you now hold in your hands is the result of all that.

From the very first episode of *The Twilight Zone,* broadcast on 2 October 1959, through the second incarnation that ran on CBS from 1985 through 1987, and the final batch of episodes produced under our jurisdiction that first aired between 25 October 1988 and 16 April 1989, *The Twilight Zone* has always been about *stories,* about ordinary people confronting extraordinary situations.

It is the sort of show that allows a writer to find what moves him to passion and write about it. There are suddenly no confines of character, no stories that can't be told, no limits except that of the thirty-minute format, no expectations except a tale well told, about something that matters.

It was, without question, an affair of the heart, born of passion and long-frustrated need, exhausting and exhilarating, a rush of days and weeks and vibrant passions.

And *that* is what working on *The Twilight Zone* was like.

A few parting observations about the stories that follow.

One of the Eternal Verities of television states that TELEVISION IS A COLLABORATIVE MEDIUM. The other, more succinct, simply says IT'S TOO LONG. Once completed, a script is entrusted to a director, and a cast, and art designers, and set decorators, and a veritable army of others. Most times, Mojo willing and the crick don't rise, you get what you wrote. Other times, scenes must be cut to fit the tick of the clock, interpretations get shaded in entirely new and unexpected ways, and directors . . .

Well, that's another discussion for another time.

For the moment, suffice it to say that these are the stories intact, freed of the constraints of time or budget or special effects, the way they were first conceived and written. What appeared on the screen is here. What might *not* have appeared on the screen is also here. With this collection, the stories are at last complete, preserved in something slightly more substantial than phosphor dots.

Second, it is my desire that these stories stand as testimony to those who, reading this, are weighing a Leap of Faith of their own.

Sometimes it works. It *is* possible.

But watch that first step. It's a doozy.

Finally, in order to answer the question I frequently get at conventions and lectures, "Where Do You Get Your Ideas?" each story includes a brief introduction that attempts to answer that question, providing a glimpse Behind The Scenes of *The Twilight Zone*.

Consider them snapshots and home movies taken while on vacation in that fabled middle ground between light and shadow, between science and superstition, that dimension of imagination we call . . . the Twilight Zone.

J. MICHAEL STRACZYNSKI

Los Angeles, California
1 March 1989

Introduction to
The Mind of Simon Foster

The year was 1983, two years since I had come to L.A. to work on my first book while simultaneously trying to make my way into TV and film writing full time. They were not easy days. We were living on maybe fifty dollars a week, after rent and bills had been paid. I lived on one Swanson ninety-nine–cent dinner per day, plus one bowl of cereal for breakfast. Our sources of income were nearly gone, the money from the book long since exhausted.

Then, one day, out of the proverbial blue, I became obsessed with having a chocolate bar. We didn't have any. And we couldn't even afford for me to go out and buy one. I tried to put it out of my thoughts. It didn't work. It wasn't that I wanted chocolate that badly . . . it was the thought that *I couldn't have it* and *why* that was making me crazy.

Finally, distracted and unable to write, I slipped outside and went to the corner supermarket.

And shoplifted a candy bar.

It was stupid. It was destructive. It was the only way I knew to keep my sanity. I returned home to find that the bar had no taste for me. It was like eating gall. I don't think I even finished it.

Three days later, when the payment for a small article came in, I went back to the corner supermarket, bought an identical bar of candy, slipped *back* into the store and put it back on the shelf. I thought at the time how wonderfully stupid it would be if I were caught with a candy bar stuffed in my jacket pocket. How could I explain that I was sneaking it *in*, not out?

It was about that same time that, driven by desperation, I began selling things.

Books, records, magazines, cassettes . . . if it wasn't nailed down or on fire, I sold it. I lost vast portions of my library, and records that have now proven almost impossible to replace. Among the possessions sold was one item—which I cannot bring myself to describe here—that has turned out to be utterly irreplaceable. A return to the shop where I sold it has proven fruitless. In the long months since buying it, they sold it to someone else. A further search resulted only in dead ends. I've had to accept that it's gone, forever, a very personal part of my life that cannot be reclaimed.

But it burns. To this day, it burns.

Flash forward four years, to one cool afternoon at the *Twilight Zone* offices. I needed to come up with a story, and my thoughts returned again to those terrible days, to that sense of utter and complete loss. I walked down Hollywood Boulevard, where our offices were located, past the stores where other people had sold off pieces of themselves over and over until there was nothing left but an empty ache and a sense of awful violation.

I took the elevator back upstairs, to our tastefully appointed offices, so many miles and years from where I'd started, and began to write. I wrote at white heat, staying late, long after everyone else had gone home. When I left the offices that evening, a first-draft script lay on the producer's desk.

And with it lay anger and bitterness and loss set finally to rest.

"The Mind of Simon Foster," production #87038, went before the cameras on October 17, 1988, starring Bruce Weitz (Simon Foster), Geza Kovacs (Quint), Rafe Mac-Pherson (Manager), Ilse Von Glatz (Unemployment Counselor), and Jennifer Griffin (Crying Woman). Directed by Douglas Jackson. First broadcast on February 26, 1989.

THE MIND OF SIMON FOSTER

There wasn't much left to sell.

Simon sat on the narrow bed that had been shoved into one corner of the dark, one-room flat. Clothes were piled on the dresser, and the curtains hung at an angle that stopped just short of the windowsill. He couldn't remember the last time he'd bothered to clean up the place. Not that it mattered. Nobody came by anymore. Not in person.

He cast a glance toward the vid. He supposed they didn't want to soil their hands by actually coming and talking to him face-to-face. No, anything but that.

He continued packing.

Shaver, cassettes, the few old coins he still possessed, a handful of books . . . and the watch. That was the hardest one of all. It was his father's watch, bought on impulse back when the old man had won a couple thousand dollars on one of the lotteries. It had been expensive, far too expensive even then, in better times. But he'd never once regretted the decision. When things had started to get bad, and he'd lost nearly everything else, the watch was his father's one remaining luxury, his last source of dignity in a world that had stripped away most the others.

On his deathbed, he had given the watch to Simon —and oh, in that moment, hadn't he been proud, though sad and shrunken and weathered? Hadn't he been so proud to have kept hold of it all those years, until he could pass it on, a real, honest-to-God legacy from the old man?

"No matter what they take away from you," his father had said, "as long as you've got this, they can never take it all away." Then he closed his eyes, and went away, and the state claimed its long overdue account.

He looked at the watch one last time before putting it into the box and closing the lid.

Don't think about it. Just do it.

He sat there for a long moment, running his hand over the rough corners of the cardboard box, when the vid rang. He let the answering machine catch the message. He knew what news it would be bringing.

"Yes, hello, Mr. Foster, this is Jennie Maloshevsky from the unemployment office returning your call." There was the sound of papers being shuffled. "I'm sorry, Mr. Foster, but as we discussed earlier, your benefits for the period two–seventeen–ninety-nine have expired as of this past week. If you wish to discuss this further, you can reach me at the usual number, but as I explained to you before, I'm afraid there's really nothing I can do."

The message cut off with a CLICK, and the screen filled with a moment of static before going black.

Simon Foster picked up the box and, careful as always to lock the door, stepped outside into the harsh sunlight. He made his way along the catwalk to the narrow stairs that led down the side of the housing complex. He wondered sometimes if during the night, little men didn't emerge from some unseen corner of the building to add more steps to the staircase. The journey down seemed to get longer with every passing day.

The year is nineteen hundred and ninety-nine. Within the box, evidence that some things do not change with the passage of time. Its contents: the collected debris of a shattered life now valuable only for the dimes and nickels they can solicit from a third party.

A familiar process and a familiar long walk that is about to lead into the unfamiliar terrain of the Twilight Zone.

The pawnshop bell rang softly as Simon stepped inside. No one was behind the counter. He looked around the shop as he waited for someone to come out. He'd never been in this one before—he rarely ranged this far downtown—but it was like all the others. Row upon row, and aisle upon aisle of brass and silver and mortgaged moments.

He started at the sound of a door closing behind the counter. "Mister Quint?" That had been the name engraved on the store window. QUINT'S PAWNSHOP— BEST PRICES IN TOWN.

He was a large man, with a square face and eyes that looked at Simon with only marginal interest. "Yes, sir? Something I can help you with?"

"Well, I'm—afraid I'm not buying."

Quint's shoulders sagged slightly. "Ah. Selling, then."

"Yes."

"Bring it here, let's see what you've got."

Simon put the box up on the counter and stepped back as Quint rummaged through it. He tried to look interested in the racks of musical instruments, tried not to notice which items were received with silence, and which elicited an occasional *hmm* or a shrug of disinterest.

He wandered back to the counter, despite his best intentions. "It's all in good condition," he said, trying to make conversation. "It's not much, I know, but I sold off most of the rest. Rent to make and everything, you know how it is. Been having some hard times, lots of— well, lots of things going wrong, you know? But I guess you hear that a lot in this business, don't you?"

"Yes, I do." Simon could see him adding up the figures in his head. "Fifty dollars."

"Fifty! The watch alone is worth at least that!"

Quint looked back inside the box, frowned. "Sixty, then. But that's as high as I'll go."

Anguished, Simon gathered up the box and started toward the door.

"You can take it somewhere else, but you won't get any more," Quint called after him. "And when you come back, the offer will be fifty. Flat."

Simon slowed, then stopped. He glanced inside the box. The watch dully reflected the overhead lights. *I'm sorry, Dad, God, I'm so sorry.*

He stepped back to the counter and set down the box. "At least—could you at least make it sixty-five?"

Quint frowned, then nodded. "Done."

He went to the cash register, rang up NO SALE, and slowly counted out the sixty-five dollars, not looking up as he said, "You're sure you've nothing else to sell, then?"

"No, nothing else."

"You weren't sent? Referred?"

"No, I—look, if I *had* anything else to sell, it'd be in that box. I've got nothing left. Just a gut full of pain. Why? You want to make me an offer? Go ahead, Mr. Pawnshop Man, tell me—what's the going price for pain these days?"

Mr. Quint said nothing.

Simon took the money and started toward the door, his hand almost on the handle as he heard Quint's voice.

"Perhaps there is something *else* we can negotiate over."

Simon hesitated, looked back at him. Mr. Quint unlocked the other door behind the counter. "Come," he said, and stepped through into another room.

Simon hesitated, then followed him in.

What the hell, he thought. *I got nowhere special to go.*

The room within was black, windowless, its contents all but invisible until Quint switched on the single bulb that hung suspended overhead. A computer console ran along one wall, bleeding off into an unsettling number of plugs hanging from a minimum of outlets. A chair squatted in the middle of the room, covered by a black sheet. He could make out bits and pieces of electronic apparatus protruding out of the cover, tenting it in places. It looked quite uncomfortable.

Quint stepped toward the chair, circling it slowly. "You are familiar, I trust, with memory dipping?"

"Only what I read in the papers. Supposed to be the big trend these days, renting people's memories."

"Yes, it's become very popular among those able to afford it." He pulled off the black sheet to reveal the chair in its entirety—the drouds, the scanning equipment, the displays, something that looked like a laser-probe, and a lot of equipment Simon didn't recognize. A series of digital relays led across the room to the bank of machines on the other side.

"The usual practice is to scan a subject's memories and copy them onto a computer chip," Quint said. "The process is very selective. You can take a skier, copy his memory of his best jump, and by plugging into that, you can experience what he felt. His thoughts, his feelings, the way the snow felt when his skis hit it, the roar of the crowd—you feel it all, as if it were you. A fascinating concept, is it not, Mr.—" He smiled a too-friendly smile.

"Foster. Simon Foster."

"Mr. Foster. As I was saying, a very trendy item. Unfortunately, *dubbed* memories aren't as vivid as some might like. It's like seeing a video that's been copied too many times: the color is washed out, the experience less than one hundred percent real. And that's the point of electronic entertainment, isn't it? To give you the feeling of actually *being there?*"

"Go on."

"So a market has developed for connoisseurs looking to sample a far more intense experience. For that, they require not dubbing, but *direct transference.*" He circled the chair, his hands passing gently over the equipment. "For that, we go in electronically and slice away memories. A minute, an hour, a year, ten years . . . we can remove those specific memories and store them for use by others." He glanced at Simon, and catching the expression there, quickly added, "The process is quite painless, of course."

"And illegal."

"Eminently. And the wonder of it all is, the product is not a distortion of reality, it is reality *distilled*. For those who buy, the risk is quite worthwhile. Love, sex, hate, the everyday experiences we take for granted, the facility to peek into someone else's life, they get it all. And for those who sell, the rewards are quite reasonable."

"I've never really done anything special—"

"Unnecessary," Quint said. "Look at the soap operas, Mr. Foster. No alien invasions, no vast sagas. But they know the value of voyeurism. And so do I."

Simon glanced at the chair and felt his mouth go dry. It was just one more piece of furniture, but being in the same room with it made him feel somehow—dirty.

Sixty-five dollars. You got sixty-five dollars for damn near everything you had left in the world. What's the difference?

"I don't know," Simon said. "I mean, how much would I get?"

"That depends upon what we find. Memory is like an old penny, Mr. Foster. You may think it's quite worthless, and to you, it may be. But to a collector, ah, that's something else again." He switched off the overhead light, and instantly the room was plunged back into darkness. Finding Simon's elbow, Quint led him out into the front room. The light from outside stung his eyes as he emerged.

"Every day we forget a little more of the past," Quint continued. "It does us no good to wallow in it. We've been there, after all. So why not let someone else enjoy it? Me, if I had to choose between remembering something that happened fifteen years ago, and eating a good meal at a fine restaurant today, well—"

Simon edged toward the door. "I'll have to think about it."

"Of course, of course," Quint said. "Wouldn't have it any other way. Do think about it. And while you're thinking about it, think on this: What have your memories done for you, lately, Mr. Foster?"

Simon looked back once, as the door closed, then moved away down the street, pulling his jacket closer about him.

Simon carried the small bag of groceries up the stairs toward his flat. The bag was depressingly light. It was amazing how little fifteen dollars bought these days. He was nearly to the top of the stairs when he heard the sound he had hoped to avoid: the door on the first floor opening. The door to the manager's apartment.

"Hey, you. Foster!"

Simon stopped. "Yes, Mr. Ferelli?"

The thin, wiry man in the jogging suit came to the bottom of the stairs. "In case you haven't heard, the rent's due first of every month. Today is the sixth. Either I get the rent from you by tomorrow, or I'm throwing you out of here right on your ass."

Simon nodded and continued up the stairs.

"Hey, you listening to me?"

Simon closed the door to his flat and leaned against it. He had heard just fine.

The nights were getting colder. The smell of chowder coming from the hot plate smelled good, even if the date on the can was a little old.

As the soup reached full boil, he shut it off and poured it into a small bowl, letting it cool as he went to the closet and pulled out a sweater. He buttoned it as he stepped back into the kitchen.

Something was floating in his bowl of chowder.

He nudged it with the spoon. It rolled over to reveal legs.

Cockroach.

Must've fallen into the soup while he was getting his sweater, he decided, the thought coming to him from somewhere far away.

Cockroach.

The can had cost him two dollars.

"Damn it!" He slammed his fist into the table so

hard that for a moment he thought it would splinter. It rocked badly, but held. *"Damn it!"*

With a kind of manic desperation, he carried the bowl over to the sink and spooned out the roach, careful not to move it around, as if by keeping it to one place he might somehow confine the germs to what he could spoon out.

He rummaged in the drawer for another spoon, then went back to the table. He closed his eyes and tried to see the chowder the way it had been earlier—warm and fragrant and inviting. He picked up the spoon, dipped it, brought the chowder toward him—

And stopped, the spoon an inch from his lips.

"It's not fair," he whispered. "It's not fair, it's just not fair. . . ."

He stood and threw the bowl into the sink. It struck with the crash of breaking glass. "It was the last can I had—it was the LAST CAN I HAD AND IT'S NOT FAIR! IT'S JUST NOT FAIR!"

Not one bit.

Simon stood nervously in the pawnshop doorway. As usual, no one was about. He pulled the door closed loudly, and a moment later Quint appeared behind the counter.

"It's not fair, you know," Simon said.

"Very little in life is, Mr. Foster."

He opened the drop leaf and ushered Simon behind the counter. Feeling numb, Simon allowed himself to be led through the curtains into the dark room just beyond.

"I've just had a very good offer from a fellow who collects high school graduations," Quint said, and closed the door behind them.

. . . *a swirl of colors and faces, twisting and bending, a sense of violation as they were seized and sucked and whirled away somewhere up there, into the darkness, all of them, Ben and Mrs. Massie, his mother and father . . . sitting on the bleachers, so proud, the sun hot but hanging in desolate emptiness, and the voices, overlapping one another like small waves . . . class of '66 . . . proud to have been a part . . . the highest grade-point average in . . . like to welcome our vale- dictorian . . . Richard Fleming, Michael Flores, Karen Ford, Simon Foster . . .*

"Mr. Foster? Mr. Foster?"

Quint's face slowly emerged from the surrounding darkness, inches from Simon's own. He was slapping Simon on the face, not hard, but firmly. Simon blinked hard, then tried to sit up, when the nausea hit him like a tidal wave. He slumped back into the chair.

"You are all right, Mister Foster?"

Simon licked his lips. They were dry, and seemed too sensitive to his tongue. "Yeah, I—I suppose so."

"The first time is always rough." He handed Simon a paper cup filled with water and helped him close his hand around it. "Drink this. For whatever reason, the process tends to dehydrate a little."

Simon drank the water in slow, grateful sips as Quint went to the bank of equipment along the far wall. *. . . for whatever reason,* Simon thought, the realiza- tion slowly coalescing in his numbed brain. *Of course he doesn't know how it works. Why should he?*

Quint flipped a row of switches, then squinted into the monitor. Colors played across his face. Simon won- dered what he was seeing, wondered in what digitized, three-dimensional, full-stereophonic form the memory of his high school graduation now existed.

Existed without him, separate from him.

He probed at his thoughts, tried without success to summon up a single image from that day. It was gone, like a phone number that just slips away, never to re- turn.

"A perfect transfer," Quint said, switching off the monitor. "How do you feel?"

"All right. I don't feel any different, except—"

"Except that there is now just a tiny gap in your memory, just *so*." He held thumb and forefinger a quarter-inch apart. "Everything between eight o'clock in the morning and eight o'clock in the evening, on the day in question. Twelve hours, poof, gone. And are you any the less for it? No. In fact, I would dare say, you are quite the richer for it."

As Quint said it, he handed across an envelope. Simon didn't need to open it to know it contained his fee. It felt sufficiently thick—not overwhelmingly so, but enough.

Quint helped him to his feet. Simon balanced and waved him away. "I think I can manage it from here."

"Excellent. Well, good doing business with you, Mr. Foster. Next time, when you—"

"No," Simon said, "there's not going to be a next time. I just needed enough to get ahead a little. That's all. I thank you for your—your *help,* but I think once is more than enough."

Quint shrugged. "As you say. But *if* you should ever change your mind, you know where to find me. I'm sure I can get you a very good price."

Quint helped him to the door, then stood aside as Simon walked off, heading in no particular direction, the envelope in his shirt pocket warm against his chest.

Twelve hours. Twelve hours he would never miss in exchange for a few weeks free of worrying about where his next meal was coming from. As deals went, it wasn't the worst he'd ever made.

So why, then, did he feel so unclean?

Simon peeled three hundred and twenty-five dollars off the roll and handed it to the manager, who accepted the money with a look that reminded Simon of a dead fish he'd once seen on the beach. It had been lying there for at least a week.

He started away when the manager put a hand out in front of him. "Plus the money for next month, too. New policy. Got a lot of transients coming through here —owner says we have to have an extra month's deposit." He paused for effect. "Helps discourage the deadbeats."

"Look, you can't do that—"

"Yeah?" he said, feigning amazement. "Look, I'll tell you what, why don't you run off to the housing commission and tell them all about it—and maybe when you get back you'll find your apartment rented. One of those clerical errors you hear so much about."

Bastard, Simon thought, but cut it off before the thought escaped . . . and began counting out more bills into the manager's open hand.

Simon paced nervously, not wanting to sit. He'd pulled his best suit out of the closet for the interview, had it cleaned and pressed. He didn't want to wrinkle it. Across the room, on top of the bureau, sat the remainder of his money, a little over thirty dollars. The rest had carried him this far, and now surely something would break. Something *had* to break.

When the vid finally rang he caught it on the first ring, and the unreadable face of his employment counselor appeared on the screen.

"Hi," Simon said, a little too cheerfully, he thought.

The counselor nodded. "You requested an interview," she said. "How may I help you?"

Simon's mouth worked. This wasn't what he'd expected to hear. "It's—well, it's time for my six-week review."

She blinked, and checked the forms in front of her. "Yes, so it is." She glanced them over briefly. "I'm sorry, Mr. Foster, but there are still no openings in your area. You'll just have to wait until something opens up."

"But I resubmitted my application two weeks ago! You told me then that something was in the works."

"Things have a habit of changing, Mr. Foster. I'm sorry, but you'll just have to wait your turn. When we're notified of a vacancy in your field, you will be notified at that time. That's all I can tell you. Good-bye."

Click and disconnect.

He walked over, switched off the vid. On his way back, he passed the bureau and glanced down at the remaining money.

Thirty dollars. Enough for another two days, and then—

You're not going to do it. You did it once only because you absolutely had to. Not again.

Five dollars.

Simon sat on the bed, near the window, angling the high school yearbook perched in his lap so that it caught the fading daylight. He paged through it, smiling at the passing faces, the pictures of pep clubs and school plays, rallies and footraces.

Five dollars.

He recognized the names, and the faces—most of them, anyway—and nodded at the familiar buildings captured in grainy photographs. Then he turned the page, to the two-page foldout he knew would be there, a panoramic photo of his high school graduation, everyone lined up on the bleachers, clad in caps and gowns, smiling for the camera. He managed to find himself in the photo. He ran his finger over the image, as though hoping to feel the memory vibrating somewhere just beneath its surface.

Nothing. The photo could have belonged to another place, another school, another Simon Foster whose similarity to him ended at the name.

". . . gone," he said, and the silent room embraced the word.

Five dollars.

Five dollars left.

He slammed shut the yearbook and walked out of the room.

As Simon stepped into the pawnshop, the improbable thought occurred to him that Quint had actually been waiting for him all this time, in the very spot he'd last seen him, there behind the counter.

"You're in luck," Quint said, picking up the conversation as though it had never been abandoned. "We just had a call from someone interested in buying birthdays."

Simon shut the door behind him. It closed with a too-loud *click*.

He sat in the chair.
Make a wish . . . how did you know? . . . It's from Aunt Sara—I bet it's socks . . . is it okay if I stay out late?
He sat in the chair.
Oh, look, darling! He's taking his first step! Look!
He sat in the chair.
And they took his college graduation. And his first year of college.
"—It's for the daughter of a client of mine. She's going to college. But who wants to study when all that information is locked away in your head? It's only a semester, six months—"
He sat in the chair.
And they took away his day at the circus, age ten. And his second year of college. And his first date.
—wanted to say it's been—you're a great dancer. Thank you. It—was very nice. But I have to go inside now. I'll never forget this, though . . . not ever.
He sat in the chair.
And they took it away.
And they paid him for it.

Simon awoke as the alarm buzzed annoyingly in his ear. He forced himself to sit up, rub the sleep from his eyes. He had an hour before the counselor would call. They were punctual. They were always punctual. He staggered into the bathroom and splashed cold water on his face. He had to be alert, had to be sharp. It had taken another six weeks to get the interview. He had a real shot at this one, he could feel it.

An hour later he sat before the vid, straightening his tie and checking himself in the mirror one last time as the vid beeped at him. He flicked it on, and the face of the counselor filled the screen. He smiled at it. The face sent back the barest flicker of a smile.

"Right on time, Mr. Foster. Very good."

"Thank you."

"As we indicated in our letter, we have a job in the repair field for which you might be qualified. We just have to ask you a few questions. What high school did you say you graduated?"

Graduated? I—no, wait. That's right.

"Clifford—ah, Cliffordville High, in—Madison."

"With two years of junior college."

"That's right."

"What was your major?"

Simon hesitated. "I think—I think it was—"

"Your resume lists engineering."

"Yes. Look, if you could just give me a minute, I think I have the records around here somewhere—"

"I'm sorry, but we're pressed for time, Mr. Foster. If you're not ready for this interview, you should have notified us."

Simon straightened. He couldn't afford to lose this one. "No, no, I'm—ready. Sorry. Go on."

She looked at the forms in front of her. "Please describe your training in that field during your college experience."

Simon fought to remember, but his thoughts kept slipping over the gap like a tongue worrying the space where a tooth had been removed. "Well, I—we worked very hard, covering a lot of different areas, it's difficult to describe."

"I require specifics, Mr. Foster."

He opened his mouth to respond, but nothing came out. He searched desperately, trying to find some fragment to throw up in front of him as a defense, but it was gone, all gone. "I—"

The face on the vid lifted and stared into his own. "I'm sorry, Mr. Foster, but if you're not going to cooperate, there's nothing I can do for you."

"I want to cooperate. It's just—it's difficult sometimes—"

"It's difficult for us all, Mr. Foster. The unemployment rate is thirty-two percent as of this Monday, and there are many applicants who are looking for this kind of job."

"Look, if you could just—it's coming back to me, really it is, you have to understand it's been a long time —if you could just give me a chance."

"I'm afraid you've used up your allotted time, Mr. Foster. If you will resubmit your application—"

Simon stood, stepped toward the vid. "No, wait a minute, please, you can't do this to me—I need this job!"

"Perhaps you will think of that prior to your next interview."

"Don't you *understand?*" He was shouting now, hardly aware that he was doing it. "I'm nearly broke! I can't go on like this! You've got to listen to me, it's not my fault!"

"If you wish to appeal the interview, that is your option, and it will be taken up at the proper time. Meanwhile, please resubmit your application to central processing. Good day, Mr. Foster."

Then the vid flickered, and she was gone. He clawed at the screen, as though by an act of will he could reach through to wherever she was, where the jobs were, and pull her back. "I can't go on like this," he cried. "Don't you see, you've got to listen to me! Come back here! Come back—damn you!"

After a while, he went back to his chair and sat down, rocking slowly in the filtered light from outside. He wouldn't get another appointment for six weeks. Six weeks.

Next time he would do better.

He would have to do better.

Simon stepped back into the pawnshop, the tiny bell overhead announcing his presence. By now he had developed an almost Pavlovian hatred for the bell.

No one stood behind the counter. "Mr. Quint?" He stepped slowly toward the counter, going over his planned statement for the third time. *I'm sorry, Mr. Quint, but I can't sell you anything more that might affect my hiring. If you want to buy something else, we'll discuss it.*

They would definitely discuss it. He had put off coming back for a long time, and now he was down to his last few dollars. But no matter how desperate he was, he wouldn't swerve from his decision. He couldn't afford to.

After a moment, the door behind the counter opened, and Mr. Quint emerged. Beside him was a young woman, about Simon's own age. She looked pale, drawn, almost feral. She clutched an empty paper cup in her hands, and when he looked at her, she avoided his gaze.

Ashamed.

Oh, God, Simon thought. No.

Quint opened the cash register, pulled out an envelope stuffed with bills, and handed it to her. She accepted them without a word and made quickly for the door. As she brushed past Simon, she glanced up. There were tears in her eyes. For a moment, he thought she was going to say something. But she quickly turned away and ran out the door, slamming it behind her.

The bell jingled softly to mark her departure.

"Good to see you, Mr. Foster," Quint said, as though nothing had happened.

Simon turned away from the door and focused on him. "My God," he said, "my *God,* how many? How many others?"

"You mean her?" Quint shrugged. "I run a business, Mr. Foster. Like any good business it depends on volume—and diversity. One must be responsive to fluctuations and changing demands in the market. Surely you didn't think you were the only one."

Simon started toward the door, toward fresh air, toward anyplace that was not this place.

"Save me your grand gestures," Quint said. "You're not going anywhere. And even if you leave, you'll be back. Your kind always comes back."

Simon turned, and he could feel his face burning. "Yeah, we come back," he said. "Because bread is three dollars a loaf and meat you can't even buy except on the black market. Matter of fact, I look around and the only person I see eating—is you."

"I pay you a fair price for what you have to sell."

"Well it's not enough! Who are you to say this minute is worth a nickel, an hour—maybe a dollar? Five, if something interesting's going on? What gives you the right to put a price tag on my life?"

"I didn't," Quint said, and walked away, toward the counter. "You did."

Simon stepped back as though slapped. He tried to find some biting response, but suddenly it didn't seem to make any difference. He was right. Damn him, he was right.

Simon looked away, nodded. "Yeah," he said at last, more softly now. "Yeah, I did, didn't I?" He crossed the room to where Quint stood. "So what'll it be today, Mr. Quint? A trip to the zoo? A ride on a roller coaster? Why don't you take my first marriage and save us both some grief?"

"Not interested," Quint said. "Market for birthdays and conventional stuff is down. It's only temporary, though, I'm assured by my people. Academics are also down, since school's out for the summer, which I'm sure you'll find of some relief. No, Mr. Foster, I'm only buying one thing today. We need a companion piece to the young lady who just left here.

"We want to buy the first time you made love to a woman."

Simon's knees went soft beneath him. He shook his head, slowly. "No. . . ."

"I'm prepared to make you a very good offer."

"No, I can't. There's got to be something else—"

"Sorry. Take it or leave it, but that's all I'm buying at the moment. Walk away and who knows if I'll buy anything else. I need a reliable supply of material. Either you're here to do business, or you're not—and if not, then get out."

With that, Quint stepped back through the door behind the counter, leaving it open just a crack.

* * *

Her name was Carolyn. Carolyn of the auburn hair, the green eyes, the ruddy Basque complexion, the dancer's legs, and the small, delicate breasts. They'd argued the night before, and he'd brought her roses the next day to apologize. She cried when she saw them. No one had ever brought her roses before. "Make love to me," she'd said, her voice small, her face still moist from tears. He'd been about to enter her when she held his face in her hands.

Tell me you love me. . . . Don't be silly, I—It's not silly. Just tell me you love me. I don't even care if it's true or not. . . . I love you . . . For always. Forever and ever . . . For always. Forever and ever and ever and ever and ever and

"That will be all."

Simon flinched, his gaze fixed at a no-place point beyond the wall, but he didn't move as Quint removed the drouds. He tried to summon Carolyn's face to mind, tried to find some trace of that evening, but it had all turned to mist behind his eyes.

Gone. All gone.

"I said that will be all, Mr. Foster. You can go now. Your payment is on the counter."

Simon took the paper cup beside the chair and knocked the water back in one swallow, his throat burning. The process did not get much easier with time. He pulled himself out of the chair and started for the door —then hesitated. He looked at the bank of equipment along the wall, then slowly made his way toward the row of scanners and readouts and digital displays.

He peered into the monitor, but all he could see was row after row of numbers, swimming in front of his eyes. "She's in there, isn't she?"

"Please stay away from the equipment," Quint said from the door, "you might damage something."

"Somebody told me once," Simon said, "that you always remember the first, you always remember the last, but nobody remembers the second. Guess now I'm the exception to the rule, aren't I?"

"Well spoken, Mr. Foster. Now if you will please step away from the equipment—"

Simon turned, faced him. "I want her back. I've changed my mind."

"Sorry. No refunds. Take your money and get out."

Simon advanced on him, backing him toward the door. "I said I want her back. I want her back in my head, where she belongs. I want my life back." He grabbed Quint before he could bolt from the room. "You've got my life. I want it back. *Give me my life back!*"

"Get away from me!" Quint said, struggling in his grip. "Let—me—go!"

Quint pushed away, ripping his shirt, and bolted from the room. Simon ran after him, found him reaching under the counter—

Gun!

He tackled Quint, and they went to the floor, struggling for the gun. Simon closed his hand over Quint's, finally managed to rip the gun out of Quint's hands. He rolled away fast and came up with the gun clenched in both hands. Quint scrambled to his feet, and Simon caught him in the crosshairs.

"I want my life back! Damn you!"

"I haven't got it! I sold it! Don't you understand? It's not here anymore!"

"Then get it!"

"I can't!"

Simon cocked the hammer. He didn't need to see his own face to know there was the light of madness in it. "Then I suggest you try," Simon said, "because right now, I haven't got much of anything to lose. I want a life. I want to be whole again. Now."

"All right!" Quint licked his lips nervously. "There—there is a way. But it's not perfect."

"Like you said, Mr. Quint—what in life is?"

Simon Foster waited in his room, sitting in his usual place in front of the vid, dressed in his best clothes. He awaited with quiet calm the beep that would announce the incoming call from the job placement bureau. When it came, he toggled the vid and smiled at the face that shimmered into view. He felt good. He felt confident. He felt whole.

The counselor returned the smile, though it looked false and without conviction. "Punctual again, I see."

"As always."

"We've received your new application, Mr. Foster. Very professionally typed. Did you have it done by a service?"

"No, ma'am. I typed it myself."

"Did you?" She glanced back down at the form. "Yes, I see you've added clerk/typist to your job goals. And a number of other occupations. Where, exactly, did you learn to type?"

"I took three years of typing at Sorworth College. It's all on the resume."

The counselor looked up at him and frowned. "But Sorworth was a women-only college at that time."

Simon nodded. "And I graduated on June twelfth, on the year shown. And then I graduated again, on July first of the following year. I attended and graduated from Lennox High School. Also Chula Vista High School. Did I mention Matawan Regional High School?"

"Mr. Foster," the counselor said, trying to interrupt. She looked concerned. But Simon kept on going. He knew that everything was going to be all right now.

"That was shortly after I returned from London. Did I tell you I have two children? I remember when they were born. It was such a moving time for me, being an only child. I remember when I turned five, my brother and my sister helped make the decorations—"

"Mr. Foster . . . ?"

"But of course the credentials are what's at issue here. I should mention that my German is quite fluent. I spent much of last year in Vienna—or was that Spain— yes, it was, and I worked as a translator, and a bus driver, and a secretary, and I interned for two years at the Institute de Neurologica. . . ."

Simon smiled as he spoke.
Everything was going to be just fine.

Exit Simon Foster, a patchwork collection of lost dreams, held together by the stolen memories of strangers—a man who discovered that in the final analysis we truly are the sum of our parts. Mister Simon Foster, a very special resident of the Twilight Zone.

Introduction to
The Curious Case of Edgar Witherspoon

A word about Haskell Barkin.

I've known Haskell—Huck, to his friends—for about five years now, as I write this. The first time we met, he was story-editing a series I was working for on-staff. He's one of those people who you would never think of as a Hollywood Writer at first glance. Quiet, soft-spoken, and self-effacing, his talent for understating his abilities is almost as considerable as his abilities themselves.

Though we never collaborated, I enjoyed working with him, and when the time came to do *The Twilight Zone*, one of the first phone calls I made was to Huck Barkin. He came in and sold us a story right off the bat: "Appointment on Route 17," a gentle and moving story about a man whose heart transplant brings him a legacy he had never considered possible.

Shortly after finishing that script, we called in Huck to pitch another. This time, nothing really grabbed us—with one exception. As near as I can remember it now, the story involved an old man, living alone, who was constantly sending letters to people pleading for help. Demons were involved in some way, as I recall, with the denouement dealing with the death of the old man, at which time the truth of his dire warnings is revealed and visited upon those who didn't listen to him.

Although the specific storyline didn't take us by storm, the image of an old man driven by urges and concerns that no one else would either believe or understand stayed with me. There was something there, and I continued to work at it the way a dog worries a bone. Later that night, lying abed, the story suddenly unraveled in front of me, and I walked down the hall to my home-office and began typing what started out as a few notes and by dawn had turned into a detailed ten-page outline.

I brought the story—which by now had *no* resemblance to the story that Huck had pitched—to the producer, who read it and liked it and approved it to script. The assumption around the office was that I would write it myself, taking sole credit, since it was by now so far from Huck's original story that certainly no one would think twice about the propriety.

In all likelihood, they were right.

In all likelihood, even Huck probably wouldn't have put the two together.

I don't work that way. The story would never have been born at all if Huck had not come into the office on a pitch. So as far as I was concerned, it was his story.

I called Huck within the hour, and when he arrived, I handed him the outline and the assignment. I made it clear that I wanted no credit on this one. The story would never have been written at all had it not been for his original pitch.

But Huck doesn't work that way, either.

When the smoke finally cleared, and the wounded were dragged off the field of battle, we agreed to share story credit, but only on my insistence that Huck would receive sole teleplay credit, and *all* residuals from the episode.

The script came in less than a week later, and turned into one of our best episodes, going through without notes. Although virtually every word in the outline is in the script, it was Huck's genius with comedy and characterization that fleshed out the story and truly brought Edgar Witherspoon to life.

For some time, there was discussion about casting Jonathan Winters in the role of Witherspoon, but in the end the one person most ideally suited for the role got it: Harry Morgan, perhaps best known for his role as Colonel Potter on *M*A*S*H*. Morgan was able to infuse Witherspoon with a delightful looniness that managed somehow to be vulnerable and utterly sympathetic. We were so pleased with the performances, the direction, and the episode overall that we decided to make this the debut episode for the new *Twilight Zone*.

In over a decade of scriptwriting, I've collaborated on only a handful of scripts. And this is one of those that I'm most proud of.

"The Curious Case of Edgar Witherspoon," story by Haskell Barkin and J. Michael Straczynski, teleplay by Haskell Barkin, production #87019, was directed by Rene Bonniere, and produced the week of May 16, 1988. It starred Harry Morgan (Edgar Witherspoon), Cedric Smith (Dr. James St. Clair), Barbara Chilcott (Mrs. Milligan), Eve Crawford (Cynthia), Pixie Bigelow (Secretary). First aired on October 25, 1988.

THE CURIOUS CASE OF EDGAR WITHERSPOON

(with Haskell Barkin)

The voice that came from Dr. James St. Clair's office spilled out into the late afternoon and across the greensward that nestled at the center of the Snug Harbor Hospital. "He's crazy! That's what he is! A loony, a nut case, a genuine wacko!"

Inside the neatly appointed office, James St. Clair nodded understandingly. Mrs. Milligan, the old man's landlady, was upset to be sure, and he'd learned long ago that the best cure for that kind of upset was a show of quiet, calm sympathy.

Cynthia Gaines, the old man's niece, chimed in next, in tones slightly more reasonable—but only slightly. "Uncle Edgar is always out *looking* for things."

"Such as?" St. Clair asked. He turned slightly in his chair to face her, careful to adjust his sleeves so that the shirt cuffs stayed the proper quarter-inch beyond his jacket.

"Things like—like three paper clips. Or a chrome coat hanger."

"Or one patent-leather tap shoe!" Mrs. Milligan added.

St. Clair nodded understandingly.

"He rummages through trash cans," Cynthia said. "He goes to garbage dumps."

"He's always bothering my other tenants," Mrs.

Milligan said. "One day it's bicycle spokes. Then it's baseball cards—needed by 3:15! And who do the tenants complain to? Yours truly!"

St. Clair nodded, though by now his neck was stiffening from looking back and forth from one to the other. It was, he decided, a little like watching a tennis match, with the old man as the ball.

Cynthia served. "He won't let anybody into his apartment. Not even me, his own niece."

Mrs. Milligan returned. "All that junk he's collecting. It's a firetrap."

"He could hurt himself."

"And other people—namely me!"

"He needs your help."

"Yesterday he wanted a yo-yo by six o'clock!"

"Please do something."

The game point went to Dr. St. Clair, who glanced once more at the manila folder on his desk with the old man's name written on it in black felt-tip pen: EDGAR WITHERSPOON. Then he nodded understandingly (just once more for good measure) and smiled.

"Of course," he said, as his watch chimed out the end of their session.

Time to go to work.

Mrs. Milligan had left an address, and a crude map, and St. Clair showed up at the apartment building promptly at nine o'clock the next morning. He checked the mailboxes on the shabby brownstone, looking for WITHERSPOON, E., and finally found it. He pressed the buzzer below it and stood back, waiting for a response.

Nothing.

He pressed it again, holding it down longer this time.

Nothing.

"His bell don't work."

St. Clair stepped back from the porch and looked up to where Mrs. Milligan leaned out of the second-story window, her hair in curlers, holding her robe closed around her. "I think he disconnected it," she continued. "He's down there."

She indicated a narrow flight of stairs that led down the side of the building to a basement entrance. He waved his thanks and proceeded down the twelve steps to the basement.

Beyond was a storage room—long, and cold, and filled with the castoffs from tenants and visitors going back at least twenty years, St. Clair estimated. A Dumpster was shoved up against one wall, and the furnace wheezed mightily just to the right of the entrance. There was no sign of Edgar Witherspoon.

He stepped forward and noticed another door at the far end of the room. Maneuvering past the junk on the floor, he stepped up to the door, straightened his jacket, and knocked—

—at the very instant that the door flew open and a tiny, distracted wrinkle of a man lunged out like someone late for a bus, locking the door behind him, addressing St. Clair over his shoulder. "Thanks anyway, Mr. Pilchick, but I already found a brass thimble."

St. Clair cleared his throat. The old man turned and appraised him with a glance.

"You're not Mr. Pilchick," Edgar said.

And as though that resolution somehow signaled the end of the conversation, Edgar padded quickly away, heading for the Dumpster.

St. Clair followed him across the room. "May I speak to you, Mr. Witherspoon?"

"Some other time, perhaps. I have to look for a doll's head." And then he dove into the nearest pile of debris, pawing through it with a stick, throwing aside cartons and suitcases and boxes and shirts and rubber tires and broken toasters in his frantic search.

Fascinating, St. Clair thought. *Absolutely fascinating.*

One old man, in a private world of irrational urgencies. For Dr. James St. Clair, an all too common sight. But Edgar Witherspoon is a most uncommon old man, with a secret that reaches out to the four corners of the Earth. As the good doctor is about to discover.

St. Clair cleared his throat again. This time Edgar seemed either not to hear or not to notice. "Your niece worries about you."

Edgar glanced up at him over a pair of Franklin glasses. "She's a very nice woman. So tell her not to worry. See? A simple solution. Thanks for coming, it's been a pleasure meeting you, but I have to get on with my work."

And he went back to his digging.

"Your work?"

"I'll bet you'd like to know what it is, wouldn't you? You've got that look."

"Well, yes, I—"

"Wrong answer," Edgar said. He straightened scratching his head and looking around. "You see a doll's head anywhere?"

St. Clair glanced about the floor and saw a patch of brown hair and plastic under an old suitcase. He picked it up and brushed it off. "Like this?"

Edgar gave it a cursory glance and shook his head "Too big. Also brunette. I need blonde and I need in—" He checked his watch. "—five minutes."

He climbed out of the Dumpster and went to one of the piles of trash shoved up against one wall.

"What do you need it for?"

"Do you want Santa Barbara to fall into the ocean?"

"No."

"Then stand aside, sir," Edgar said, rushing past him to another pile, "stand aside!"

Edgar bent to peer behind the pile, and with a sudden whoop of delight dove into the debris, coming up a moment later with a small blonde doll's head "Hoo-hoo!" he yelled, holding it with undisguised pleasure and relief. "And not a second to spare!"

Clutching the doll's head to his chest, Edgar raced back across the room to the door of his apartment. St. Clair rushed to follow, but arrived a moment too late

Edgar dashed inside and slammed the door, like some half-mad rabbit from *Alice in Wonderland* diving back into its hole, late for a very important appointment. St. Clair caught the sound of multiple locks being clicked shut.

"Mr. Witherspoon?" He leaned against the door, listening for any sound inside. The door was thick, but he thought he could just make out a curious whirr-click-whirr-*sproing* sound from inside. "Mr. Withersp—"

The door suddenly jerked open again. Edgar stood in the opening, blocking St. Clair's view of the room beyond. "I'm sorry. I shouldn't be rude. You've come all this way to see me."

St. Clair smiled. "May I come in?"

"And it was so nice," Edgar continued, as though not having heard. "A pleasure meeting you. Tell my niece hello. Now if you'll excuse me, I have to stop the shaking in Santa Barbara."

"Mr. Witherspoon—"

Slam!

Then the door opened again, and Edgar thrust a large plastic garbage bag into St. Clair's hands. "Oh, and could you dump this on your way out?"

Then a final, definitive *slam!*

St. Clair looked at the bag in his hand, at the door, which showed no signs of opening again anytime in the near future (pending another sudden desire for dolls' heads or bicycle pumps), and headed away, pausing only to listen one last time at the door.

Whirr-click-whirr-*sproing*.

Fascinating, he thought, and dropped the bag into the Dumpster on his way out of the building.

The radio was playing Mozart's *La Clemenza di Tito* softly in the background when Cynthia Gaines appeared in the door to St. Clair's office. "Well? Did you see Uncle Edgar?"

"This morning. It wasn't exactly what you would call a long conversation."

"But long enough? To realize that he's—"

"Oh, absolutely. But on the other hand, Mr. Witherspoon appears happy and quite harmless."

"Harmless? He pesters strangers on the street. He runs after garbage trucks. That is far from harmless. Someone saw him take a baby's bottle out of its carriage. I'm afraid he'll get arrested next time. Doctor, I will sign anything, cooperate in any way necessary."

St. Clair tapped his fingers on the top of his desk, then finally nodded. "Well . . . I could have another chat with him. A longer one this time. Although you must realize that I can only go so far without written permission from you for a period of observation, if it becomes necessary, and—"

He slowed, stopped, gradually becoming aware of the news announcer whose voice had replaced Mozart on the radio. A moment ago, it had been mentioning new legislation dealing with the acid rain problem.

But now—

". . . and in the city of Santa Barbara, a small earthquake tremblor was felt shortly before noon today. No injuries were reported, and damage is said to be minimal. In the international news . . ."

"Dr. St. Clair?"

He looked up at her, then glanced at the radio. "Did you hear that?"

She shrugged. "Hear what?"

"Something about a—" He pushed the thought away. "Never mind. It's not important. Don't know what I was thinking. I'll have a look-in on Mr. Witherspoon first chance I get, Ms. Gaines, and give you a full report as soon as possible."

She smiled.

Exactly one week later (the press of other business being what it was, which was generally busy, and generally prosperous, which was how he liked it), St. Clair once again stood before Edgar Witherspoon's door, which was bolted-up just as tightly as it had been the week before. He rapped lightly at the door.

Nothing.

He knocked again.

Still nothing.

I seem to recall having gone through this once already, St. Clair thought, and decided to abandon knocking in favor of a more direct approach. "Mr. Witherspoon?" he called through the door.

From inside: "Go away, I'm not home."

"This is Dr. St. Clair, Mr. Witherspoon. I was here last week. Remember?"

"Sorry," the muffled voice continued. "I wasn't home last week, either."

St. Clair sighed with infinite patience and leaned against the door. "Mr. Witherspoon, I could legally force you to open this door to me. Is that what you want?"

A moment passed, followed by the click and rattle of locks being unlocked and bolts being thrown on the other side of the door. It cracked open just enough for Edgar to peer through, the by-now familiar whirr-click-whirr-*sproing* filtering through the opening past him. "Back one foot," Edgar said.

St. Clair stepped back the suggested distance.

Moving quickly, careful to keep himself between St. Clair and a clear view of the room beyond, Edgar slipped out, hurriedly shutting the door behind him. "You're a curious one."

" 'Odd,' you mean?"

"I mean nosy."

"I'm paid to be nosy," St. Clair said, then caught himself. "That is, curious."

"Really? Don't you find that odd? Most people are curious for nothing. That's very nice for you. Are the hours good?"

St. Clair smiled. He would not let his purpose be distracted again. "Mr. Witherspoon, why do you collect dolls' heads and shoes and paper clips?"

"Because I can't afford Rembrandts," Edgar said, as though it were the most obvious reason in the world. He seemed about to go on when he abruptly stiffened. He glanced up toward the ceiling, a look of sudden dismay crossing his features. "What?" he said.

Edgar paused, as though listening to a response in the silent room. "Oh, no," he said, and turned his attention back to St. Clair. "As usual, it's been lovely. Please don't call again."

He turned to rabbit-back into his apartment. Having seen this routine before, St. Clair moved quickly, sticking his arm out and blocking the door before it could slam shut in his face again.

"I'll have to come back," he said. "And next time it might not be so lovely. Do you understand me, Mr. Witherspoon? Wouldn't you rather invite me in of your own free will?"

Edgar glanced at his watch, fidgeting with anxiety and a sense of urgency. "So you're saying you won't go away?"

"No."

Edgar nodded, and seemed to sag a little. "All right," he said. "If you must, you must."

He pulled the door open and allowed St. Clair to step through. "But be very, *very* careful where you walk!"

WHIRR!-CLICK!-WHIRR!-*SPROING!*

It was much louder in here, St. Clair decided, as his eyes adjusted to the dim light inside.

Then he saw it and instantly understood the warning.

There were only a few sticks of furniture, an oven, and a sink shoved against one wall. The rest of the apartment was filled by—*it:*

A nightmare construct made up of springs, inner tubes, old shoes, paper clips, yo-yos, balls of string, aluminum foil, TV antennas, clocks by the barrel (only a few of which seemed to be working), old newspapers, toys, tops, radiator parts, cogs, clogs, baby bottles, steam pipes, suspenders, pendulums, rocks and putty and Christmas tree lights and on and on and on, all strung together with string and springs and chicken wire and bits of metal, all moving, all whirring and clicking and going *sproing* in a thoroughly mad junkman's ballet.

St. Clair gradually realized that his jaw was hanging open.

Building something this complex must have taken years, *years!*

He searched for Edgar amid the noise and movement and crying dolls' heads and plastic butterflies, and finally found him making his way carefully to the back of the construct, where he poured water from a copper tea kettle into a pair of teacups balanced precariously on a tennis racket. The racket shifted as the two cups came more closely into balance, and the *sproinging* moved up the spectrum, sounding almost like a guitar being tuned into a frequency that only dogs could hear.

Measuring out the final drop with incredible precision, Edgar stepped back and smiled with relief across the construct. "Phew. That was a close one."

St. Clair took a tentative step forward, careful not to step on anything that might be moving. "Very . . . interesting, Mr. Witherspoon," he said, nodding. "What is it?"

Though he would not have thought it possible, it seemed Edgar smiled even more broadly, stood a little straighter, and when he spoke, it was with the pride of accomplishment. "This," Edgar said, *"this* is the only thing that keeps the world from going POOF!"

St. Clair nodded.

It occurred to him after a while that he had been nodding for a long time without saying anything, and he supposed that it would be a good idea if he did. "Let me understand you, Mr. Witherspoon. You say that this—" *This what?* Never mind, he decided. It didn't matter. "That *this* is what keeps the world from going . . . poof?"

Edgar set down the tea kettle and brushed his hands off on his pants. "And it's not easy. Some things are nearly impossible to find. Where would *you* look for a skate key these days?"

"I can't imagine."

"I found one though," Edgar said proudly. "You think that's crazy?"

"Well—"

Edgar looked straight into his eyes, suddenly attentive. "You wouldn't by any chance have a business card, would you?"

At last, a statement he could deal with. "Yes, of course," St. Clair said. He reached into his vest pocket and produced a crisply printed card, handing it across to Edgar.

"Thanks," Edgar said, and with tremendous care and deliberateness, placed it on a string that ran through the construct, pulled by a tiny motor somewhere inside. St. Clair watched his card disappear into the belly of the construct.

"That was an easy one," Edgar said, and moved back around the construct, prodding and poking and adjusting as he spoke.

"I used to be an engineer," he continued. "Earned lots of money. Then I retired. Worst mistake I ever made. Life was so damned boring! And then one day the Voice spoke to me."

"Oh? You also hear voices?"

Edgar perked up. "You too?"

"No, I'm . . . afraid not. Can you tell me about the voice, Mr. Witherspoon?"

"Well, it was a Sunday, and I was on a park bench feeding the pigeons. Then, suddenly, there it was. The Voice. 'Edgar,' it said, 'have you ever been to England?'

"I said no, of course not, and that any decent, self-respecting Voice talking in my head should know that. I think that must've annoyed it, because it didn't say anything for a minute. Then it went on.

" 'Edgar,' it said, 'in the heart of Big Ben there is a pendulum that tells the clock how fast to tick. At the bottom of that pendulum, on top of the big weight, is a stack of pennies. Every so often they take one penny off. The clock speeds up. Or they put one on. The clock slows down. The pennies change the balance just a little, but enough to keep the whole mechanism running perfectly.' "

St. Clair nodded, surveying the construct. "Then what you have here is some kind of clock?"

"Of course not. Why would I build a clock?" He tapped the digital watch on his wrist. "Three dollars. Any drugstore. Doesn't lose ten seconds in a year. Anyway, the Voice said, 'Edgar, the world's a funny place. Little wars here, big wars there, volcanoes going off, storms, tornadoes, a terrific amount of noise and bother. You have to build something that will keep the world from going too far, maybe even going poof.' "

Edgar indicated the mechanism whirring and clicking around them with a sweep of his arms. "What the pennies do for Big Ben, *this* does for the world."

"Ah," St. Clair said, quietly wishing he had brought his tape recorder along. "Tell me, Mr. Witherspoon, do you believe it is God talking to you?"

Edgar shrugged. "Sometimes, I think it's God. Then I think, no, God would have a much deeper voice. Would you care for a prune, Doctor?"

"No, thank you," St. Clair said, and started for the door. "I'm just leaving."

Edgar followed close at his heels, talking faster now. "I have no idea how the thing works. All I know is that the Voice tells me what it needs, where it's supposed to fit, and I get it."

At the door, St. Clair turned to look back at Edgar, and saw there a nervousness that had not been present earlier. For a moment, Edgar seemed less the eccentric and more just a lonely old man, frightened and very much alone in his beliefs. He felt a moment of compassion for him and summoned up a sympathetic smile. "Good-bye, Mr. Witherspoon. Keep up the good work."

He stepped out into the storage room.

Edgar followed as far as the doorway. "We could call it a sculpture," he said. "Would that make my niece happy?"

St. Clair continued walking.

Then, suddenly, Edgar glanced back up at the ceiling. "What? Oh, no."

The last thing St. Clair heard as he stepped out of the storage room and into the daylight beyond was Edgar's voice, calling out to him. "If you happen to see an old tuba, could you bring it around? I need it by five o'clock."

Slam!

It took only a few hours to sign all the right papers, call all the right people, and arrange for a seventy-two-hour observation period at the hospital. One of those calls was to an intern St. Clair knew. A very large and very strong intern.

He suspected that Edgar would not go easily, or quietly.

He was right on both counts.

"Don't let them do this to me, Cynthia," Edgar said, as the intern maneuvered him as gently as possible out from behind the construct. His niece hovered near St. Clair, fighting tears.

"Please, Uncle Edgar," she said, "don't fight them It's only for three days."

"That's too long! Don't you understand? It has to be maintained, kept in balance! I have to be here!"

"Mr. Witherspoon, you hear voices," St. Clair said. "That isn't normal. Even you must realize that."

"You hear voices, don't you?" Edgar said, struggling with the intern. "You hear me, right?"

"Yes."

"So what's the difference between a sane man hearing a crazy voice, and a crazy man hearing a sane voice? I think Truth is somewhere in the middle."

That one stopped even the intern.

But only for a moment.

Finally getting a good grip on Edgar, the intern hustled him toward the door, past the last edge of the construct. "You don't understand what you're risking!" Edgar said, struggling to break free.

The intern moved to catch his arm, and off-balance,

slipped backward, knocking into the front of the construct. A bicycle chain and two yo-yos clattered to the floor.

"I knew it!" Edgar said, panic in his voice. "There goes Tatoa!"

His grip restored, the intern hustled Edgar out of the room and up the basement stairs.

"Tatoa?" St. Clair said.

"A tiny island in the South Pacific!" Edgar called back at them. "What's the time?"

Cynthia glanced automatically at her watch. "Three-seventeen."

"At three-seventeen in the afternoon, Tatoa became history. And it's all because of you!"

Edgar tried one last time to lunge back—whether for St. Clair or the safety of his room, the doctor could not determine—before being hauled up the stairs past Mrs. Milligan.

"A case of classic psychosis," St. Clair said quietly to Cynthia. "Retired, feeling useless, he created a typical delusion of grandeur—that he was vital to the world's survival."

Mrs. Milligan looked past them and into the apartment, shaking her head. "Will you look at this! It'll take me days to clean out this junk!"

And as the intern hustled Edgar into the waiting ambulance, he was still shouting. "Keep her away from it!" he said, pointing at Mrs. Milligan. "Remember Tatoa! Remember Tatoa!"

Then the ambulance pulled away, and Edgar's voice faded into the distance.

Mahler, St. Clair decided, listening to the radio as he finished his recommendations for the examining psychologist who'd been assigned to handle Witherspoon. The music filtering through the office was definitely Mahler, but he couldn't quite put his finger on which piece.

After a moment, and a final poignant crescendo, the music subsided. But instead of the usual announcer, the voice of the station's newscaster came on. St. Clair frowned. They must have announced the title prior to playing it, and he'd just missed it.

He reached for the radio to turn down the volume, then decided to wait just long enough to hear the headlines that were always given at the top of the hour.

"Coming up: Mideast stalemate continues. New hostages taken in Paris siege. Congress passes transportation act. And in the South Pacific, the tiny island of Tatoa is destroyed by a tidal wave. Details on this and all the news in sixty seconds."

St. Clair stared at the radio.

Tatoa?

He couldn't have said Tatoa.

Could he?

Deciding that sixty seconds was too long to wait—and it would probably be late in the broadcast anyway—St. Clair reached for the phone and dialed information for the number of the *Herald Chronicle*.

The phone rang six times before someone at the editorial desk answered. "Yes, hello," he said, "I'd like to check out a news story. I just heard something on the radio about an island being destroyed by a tidal wave."

"Tatoa," the voice at the other end confirmed.

"Yes, that's it. Are there any details yet?"

St. Clair listened as a tableau of utter destruction was painted in words at the other end of the phone. "Would've been a lot worse if it'd been one of the bigger islands. As it was, the place had a population of about a thousand, so it's still pretty grim."

"Do you know when the tidal wave hit? I mean, exactly what time?"

Papers shuffled at the other end of the phone. "Three-seventeen, on the button."

St. Clair nodded for what felt like a long time. "Thank you," he said at last, and let the phone slip from his hand into the cradle.

Tatoa.

Three-seventeen.

"Miss Bigelow!"

His secretary appeared at the office door. "Yes, Doctor?"

"Miss Bigelow, Tatoa was destroyed at three-seventeen this afternoon!"

She considered this, then shrugged. "Is that bad?"

He stood, coming around the desk. "And last week there was an earthquake in Santa Barbara! We can't afford to take any chances. We've got to—"

Then he remembered.

Mrs. Milligan.

The floor seemed to tilt under him with the realization. "Omigod. The landlady. She's going to destroy it!"

"Santa Barbara?"

"No, it's—look, never mind. Just call admissions, right now. Have them release Mr. Witherspoon immediately, on my authority! Then drive him home! You. *Personally.* As fast as you can!"

He rushed past her, paying no attention to the puzzled expression on her face. He had to move fast. He had to get to the apartment before Mrs. Milligan began cleaning.

The traffic was infuriatingly, maddeningly slow.

Finally, he pulled up in front of the apartment building and rushed out of the car toward the basement steps. He hit the bottom just in time to see Mrs. Milligan inside the room, aiming a broom at the construct as though it were a spider web she was about to smash into oblivion.

"Stop!" he yelled, breathless. "Don't touch a thing!"

She turned to him, broom still in hand. "Doctor?"

He surveyed the room nervously. "You didn't, did you? Touch anything? Move anything? *Remove* anything?"

"Not yet. Why?"

Why, indeed? he thought, and thought faster. "Because—because this is the creation of a disordered mind. By analyzing this—exactly as he left it—I can get a deeper insight into Mr. Witherspoon's problem."

She looked at her feet, thinking this over. Then shook her head. "He's a loony. What else do you have to know?"

She raised the broom for a tactical strike on the construct.

"No!" he said, and grabbed the broom. She backed up, startled. "Please," he said, more softly this time, "you have to understand, it's not that simple."

"But I can't rent this place with garbage in it."

"Then I'll rent it."

She studied his face. "You?"

"Absolutely. To preserve it for study. Is that all right?"

"Well, I suppose so. . . ."

"Excellent," he said, and hustled her toward the door. "I'll be up later with a check."

Before she could say anything else, he closed the door, then leaned up against it, aware now of just how fast his heart was beating. *That should take care of her for now,* he thought.

Then she pushed open the door from the other side. "He's escaped!" she said, and shrank back as Edgar whizzed past her into the room. "Should I call the cops?"

"No, I don't think that'll be necessary," St. Clair said. "Everything's just fine. I'll see you in a minute."

He closed the door again and glanced to where Edgar was picking his way through the construct to the other side. He couldn't see what Edgar was doing, only that he was working at something in his closet.

"Mr. Witherspoon," St. Clair said, approaching, "I don't know how to begin to apologize. Nothing in my training has prepared me for a case like yours."

"I'm sure," Edgar said, and turned toward the construct. He frowned. "You got a handkerchief?"

"A handkerchief? Yes," St. Clair said, frantically digging a silk handkerchief out of his jacket pocket, "here!"

"Thanks," Edgar said, then blew his nose into the handkerchief and stuffed it into his pocket. "That woman at the hospital had me dress so fast I left mine behind."

That done, he turned back to the closet, and now St. Clair could see what he was working on. A suitcase.

Why was he packing a suitcase?

"Well, it's been nice meeting you," Edgar said, taking the suitcase and picking his way through the construct toward the door.

"Wait a minute—where are you going?"

"Away. Finally. After eleven years."

"But what about all this? What about—poof?"

Edgar smiled. "The Voice spoke to me while I was in your hospital. It said, 'Edgar, you ever been to Miami?'

" 'No,' I said, 'but I always thought it would be a nice place to retire.'

" 'Then go for it,' the Voice said, 'you're off duty.' "

"That's it?" St. Clair said, looking around at all the bits and pieces rotating and beeping and whirring around him. "You mean all this isn't necessary anymore?"

"Sure it is. It's absolutely essential. The world still has to be kept in balance."

"But then who's going to—"

Suddenly, behind him, a spring that was supposed to go *spring* went *sproing*.

The tennis racket was leaning ten degrees to starboard.

"There!" St. Clair said. "You see! It already needs adjusting!"

Snatching up the tea kettle, St. Clair picked his way through the maze of moving bits and pieces, pouring water into the two cups until they balanced perfectly on the tennis racket.

"Got it," St. Clair said, nodding. "Now if I can just get a Ping-Pong ball in there by seven-thirteen—"

He stopped.

A Ping-Pong ball.

He knew exactly what it needed.

He knew when he had to have it by.

And without trying, he knew exactly where it should go.

He looked up to see Edgar Witherspoon smiling at him.

"Well, I guess we've solved *that* little problem," Edgar said, and glanced at his watch. "Six-thirty. I'd get crackin' if I was you."

"No! I refuse!"

"Now, don't panic," Edgar said, "you'll get used to it after a while. Really." He stood in the doorway and slipped on a fishing cap. "So long, Dr. St. Clair. Don't take any wooden nickels." Then, almost as an after-thought, he added, "Unless you really need 'em, of course."

Slam!

"Mr. Witherspoon! *Mr. Witherspoon!*" He rushed toward the closed door, but the old man was already gone.

Whirr-click-whirr-*sproing.*

Whirr-click-whirr-*sproinggggggggg.*

Dr. St. Clair closed the door, and shut his eyes, and tried mightily to ignore the sudden, insisting voice in the back of his head that was telling him he needed to get a tambourine by 9:42 or they'd lose Detroit.

They didn't understand.

None of them understood.

He ran from one door to another down the long hallway in the apartment building.

"Excuse me, do you have a ballpoint pen spring?"

Slam!

"I'm sorry to bother you, but I've got to have a kazoo, please, if you could just check."

Slam!

He checked his watch. He was running out of time.

He would have to go back down to the Dumpster and check it again, just one more time.

Five minutes left.

Then again, would anyone really *miss* Washington, D.C.?

* * *

If in the next few months you notice that there has been a spate of catastrophes, or things are just not going right, remember that Edgar Witherspoon's replacement is learning how to make some very precise adjustments. Don't worry, though—his education will not last long, and then you might give thanks to Dr. James St. Clair, a physician whose practice is limited to the well-being of the entire planet. Dr. St. Clair offers a unique form of preventive medicine found only in—the Twilight Zone.

Introduction to Dream Me a Life

I've rarely had recurring dreams. When they've come, it's usually been in response to stress or over-work. They're almost never alike. But there was one set of recurring dreams that came back twice. And what was singularly unusual about them was what happened in the course of time.

The dream was always the same. I am in a darkened room, lit only by candles. The floor tilts crazily beneath my feet. Over it all is a pounding, fierce and frantic. And there, before me, a door suddenly appears. And something is just outside, trying desperately, frantically, to get in. Fingernails scrabbling against the surface, wood splintering, hinges rocking on their nails. Beside the door is a calendar, the kind where you tear off one page to reveal the next beneath.

The calendar page on the first night of the dream read *ten*.

The next time the dream came, the page read *nine*.

And the door was open a little further.

Next time: *Eight*.

And the door was open still further, enough to get a sense of *presence* beyond it, something massive, frightening, and terrible.

The dream progressed.

Both times, the dreams suddenly halted on *two*. Halted just before I could see what, or who, was on the other side.

The first time it happened, I was mugged and nearly beaten to death on the night that would have been one on the calendar.

The second time it happened, my grandmother died on the night that would have been one on the calendar.

Both incidents rocked me to my insteps, and though the dreams haven't returned since then—not in ten years—I dreaded their return.

Because, you see, I *know* what's behind the door.

When it finally came time to translate that dream into a story, I decided to take a different approach, using the dream as a springboard into, oddly, a more positive story. But no matter how I tried, I couldn't seem to come up with the right angle. I labored at it day and night, and still it eluded me. The problem, I realized, was that I knew what was behind *my* door—but what was behind Laurel Kincaid's door? It took my wife Kathryn to prod me and poke me into confronting some of my own losses, some of the people and relationships that I had lost to the darkness over the years, until I finally was able to answer the question.

It was a revelation, and a final scene, that had me crying behind the keyboard. It had a similar effect on just about everyone who read the script, or saw the episode.

But the story doesn't end there.

Eddie Albert was cast in the role of Roger Simpson Leeds, a particularly poignant choice because, like Roger, Albert's wife had passed away a few years previously. He loved her very much and wanted to make the role a testimony to her memory. At times, according to the director, the role became very hard for him.

There were many things he didn't want to face. The director eased him through it and brought the pain out to the surface where Albert could deal with it.

The performance was a moving one and gave the story a deeper context than most people would ever know was there.

One other positive result came out of the episode.

I think that the very act of writing this story has forever closed the door to that room. It's hard to put it into words, but I don't think the dreams will be coming back again.

That, at least, is my hope.

Which, along with the permanence of love, is what this story is all about.

"Dream Me a Life," production #87003, went into production on May 23, 1988, and was first broadcast on October 16, 1988. It starred Eddie Albert (Roger Simpson Leeds), Barry Morse (Frank), Frances Hyland (Laurel), Joseph Shaw (Husband), Michelyn Emelle (Nurse), Jack Mather (Boarder #1), and Warren Van Evera (Boarder #2). Allan King was the director.

DREAM ME A LIFE

Roger Simpson Leeds didn't belong here. Everything about the room was wrong. The walls bled out into infinite midnight. Angles refused to meet at conventional places. He blinked, but his eyes were unable to focus on anything, his gaze sliding off walls and chairs and bed as though they were pushing it away, refusing his attempt to bring them into clarity.

And everywhere, for as far as he could see, there were candles, candles on the walls and on the floor and ascending candelabra like glowing steps; candles surrounding framed pictures on the wall, creating brilliant islands amid the overwhelming darkness. And in the middle of those islands, a face, the same face, over and over. . . .

He didn't belong here.

He stumbled as the shadows were split by a sudden shaft of brilliant light from somewhere straight ahead. With it came a wind that chilled him to his marrow. He thrust up one hand, futilely squinting against the brilliance, and in that light he saw her. Again.

I don't belong here.

She spotted him, as she always did, and cried out, a mournful sound born of pain and fear and desperation. "Please," she cried, arms outstretched, "You've got to help me!" She was old, trembling with fear, the lines in her face deepened by the glare from behind, her long grey hair whipped by the furious wind. In her eyes was a fear that seemed almost palpable.

She rushed to his side, clutching at his hands, his arms, trying to draw him toward the source of the terror. "You've got to stop him! If he gets through, I'll die!"

"No," Roger said, and pulled away from her. He didn't want to look, didn't want to know the reason for her terror, but as he lunged away from her, he saw it: a door, the source of the blinding light, held partly closed only by a fragile chain-lock. The door bounced furiously against the chain as someone or something pounded on the other side. Light and wind roared through the narrow gap that had been forced in the doorway. The pounding grew louder, ear-shattering, like invisible cannonballs slamming into the wood, splintering it, a rhythmic sound punctuated by a scrabbling and a scraping and a scratching from the other side.

Somehow the door was holding, but it wouldn't, not for long.

The old woman tugged at him again, frantically trying to draw him toward the door. "You've got to do something!" she screamed over the noise. "Please! Don't you understand? If he gets through, I'll die! *I'll die!*"

"Let me go!" Roger cried. He pulled away, back toward the darkness, back where it was safe. "Get away from me! Leave me alone! I don't want to be here! LEAVE ME ALONE!"

She screamed.

And then the room was silent.

But it wasn't her room any longer.

It was his room. Silent except for his labored breathing as he sat up, forcing his legs out of bed and onto the floor. He stood, unsteadily, and leaned against the nightstand, fighting down the panic and the fear, fighting to slow his heartbeat to less than trip-hammer pace. He staggered to the window and looked out onto the darkened backyard, wiping at his face with the back of his hand.

Again, he thought. *God help me, I don't know how much more of this I can stand.*

"Please, God," he whispered, "make it stop."

* * *

Portrait of a man having a bad dream. His name: Roger Simpson Leeds. Place of residence: a retirement home. Roger Simpson Leeds, who since the death of his wife three years ago has dedicated himself to living a life in which he touches no one, and no one touches him. But now contact has been made, and Mr. Leeds is about to find himself touched—by the Twilight Zone.

"Get anything interesting?"

Roger poked through the mailbox, finding the usual assortment of bills and advertisements and envelopes addressed only to OCCUPANT. He tore them up and walked back toward the front porch of the retirement home. Down the street a bunch of kids were playing touch football. Loudly. Frank Weatherby stayed at his elbow, following him back inside. As always. And just about as loudly.

"Shall I take that as a no?" Frank asked.

"You may." He'd known Frank for twenty years, and now at seventy, two years older than Roger was, Frank seemed to have decided to adopt him. Sometimes he wondered why. And sometimes he wondered if Frank wondered why.

Oblivious to his indifference, Frank paged through the letters in his hand. "Got a postcard from my sister in Detroit. Ruth. You met her, must've been around Christmas, seventy-nine. She says hello, asks if your mood has improved any."

"Hmm."

"Hmm. Good. Eminently quotable. So how's with that son of yours, and the kids?"

"Fine, I suppose."

"You suppose? I thought they were coming up to visit this weekend."

Roger shrugged. Some days he suspected that Frank had a little radar dish in his head, some sort of souped-up range finder that enabled him to know with unfailing accuracy when Roger most wanted to be left alone . . . and instinctively to do the opposite. "Yeah, well, I told them I just—you know how it is, Frank. I don't have time for a bunch of kids running around all over the place."

"Of course not," Frank said, nodding. "What with the photographers, the mad social whirl, the state dinners—why, it just doesn't leave *time* for anything else. I'm sure they understand. And speaking of which, how *are* Charles and Di these days? They seemed, I don't know, crabby the last time they stopped by."

"You're an evil man," Roger said, moving through the sun-flecked porch and into the cool front room. Someone was watching television, an old sitcom by the sound of it. He supposed eventually he'd have to start learning some names around here. "You're evil from toe to follicle. Have I ever told you that?"

"Frequently, and with great enthusiasm. But then, I'm not the one with the nightmares."

Roger stopped, turned toward him. "You're prying again, Frank. I told you if you did that again, I'd have to hire somebody to hurt you."

"I wasn't prying. I just overheard one of the nurses talking about it a little while ago. They said they heard you again last night. That's three times this week, Roger."

A reply started in Roger's throat, but he bit it off before it hit the air. What could he say? *Sorry I've been waking everybody up lately, but there's this woman who keeps appearing in my dreams, and she's scared, and she says she'll die if I don't help her keep some door shut, and I really don't want to deal with this, or you, or anyone else at the moment?*

He said nothing. Only shook his head and started up the stairs, toward his room.

Frank followed as far as the bottom step. "We're meeting in the rec room at seven for poker."

"Pass."

"I can hold a place for you—"

Roger stopped at the second-floor landing and peered back down at Frank in a way he hoped would be intimidating. Frank looked so small down there, except for the big, hopeful smile he seemed to wear all the time. He hated it when Frank forced him to be harsh. "Frank—the answer is no. You want it any clearer than that, go ask one of the nurses. They seem to know everything around here."

"All right," Frank said, and after a moment, when it seemed safe to assume that the conversation was indeed over, Roger continued on toward his room.

"By the way," Frank called up the stairs, "I hear you're getting a new neighbor. Someone's finally taken that room next to yours."

"As long as he doesn't snore."

Roger wasn't sure—his hearing wasn't what it used to be—but he was reasonably confident he heard Frank mutter, "Who said it was a he?" before heading back into the television room.

Roger hit the top of the stairs and crossed to the closed door to his room, fumbling with his keys as he went. He'd long ago forgotten what most of them were for, but was loathe to throw any of them away, knowing full well that he'd discover he needed them within twenty-four hours.

Someone behind him called, "Good morning, Mr. Leeds."

Roger turned, nodded perfunctorily toward the nurse—and froze at the sight of the elderly woman being wheeled ahead of her down the hall, toward him: grey hair, pulled back so tight he thought it might scream. Eyes vacant, unfocused, fixed on the private domain of her own thoughts. Hands clasped tightly in her lap.

She was silent, seemed not even to note his existence. But in his mind, Roger saw her as he had the night before, in his dream, clutching at him, screaming into his ear. . . .

The nurse smiled at him as she wheeled the chair past him. He crowded back against the door, as though with sufficient effort he could melt into it, away from that chair and its terrible, impossible occupant.

The nurse came to the corner and reached across

the chair to open the door to the room next to his. As she maneuvered the chair inside, she glanced back at him. "Well, aren't you going to say hello to our new guest?"

Roger stepped into the television room, knowing even before he arrived that she would be there. But the rec room, and Frank, were on the other side, and there was no other way through. The television was on, as always, and a few others were watching, barely paying attention. The only eyes that never wavered from the screen were *hers.* Her wheelchair had been deposited right in front of the TV, and somehow the effect of canned laughter and those staring, unwavering eyes made his skin go cold.

He walked quickly, glancing down at her as he crossed in front of her chair. Her hands were still clasped tightly together in her lap—so tightly, in fact, that he could see her knuckles whiten from effort. And yet her face remained utterly without expression.

When he reached the rec room, Roger realized he hadn't taken a breath since walking into the other room. Frank was at his usual place at the poker table. He glanced up at Roger and smiled. "Here, pull up a chair," Frank said. "I need another witness—these guys cheat."

The player on his right bristled. *"We* cheat!"

"Good for you," Frank said. "It takes a big man to admit a thing like that." He motioned for another player to continue dealing. "So what do you say, Roger? Sit in on a hand or two?"

"No, I—don't think so."

The other boarder snorted. "Told you," he said.

"So who asked you?" Frank said, and checked the hand he'd been dealt. "Give me two."

"Frank," Roger said, trying to sound casual, "who is that?" He pointed back into the television room. They could just see the wheelchair from where they sat.

Frank glanced up over the rim of his glasses, then went back to his cards. "How should I know? I get my information from nurses." He dropped his cards. "Fold."

"Frank—"

"Okay, okay." He lit a cigarette, sat back in his chair. "Her name's Laurel Kincaid. Word is she hasn't talked to anyone in ten years, ever since her husband died." He shook his head. "She went—*away*. You look in her eyes, all you see is a reflection. Nothing goes in."

"What else?"

"That's it. What do I look like, an encyclopedia? Look, you sure you don't want to sit in on a hand?"

"Positive," Roger said, barely paying attention. "Thanks."

Almost immediately afterward, he wondered if he shouldn't have accepted Frank's offer after all. His business finished, he had no reason now to hang around in the rec room.

But leaving meant walking past Laurel Kincaid again.

What the hell, he thought. *What's she going to do? Bite me?*

Very possibly, he thought, and pushed away the thought as he headed out of the rec room.

"Roger? You okay?"

Roger looked up to see Frank standing in the doorway of the reading room. It was late. He was sitting in his favorite spot, on the winged chair beside the window, trying not to think about sleep. "I'm fine," he said, quietly. The room didn't seem to appreciate noise.

"Surprised you're not asleep," Frank said, glancing at his watch. "You're usually upstairs by ten—"

Roger looked away. "I don't feel much like sleeping."

"You want to talk about it?"

"No, I don't. Look, Frank, why don't you just go away and leave me alone?"

"Because I'm your friend, damn it!" He stepped into the room, came toward him. "We used to *talk,* remember? Twenty *years*, Roger, that should count for something."

Roger said nothing, only stared out the window into the darkness just beyond the frosted glass. He was tired. So completely, bone tired. But he couldn't sleep. Couldn't *let* himself sleep.

Frank sat in the chair next to him, and after a moment he leaned forward, tried to catch Roger's eye. "Nothing's been the same, has it? Not since—" He hesitated, then drew himself up in his chair. "Roger," he said finally, "it's been three years."

"No," Roger said. "It was yesterday." There was no question what Frank was referring to. *Why wouldn't he let it go? Why wouldn't he let him alone?*

It was all so stupid, so—wrong.

"You know," Roger said, and smiled faintly at the memory, "I was thinking the other day about her. We never could get it straight between us, jam or jelly. I'd say, 'Pass me the jam, please,' and she'd say, 'Here's the jelly, dear.' It was a game, I guess. Then one day I was in a bad mood, I guess, and we got into an argument about it. Can you believe it? The stupid, petty little things people argue about—"

He looked away, his eyes burning, moist. *So stupid. So wrong.* "God, Frank, I miss her so much."

"I know. Rachel was a fine woman. But you can't keep pushing everyone away."

Roger turned to gaze back out the window. "I never knew how much I needed her until she was gone. Just—gone. When I had my first heart attack, she held my hand. She said she wouldn't let go, no matter what happened, as long as I held on. She held my hand in the ambulance, and in the emergency room, and she never let go. I think she would've held on till the end of the world if she had to."

He wiped at his face with the back of his hand. "She believed in me, Frank. When I looked in those eyes, all I saw was love. I felt like I could do *anything*. Because she believed in me." He shook his head. "I wonder—I wonder what she would think of me now."

"Why? What's happening now? Come on, Roger— talk to me."

Roger looked at him, but in his thoughts he saw only that closed, dark room, no way in, no way out, heard only that terrible pounding behind the door, that voice, *Help me, please, if he gets through, I'll die!*

"No. You'd think I was crazy. I'm halfway convinced myself."

Frank briefly looked as though he might push the subject. But he didn't. He only clasped his hands and, leaning forward, smiled a little ruefully. "My old father, he never said much of anything useful. But he did tell me two things. First, love never dies. And second, that we're never given anything we can't handle."

"You don't know the situation."

"No, I don't. But I know you. And I knew Rachel. And you don't have anything to be ashamed of."

Roger shrugged, not knowing what else to do, awkward as he always was when he talked to Frank like this. He checked his watch. "It's getting late."

"Roger, I—"

"Look, Frank, I'll be okay," Roger said, cutting him off. "Don't worry, all right? You know how I hate it when you make a fuss."

He walked toward the door, and Frank followed him out. "All right," Frank said. "But if you change your mind, if you need me, you know where to find me."

They stopped beside the stairwell. "You know," Frank said, "this is the longest we've talked in almost a year. I think we should do it more often."

"Good night, Frank," Roger said, hoping it sounded final.

"Good night," Frank said, and headed off toward the TV room.

Roger took a step up the stairs—and hesitated.

She was up there, somewhere, in the room next door to his.

I don't want to sleep, he thought. But the fatigue in his bones told him otherwise. He continued up the stairs, pausing only to glance in the partially open door to her room. Laurel Kincaid slept quietly. Her room was spare, the only obvious decoration a photograph on her bedside table. A man, his hair almost gone, his face weathered by the years. It was, Roger decided, a pleasant enough face. And there was something passingly familiar about it—

Go to bed, he thought, and turned away. Maybe it wouldn't happen this time. Maybe tonight the dream wouldn't come.

He hoped so. He didn't know how much more of this he could take before losing his mind.

"Whoever you are—please—you've got to help me! If he gets through, I'll die! You've *got* to *do* something! *Please!*"

Roger squeezed his eyes shut. It was the same. Starting all over again.

She snatched at his arm, and he pulled back. "I can't help you. Don't you understand? I don't want to be here, I don't even know what I'm *doing* here!"

"Please—"

She reached for him again, more insistently than before, and caught his wrist.

"I said *no!* Leave me *alone!*"

He ripped out of her grip with such force that he fell backwards, toward a table strewn with photos and candles. He twisted around, reaching out, trying to break his fall. Glass scattered and crashed soundlessly to the floor. His hand brushed against a lit candle, and he smelled burnt flesh, felt a searing pain lance up from the palm of his hand. He cried out in agony—

And found the cry still on his lips as he sat up in bed, head throbbing with the sight of that other place.

Then like a sudden tide there came the other pain, spiraling up from his palm, and the smell of singed flesh. Trembling, hardly even aware now of the nurses knocking at the door, drawn by his cry, he switched on the bedside lamp.

A black smear, like soot, marked the burn that was already blistering in his palm.

"Dear God," Roger whispered, "dear sweet God."

Bright sunlight flooded the dining room, accompanied by the clatter of dishes and the chatter of voices, and Roger wondered why, why on *earth* they all seemed incapable of eating their breakfasts quietly. Couldn't they see he hadn't slept? Couldn't they see he was dying inside?

No, he thought. They couldn't. Which, on balance, was probably all for the best.

He shifted the fork to his left hand, the one that wasn't bandaged. He was right-handed, but could only bear the discomfort of holding the fork for a few minutes in that hand before turning it over.

He looked up as a nurse stepped up to his table. "How's the hand?"

"Better."

She nodded. "Good. And I'm sure we won't have a problem like that in the future, but I did want to remind you again that we have very strict policies concerning smoking in bed."

Roger put down his fork, letting it clatter loudly on his plate. "If you'll read your chart you'll see I don't smoke. It just—it was an accident, all right? Now, is there some other rule I should be aware of?"

Her expression didn't so much as flicker. "No, Mr. Leeds, that will be quite sufficient. As long as you *are* aware of our policies. I'll check on the dressing later."

She walked away. Roger watched her as she stepped out of the dining room just as another nurse wheeled in Laurel.

He went back to his eggs, hoping the nurse would continue to wheel her through the dining room and out onto the patio behind the house, hoping that perhaps she had already been fed, hoping not to have to look into those vacant eyes one more time.

The patio door rattled shut behind him. She was

gone. He let out a long, slow breath, and realized that his hands were trembling.

"Roger! Have you been outside yet?" Frank came over to his table, rubbing his hands and looking flushed. "It's glorious. After breakfast, what do you say we go for a walk, get a little sun, hmm? You know you're awfully pale these days, you could use some sun."

Roger tried to wave him away. "No, I—"

"Say, what happened to your hand?"

Roger tried to tuck it away, under the table. "Nothing."

"Oh, no. Nothing I can't see. *This* I can see. Therefore this is something. I've been reading Socrates again. You can tell, can't you?"

Roger slammed his fist into the table, bolted up out of his chair. "Jesus, Frank—can't you ever *shut up?*"

He charged past Frank, not knowing, not caring where he was going until he realized he was outside.

Where she was. Sitting in her chair in the shade of a eucalyptus tree, next to the shuffleboard court. Not moving. Staring, but not seeing.

He started to turn away, to go back inside, but stopped at the memory of his outburst. Frank would be hurt. He'd find a way to make it up, later, but now was not the right time. He looked back at Laurel, and hesitated.

I've got to do something, he thought, *anything, or I'm going to go mad.*

Pulling his feet as though they were held in concrete, he forced himself to walk across the patio and sit in the chair facing her. He looked into her vacant eyes, and for a moment said nothing, not knowing how to begin.

How else? he thought.

"Hello. My name—my name's Roger. I think we've met."

Nothing.

"I don't mean to bother you, but it's just that—I'd like some answers. I need to know . . . am I losing my mind? That *is* you, isn't it? In my dreams. Even before you got here, even before I saw you—you were there, weren't you?"

Nothing.

"Look, you must be able to hear me. You picked me —called me—somehow. What I can't figure is, why me? They tell me you haven't talked to anyone since your husband died. So what do you want from *me*? You want me to protect you from that—thing behind the door, whatever it is? Is that it? Because if it is, then you'll have to find someone else. There's nothing I can do for you, Mrs. Kincaid. I can't protect you. Hell, I couldn't even protect my own wife, when she—"

Oh God, he thought, and stopped. The familiar pain lanced through his heart. He stood, walked around the chair, trying to throw it off, trying not to deal with it. He couldn't deal with it, not yet. Better to remember the other moments.

"She was a good woman. Kind, decent—she took in every stray cat on the block. You would've liked her. Hell, everyone did. And Sundays, when the kids would come over—"

The kids.

How long had it been?

His mind turned away again, but this time there was nothing else to focus on, nothing but the one thing he wanted most to avoid. He sat back in the chair, suddenly feeling old, so very old. It still hurt. God, how it hurt.

He began slowly.

"Toward the end, she started to—we were in the hospital, and she could barely see, and oh God, she was in such pain, and she kept calling out for me, and I was right there but she couldn't *see* me and she kept pleading with me, please, God, stop the pain, help me, calling my name over and over, and *I couldn't do anything!* I just—held her hand and I said I wouldn't let go. Just like she did. But then I felt her hand tighten once, on mine —and that was all.

"God help me, I'm still not sure she even knew I was there."

He reached for a handkerchief to wipe at his face. The woman opposite him was unmoved. She stared ahead as though he weren't even there.

Just like Rachel, he thought, and his cheeks flushed hotly. This wasn't fair. This wasn't right. Why was she *doing* this to him?

To hell with her, he thought, with a flash of anger. To hell with her for making him feel that pain all over again, feel this useless and old and impotent.

"Mrs. Kincaid, that thing, behind the door, whoever, whatever it is—it's going to come through soon, isn't it? Look, I don't know what you're afraid of, but it's not my problem. I just want everyone to leave me alone. Get out of my head! *Leave me alone!*"

He stood, knocking the chair backward, and fled from the patio, away from those terrible, vacant eyes, not looking back, but knowing she was still staring, staring, staring. . . .

Leave me alone!

The television was no help.

Roger stared at the screen through slitted lids. He'd found the old black-and-white in his closet and had propped it up on the dresser, where he could watch it from his bed. Carson had come and gone, as had the repeat broadcast of the local news. He'd switched around until finally finding an old Rock Hudson movie whose name he couldn't remember, and he felt too tired to get up and check the *TV Guide.*

He rubbed at his face, trying to keep alert. Somehow watching the flickering grey and white and black images seemed to make his eyes even more tired. Since it was so late, he had to keep the volume down, reducing the dialogue to a soft murmur that soothed more than awakened.

I won't go to sleep, he thought, *I won't.* Everything inside him said that tonight was the night when all hell was going to break out with Laurel, and he was determined not to be a part of it.

He palmed his eyes. They were dry and sore. Just a

little longer. Just until daylight. Then he'd be safe. The nurses would come to wake her, and he'd get his sleep then, pleading a cold or bug of some sort or other. The television murmured somewhere far away, outside his closed eyes. Just a little longer—

—and it was cold, and dark, and she was there, screaming at him, "Help me! You've got to help me! If he gets through I'll die! You've got to—"

Roger jerked upright in bed, heart slamming against his ribcage. He'd dropped off. Just for a moment, but it had been enough for her to drag him into her dream. He sat up, letting his feet find the floor. He couldn't risk it happening again.

He found his slippers and robe and stepped out into the hall. The place was quiet. Hoping not to be discovered by the nurses, he made his way downstairs to the kitchen. He chose a clean pan instead of the tea kettle. Less noise.

While the water heated, he spooned out a double dose of instant coffee into a big mug. Warmed his hands over the heating coils. Rubbing his arms to spread the warmth, he wandered into the sitting room. There, across the room, was his favorite chair, and beside it, Frank's chair.

I never knew how much I needed her until she was gone.

The words seemed to linger in the cool night air. He could almost see Frank in his usual place, looking at Roger as he had earlier, full of sadness.

And it was nothing compared to his own.

She kept calling my name over and over, and I couldn't do anything!

There are times I'm afraid, Frank. And I think of her, and I'm ashamed. Ashamed of what she'd think of me.

What indeed? he thought. *What indeed?*

Behind him, from the kitchen, he could hear the water coming to a boil. He padded back to the stove and stared into the churning water for a moment before turning off the heat.

I couldn't do anything!

Not then. No, not then.

He picked up the pan and emptied the water into the sink, returning it to its usual place before switching off the light and heading back up the stairs.

Rachel would want him to do it, he thought, as he closed the door to his room. To try, at least, as he hadn't been able to try for her.

God help me, he thought, then lay down and closed his eyes.

The wind screamed all around him. It clawed at him like a living thing, and she was there, in the middle of it all, clutching at his sleeve, her face desperate, frightened.

"Help me—please—you've got to *do* something!"

Then the light.

And the door.

And the pounding.

Wood splintered, the door bounced frenziedly back and forth on the chain-lock, and over it all, over the noise and the wind, there was her terrified voice.

"Please!"

And the photographs. Everywhere. He could see them in more detail now than before. Some were of Laurel with another man, and some of the man alone. A familiar face.

"You've got to stop him! Please! If he gets through, I'll die! Don't you understand? I'll *die!*"

He charged the door and slammed into it, bracing it with his shoulder. He pushed, pushed for all he was worth, pushed for Rachel and the memory of his helplessness. He shoved with everything he had, and the door went back only the barest fraction of an inch. The pounding now was so loud he thought it would deafen him. He could feel it, feel him, on the other side, pounding the door with cannonball force.

He looked back over his shoulder at Laurel, who hung back, watching through wide eyes. "Help me! Give me a hand!"

Laurel shook her head, stepped back a pace. "I—I can't! Please, you've got to hurry! He's getting through!"

He pushed.

The door pushed back.

The photographs on the wall bounced and swayed with each impact.

Whatever it was, it was powerful. And determined.

"What is it?" he cried back to her. "What's behind here?"

She said nothing. Only watched, as silent as if she were in her wheelchair.

She hasn't talked to anyone since her husband died, Frank had said.

The words reverberated outside his head as well as within. She glanced around furtively, frightened. Could she hear them as well?

The pounding grew louder.

Then his own words, caught in the wind and whirled around him. *You haven't talked to anyone since your husband died.*

She clamped her hands to her ears, closed her eyes. "Shut up!" she cried. "Shut up! SHUT UP!"

He looked back at her, and his grip on the door loosened.

The candles.

The photographs.

The door.

Dear Lord, he thought.

"My God," he said. "You're not keeping someone out, are you? You're—you're *keeping someone in!*"

The wind and sound reached deafening proportions. The pounding at the door became one prolonged hammering.

She looked at him, and Roger thought that he had never seen anything, or anyone, more pitiable. "Please," she said, her voice small and frightened, "if he gets through . . . I'll die!"

"Then pray I'm doing the right thing," Roger said —and let go of the door. He staggered back, seized one of the brass candlesticks, and brought it crashing down on the chain-lock.

"No!" she cried out. "Nooooooo!"

It was suddenly the only sound in the room.

The door stood open. For a moment, there was only a brilliant light, then a form appeared in the doorway, silhouetted against the light.

The man in the photographs.

Without looking at Roger, he stepped across to where Laurel turned away and sat on the bed, not meeting his gaze. He sat beside her. "Laurel—"

"No," she said, her voice tight with pain.

"It's time for me to go."

"No, you can't go. Please—"

"It's been long enough. Too long. You have to let me go. This isn't even me anymore—it's just a shadow, a memory."

"I can't live without you. If you go, I'll die."

"No, Laurel, listen to me. I love you. I want you to go on, I *need* you to go on, so that my life will have meant something. Live, Laurel, for me, for the kids, for what we had, forty beautiful years."

"No," she moaned, but the protest was gone from her voice, leaving only resignation and weariness. She leaned forward, laying her head on his shoulder.

He brushed her hair away from her face. "You were always so strong, you were always there for me. Now I need for you to be strong for me one last time."

She sobbed something into his shoulder, and Roger could see her pain reflected in his eyes. "It's all right," he said, holding her. "It'll be all right. But I need—I need you to let me go, Laurel. Live. Please."

She said nothing for a moment, then sat back a little, still refusing to look into his eyes. "How can I let you go," she said, her lips trembling, "when you never even said good-bye?" She tried to smile, just a little, for him—but it faded as she finally met his gaze.

He ran the back of his fingers along her cheek. "Good-bye, Laurel, my true, my greatest love."

Then he stood, touched her hair, and started to

walk away, toward the darkness just beyond her room. Roger took a step toward him, but stopped. Where he was going, Roger couldn't follow.

"It was you who called me here," Roger said, "not her, wasn't it?" The figure nodded without looking back at him. "Why? Why me?"

He looked back, just once. "I think you know."

Then he continued on toward the darkness, which seemed to stretch out before him, the room becoming elastic, as though it were leaving him more than he was leaving it. Then, gradually, the candles went out, one by one. The last thing Roger saw was Laurel sitting alone on the bed, face turned to catch one final glimpse of the figure before it vanished at last.

Alone, so terribly alone.

And then nothing . . . only the faint traces of pre-dawn glow that seeped into his room.

It took Roger a moment to realize that he was crying.

The dining room was its usual flurry of noise, the smell of eggs and bacon filtering out into the hall. Roger searched for Frank in the line of others waiting at the buffet. He straightened his collar. It had been a long time since he'd last worn a suit.

"Frank," he said, spotting his quarry at the bacon bin, "have you seen Laurel?"

"Hey, look at you!" Frank said. "Nice suit, Roger."

"Frank—"

Frank gestured with a slice of burnt bacon. "She's out back, I think."

"Thanks." He headed for the patio door.

"No problem," Frank called after him. "By the way, we're having a poker game tonight at seven, I'll hold a place for you!"

Roger didn't answer. Later, there would be time. Just before he stepped out the door, he heard one of the boarders turn to Frank. "Why bother? You know he never comes."

"Ah, eat your corn flakes," Frank said.

Roger smiled, and let the door clatter shut behind him, searching for the familiar wheelchair.

He found it, and for a moment, his heart sank within him. She sat in her usual place, staring without seeing toward the shuffleboard courts, hands folded together in her lap.

He crossed the patio, and sat down in the chair opposite her, searching her face for some clue that what he'd seen and heard the night before had been more than just a dream. But he saw nothing in her eyes but his own reflection.

"Hello," he said at last.

No response.

"I know you're there. I know you can hear me. And I can wait." He folded his arms and sat back in the chair. "I can wait as long as I have to."

For a moment, there was nothing. Then, slowly, her gaze tracked up from the ground, pausing just a moment at his bandaged hand, then slowly fixing on him, as though it took an effort to focus on anything outside her own thoughts. She licked her lips, and when she spoke, it was little more than a whisper.

"You've burned your hand."

Roger sat forward, glanced at the bandage. "Yes."

"On a—candle."

"Yes."

She met his gaze. "I'm sorry."

He was about to respond when the breakfast bell chimed from inside the kitchen. He smiled across at her. "Last call for breakfast. Would you like something to eat?"

She hesitated a moment and then smiled. It was faint, and small, but Roger thought he had never seen anything more glorious. "Breakfast—would be very nice, I think."

Rubbing his hands, Roger stood up and went behind the wheelchair, pushing it toward the patio door. "An excellent decision. Now let's see—we've got bacon, we've got eggs, and toast, and marmalade—I mean, *jam* and *jelly*—and we've got hash browns, but I wouldn't go near them if I were you—and I hear there's a poker game every day at seven. . . ."

He opened the door and helped maneuver her through. It was going to be a good day, he decided, a very good day indeed.

Mr. Roger Simpson Leeds, lately returned from a journey into shadow, who found that there is no darkness so complete that it cannot be penetrated by the human heart—or the Twilight Zone.

Introduction to
The Call

So there's this woman I've known as a friend for many years. An attractive and giving woman, she has been ill-served by relationships, and men. We had what can best be described as an on-again, off-again, on-again, off-again, on-again, off-again, on-again, off-again relationship. We both liked each other enormously as friends, but could never quite seem to make it work as anything more than that.

The friendship continued even after I got married, through occasional letters and phone calls. Mainly phone calls. The curious thing that I discovered was that even though years would go by without seeing her, I always knew what she looked like when we spoke— her expressions, gestures, shrugs, and glances, they all came through the phone line as clearly as if they'd been narrated. It is, I suppose, one of the perks that comes with years of familiarity.

Given that several years would sometimes pass before running into her again, perhaps it's not surprising that the idea of a relationship born, and perpetuated on the telephone would come burbling up one sunny afternoon. Besides, telephones are traditionally magical creatures, push-button oracles connected by nervous systems of wire and steel and fiber optics. You may be thousands of miles away, but you can be found, and your life changed—for good or ill—by one single telephone call.

Or one misdialed number.

Once I had a handle on the story, the script wrote itself in one sitting, the characters taking over and the words coming with unexpected clarity. Interestingly, one of the first persons to read the script—our reader at the Zone offices—had once fallen in love with someone without ever having met her, only talking with her on the phone. After it was produced, others came to me with similar stories. So perhaps there's something to Norman's reaction after all.

There is only one regret with this particular story. When I heard of the final decision on casting, I knew we were effectively dead in the water. The actor—William Sanderson, most widely known as Larry, the middle brother on *Newhart* ("Hi, my name's Larry, and these are my brothers, Darryl and Darryl")—tried desperately to disappear into the role, and may have done too good a job, in my view. Still, a number of people have told me that they consider this one of their favorite episodes, and I suppose that's not too bad. It touched them, and that was the main objective.

And it didn't even run up any long-distance charges in the process.

"The Call," production #87020, went into production on June 27, 1988. Directed by Gilbert Shilton, the episode starred William Sanderson (Norman Blair), Jill Frappier (patron), Dan Redican (Richard), Julie Khaner (Mary Ann), Djanet Sears (Clerk), Ian Northnagel (Museum Attendant). Originally broadcast on November 20, 1988.

THE CALL

Norman Blair unlocked the front door of his apartment and shouldered past the door, careful not to drop the shopping bags or step on the cat or trip over something the cat might have left there as a greeting for him when he came back from the office.

He made it to the kitchen safely, and Catt blinked down at him from his perch atop the refrigerator. "Hi," Norman said. The cat looked at him as cats sometimes will when they're momentarily unsure who this person in their kitchen is, what he's doing here, and if there's food involved. Doubtful that it was worth the effort to find out, Catt yawned and closed his eyes.

Must've had a hard day, Norman decided, and began unpacking the groceries.

Sofa, coffee table, chair, and cat—solitary decorations in a life noted chiefly for its isolation. Point of origin and point of destination for Norman Blair, whose days and nights are routinely swallowed into unhappy silence. Norman Blair, whose greatest fear is that if he were to vanish from the Earth tomorrow, no one would notice, or mourn, or question; and whose greatest sadness is the realization that he is probably right.

Norman jerked awake to the sound of applause. He rubbed sleepily at his eyes, squinting at the television, where the end credits of some sitcom or other were rolling past. The aluminum tray from his TV dinner was still on the coffee table, and he had forgotten to change out of his good shirt.

He glanced at the clock. A little past midnight. *Got to get to sleep,* he thought, and forced himself to stand and put away the debris from dinner. Letting the television drone on in the background, he cleared the sofa and pulled out the hidden bed, getting the pillows from their usual shelf in the linen closet.

He perked up a little at the sound of big band music coming from the television. Norman recognized it instantly as Glenn Miller's 'Sliphorn Jive.' A moment later, the music gave way to an announcer's voice. "Tommy Dorsey! Glenn Miller! Artie Shaw and Benny Goodman! Finally a collection of their biggest hits. Songs from the big band era, from 'Moonlight Serenade' to 'Pennsylvania 6-5000,' a gathering of the finest of swing by the finest performers. Only a limited number of these special-edition sets will be made available to the public, so call 727-4221 and order while supplies last. Operators are standing by twenty-four hours a day."

Norman scrambled frantically for a pencil and something to write on. He'd been a fan of big band music for years, ever since high school, when it was so far from fashionable that he had gotten strange looks even from the class nerds. The collection sounded perfect—just the sort of thing he could turn on and leave going in the background while he ate or read.

He found a pencil and quickly scribbled the number on the back of an envelope before dialing. He waited as the line connected, and he heard a ringing from the other end. It rang for a long time. *Must be getting a lot of orders,* he thought, and turned his attention back to the television, and the announcer.

"A special set for those who still remember," the announcer was saying, "or who want to discover for themselves some of the very best. Includes Harry James, Woody Herman, and Kay Kyser, and such classic hits as 'Begin the Beguine,' 'String of Pearls,' and 'I'm

Getting Sentimental Over You.' For immediate service call 727-4221."

As the phone at the other end rang for the tenth time, Norman glanced down at the number he had scribbled down.

727-4212.

Oh, jeez, he thought, and pulled the phone away, about to hang up when there was a *click* on the other end of the line.

"Hello?" It was a woman's voice, small, tentative. *Must've been sleeping,* Norman thought.

"Uh, yeah, hi," Norman said. "I—um—I'm sorry, I think I dialed the wrong number."

"Excuse me?"

"I—listen, I'm really sorry, it's just a wrong number, and I probably woke you up—"

"No, it's—okay." She paused for just a moment, then continued, her voice a little firmer. "I was just sitting here and I heard the phone ring. For a minute I was afraid whoever was calling would hang up before I got here."

"Yeah, I know what you mean. I hate it when that happens. Really, um, annoying."

What a charming conversationalist you are, Norman, he thought. He always seemed to run out of steam two minutes into a conversation with a woman.

He was still trying to think of what to say next when her voice drifted across the line to him again. "What's your name?"

"Norman. Norman Blair."

"You have a—very nice voice."

She said it softly, sounding almost as shy as he felt. He lowered his eyes instinctively, even though there was no one's gaze to avoid. "Thank you. So do you. What's your name? I mean, if you don't mind my asking."

"Mary Ann."

"Mary Ann. It's a good name." *Just be casual,* he thought, *she doesn't seem in any hurry to get off the phone.* "Listen, would you like to talk a bit? If you're not busy or something."

"No," she said, "that would be nice."

For the first time that night, Norman smiled.

Norman's office was fifteen feet long by twelve feet wide, with one window at the far end (looking out onto another building across the breezeway), two identical desks, two identical lamps, two identical computers, running two identical accounts payable programs, and two identical filing cabinets. The only thing that was not identical to anything else was Norman's office mate, Richard Leeks.

"So where was I?" Norman said.

"Talking to some strange woman for an hour." When Richard spoke to him at all it was reluctantly, and almost always without looking at him. There were times Norman wondered if Richard was entirely aware of his existence. Today, though, Norman hardly noticed.

"An hour and a half," Norman corrected him. "That's the amazing thing about it. It wasn't like she was a stranger at all. It was—I don't know—*special*, somehow. I mean, she was a little nervous at first, but after a while she started talking, and I started talking, like we were old friends, and next thing I knew—"

"It was an hour and a half later."

"Exactly. She was friendly, and funny—God, I haven't had that much fun in ages. Now I can't decide what to do next. I mean, she said I could call her back tonight, after seven. I guess she works late. But I'd really like to meet her, I just don't know how."

With a look of long-suffering patience, Richard put down his pencil and turned in his swivel chair. "Norman, a year and two months we've been sharing this office. For a year and two months I've been able to come in here, and sit at my desk, and pretend that I was all by myself, because from *that* side of the room came only a blissful silence. I like silence. I have five kids. I'm sitting here with this terrific urge to give you five dollars and send you to the movies. Alone.

"Look," he said, and sighed, "you want my advice? Ask her out. Suggest lunch, dinner, ice cream, and a trip to the zoo, go crazy. Fact is, she wouldn't be spending that much time talking to somebody she didn't want to meet. Simple problem, simple solution. Yes?"

Norman considered it, nodded.

Richard smiled. "Good. Now, you're a nice man, Norman, but for the next hour, I would very much like to have no noise. It would make me a very happy man."

With that, Richard picked up his pencil and turned back to his figures. Norman swiveled around in his chair, once again facing the wall.

"Thank you," Norman said.

"That was a noise."

Norman checked his watch. Again. 6:59 P.M. He wasn't supposed to call until seven. He paced the room slowly, having worked out that each circuit, properly paced, was equal to one minute. It made the time go faster, and let him check the room for dust bunnies at the same time.

As he finished his circuit, he noticed Catt standing in the doorway to the kitchen looking at him in *that* way again. But now it was 7:01 P.M., and Catt could look at him as though he had three heads and feathers, for all he cared.

He picked up the phone, dialed. It rang five times, then six, before there was a *click* at the other end.

"Hello," she said.

Norman smiled. "Hi. It's me."

"I know."

When Norman looked up again, it was 10:30 P.M. He was sitting on the couch at one end, his arm running along the back of the sofa. Embarrassed, he realized that he was sitting as he would to make room for somebody else. He changed position and shifted the phone to his right ear; the left one was getting uncomfortably warm against the hard plastic.

"That's when I left Fayetteville for Los Angeles," he was saying, in answer to her question about his background. She'd recognized the faint Southern accent in his voice. Most folks didn't notice it. She did. "That was about a year after my brother died. Things just weren't the same anymore. I don't think my mother ever got over it. So I figured I'd come out here and try to find a job."

"You never did tell me exactly what you do."

"Nothing that would interest you. Just—work, you know how it is."

"No, really," she said, her voice sincere. "I'd love to hear. I have time."

Time, he thought, and glanced again at his watch. It had been over three hours. "Well, it's late, though, and I probably should let you go."

"All right," she said, and Norman thought her voice sounded genuinely regretful. "Just one more thing. I just want you to know, Norman—I really enjoyed our talk last night. And tonight. I wanted to thank you."

"Well, same here," Norman said. He took a deep breath. "In fact, I was thinking, and I was wondering if maybe you'd like to get together some time, maybe lunch or dinner, a movie—anything you want."

"Oh, Norman," she said, and he could hear rejection imminent in her voice.

"No rush," he said, talking quickly. "I mean anytime you want, it's okay."

"You're sweet, but . . . no, I really can't. We have so much fun just *talking*, why do we have to change it? I've been disappointed by people so often—can't we just leave it at this?"

Norman closed his eyes. *Damn*. It always happened like this. "Sure," he said, "I guess so."

"I've hurt you, haven't I?"

"No," he said, again too quickly. "Really, it's okay. Like I said, I just enjoy talking to you. If you want to leave it at that, it's all right with me. Honest."

There was a long pause from the other end. "Promise you'll call me tomorrow?"

"I promise."

* * *

Norman reached forward, picking up another folder from the pile on his desk. The chair squeaked. He sat back again to read it. The chair squeaked. He shook his foot as he read. The chair emitted a series of short, mouse-soft squeaks. He realized he didn't have the right file. The one he wanted was on the far end of the desk. He reached as far across as he could.

His chair SQUEAKED.

"All right, Norman," Richard said, exasperation in his voice. "Give."

"What?"

"Five days now, and you've been absolutely quiet. Not a word."

"I thought you liked it quiet."

"It's the *way* you're being quiet. It's a very *loud* kind of quiet, Norman, like sitting next to a tuning fork vibrating just on the edge of what you can hear. Makes my ears itch." He sighed, and it suddenly occurred to Norman that Richard talked to him in about the same way that Catt looked at him. "It's that woman on the telephone. She turned you down, right?"

Norman nodded.

"So big deal. It's just one person. So what?"

Norman struggled to find a reply, then finally opted for the truth. "Do you think it's possible to fall in love with someone over the telephone?"

Richard considered it. "No," he said, and returned to his computer.

Norman waited to see if anything else was forthcoming, then turned back to his work. His chair *squeaked*.

Twice.

"Okay," Richard said, "you win. I can see right now I'm not going to get any peace, so can I give you a piece of advice? You say you want to meet this woman, but you don't know who she is or where she lives. All you have is a phone number. Have I got it surrounded?"

"Yes."

"All right. You ever heard of reverse listings? You call the operator, you say you've got this number, you think it's the one you have to call, say it's an emergency or something, and you ask the operator to tell you who belongs to that number. Say anything you have to. Once you get the address, you cruise by her place and just sort of run into her by accident. After that, you're on your own. Okay? Can we have some quiet now?"

Norman nodded and turned back to his work, careful not to let the chair squeak beneath him. Then, remembering his manners, he started to swivel back—

"Don't say *thank you*, Norman," Richard said without looking up. "I don't think I could stand it."

It had taken him most of his lunch hour to find the address, and now that he had arrived, Norman still wasn't sure this was the right place. He looked at the address on the side of the building, at the address on the paper in his hand, and back at the wall again. They matched—but it was not what he had expected.

The white-on-black sign at the front door announced this as the William L. Feist Museum of Contemporary Art. Not at all what he had anticipated. He had imagined a small white house, with plants hung from the porch and ivy growing on a window terrace.

Not that it mattered, he supposed, and pushed through the heavy glass door. The operator had promised him that 727-4212 was inside here somewhere, and that meant Mary Ann would be here too.

Inside the lobby, he looked around. Halls crowded with paintings of oil and acrylic, statues, and kinetic art in an explosion of colors and shapes spilled out away from him in every direction. Only a few couples and what looked like art students punctuated the carefully arranged displays.

"May I help you?" came a woman's voice at his elbow.

He turned, half expecting to find Mary Ann, but the voice was different, and the name tag the clerk wore read SHARON. "Yes," he said, "do you know if a Mary Ann works here?"

She said the name aloud a few times, then shook

her head. "I don't think so—but it could be one of our student interns. We bring in a lot of them from the junior college."

"Do they work late?"

"Sometimes. I'm not sure who you would check with, though. The assistant director should be back from lunch soon. He might be able to help you."

"I'll wait, then," Norman said. "Thank you."

He stepped down the hall nearest him and wandered among the artwork. Most of it was a puzzle to him; Norman found modern art as generally incomprehensible as cuneiform, but as he passed others examining the displays he tried to look dutifully impressed.

It was as he passed an extension phone in one of the adjoining rooms that the idea occurred to him.

He went over to the phone, checked to make sure the room was empty, then lifted the receiver. The number on the extension was 4209. He reasoned that if he dialed 4212, then the correct extension should ring. Then it was just a matter of following the sound back to the correct department. Surely they would know something about Mary Ann.

He punched in the numbers, and almost instantly he could hear the ringing in the receiver. He pulled the phone away, and listened. He could just make out the sound of another phone ringing in rhythm down the hall.

Leaving the phone off its cradle, he followed the ringing back to a room at the far end of the building, just off the main hall. He went to the phone, picked it up, and pressed the plunger to cut off the ring. The number of the extension was 4212.

He hung up, and looked around the room. It was one of the least crowded with displays. A few paintings lined the walls on either side of a neon-and-glass-and-stone thing that crouched in the corner like a brooding galaxy. A handful of masks that looked distantly African were tastefully arranged in the far corner. The closest display was a statue that sat less than a foot from him.

There was no one about. Which didn't much matter. He'd wait. He'd never been late coming back from lunch before, not in five years. Surely he was due at least one. Eventually someone would show up. Maybe even Mary Ann herself.

His attention turned again to the statue. It was a full-size sculpture (bronze, from the look of it) of a young woman, attractive, sitting forward with eyes downcast, as though in deep thought or prayer. One of her hands was outstretched in supplication, and it had been shunted up against the wall so that its hand was barely inches away. He felt his gaze drawn to it almost in spite of himself. There was a compelling sadness about her features.

"I see you're admiring the sculpture," someone said.

He looked up to see a woman standing beside him, clutching a museum pamphlet. He nodded, then noticed that she wasn't looking at him, only at the statue. "It's very nice."

"Yes," she said, her voice tinged with regret. "Terrible story, that one. Last thing she ever did. A self-portrait. I never met her myself, but if this is any indication, she must really have been something."

She shook her head, frowning. "Why on earth a woman as talented as that would kill herself I don't know. Oh, there were the usual rumors, of course, lover's quarrel and all that. Damn shame. To think that we'll never see anything else from Mary Ann Lindeby."

She sighed, then moved on to the next room. She might have said something more, but Norman didn't hear it. There was a curious rushing in his ears that he distantly recognized as his own heartbeat.

He bent down to examine the brass plaque screwed into the base of the sculpture. It read *MARY ANN LINDEBY—SELF-PORTRAIT IN BRONZE.*

He followed the subtle lines up to her face, and then away to her hand. The hand that was outstretched so that it nearly touched the wall.

The hand that was barely inches from the telephone.

* * *

He had been late getting back to the office. Late arriving home from work, most of which was now a blur to him. Late getting Catt's dinner out of the can.

And now it was 8:30 P.M., and he was late in calling her. He paced the room nervously. He didn't have to call at all. He could just forget the whole thing. But then he would never know for sure. Could he live with that?

No, he decided, and reached for the phone.

It rang for a long time before she answered.

"Hello, Norman."

"Hello, Mary Ann."

"I—didn't think you were going to call," she said, more hesitant than he had ever heard her before. Almost afraid. She was quiet for a long moment before continuing.

"I saw you today, Norman," she said. "You came by." And now, suddenly, as though her resolve had finally failed, she was crying on the phone. "Oh, why did you have to do that? You've ruined everything."

"Then—it was you? That—"

Quietly: "Yes, Norman, it was."

Norman felt as though he had been kicked in the stomach. The floor seemed to tilt beneath him. He was aware of a sound from the receiver, but he couldn't make any sense of it. Nothing made sense.

"No," he said, somehow finding his voice. "I can't deal with this. I can't. This isn't happening!"

He slammed down the receiver. Got up. Paced the room.

It was crazy.

But he knew in his heart that he couldn't leave it at this.

Couldn't leave *her* like this.

It would be rude.

Steeling himself, he went back to the phone and dialed.

This time it rang only once before her voice came on the other end. She was still crying, great, gasping sobs that tore him apart to hear.

"I'm sorry, Mary Ann," he said.

"No, it's me," she said, and there was such pain in her voice, such hurt. "I'm the one who should be sorry. For putting you in this position. I never should have answered the phone. But—it's been so *long*, Norman, so long since I've talked to anyone. It was dark, and I was alone, and I was so lonely."

"I know," Norman said, his voice small in the receiver. "So was I."

Silence hung between them for a moment. "I should go now," she said.

"No—wait, I mean . . . you can't just go away like that."

"It's for your own good, Norman. Forget about me. It never happened." He could hear her control breaking over the phone, and in a voice thin with effort and strained with tears, he could barely hear her say, "I'm sorry, Norman. Good-bye."

Then before he could say anything, there was the *click* of a disconnect at the other end of the line.

He dialed again.

It rang without answer.

He let it ring anyway.

Finally, after he had lost count of the rings, he set the receiver back in its cradle and sat back on the couch, peering into the dark.

She was gone.

At 5:01 P.M., Richard switched off his computer, grabbed his jacket, and with a nod in Norman's direction, headed out into the cool evening. He was smiling.

The office had been blissfully quiet for three whole days.

Norman came home with the usual two bags of groceries and set them on the counter. He opened a can of cat food and set it out on the floor. Catt rushed by him and began lapping it up. Norman watched the cat for a while—it hardly ever seemed to mind if he watched—then went into the other room.

He sat down on the couch and switched on the television, leaving the sound off. Somehow, the voices on the TV bothered him; the tiny speaker filtered the voices, reminding him of things he didn't want to think about.

Besides, Catt seemed to like the quiet.

Norman lay without sleeping. The digital clock beside the bed glowed 2:37 A.M. The thin light reflected off the pamphlet that had arrived in the mail that day, the one he had requested over the phone two days earlier. It was a guide to the current exhibits on display at the museum.

The green glow from the clock shone off the picture of a sculpture. A self-portrait by Mary Ann Lindeby. Somehow the light made it look gloomy, not at all as real or as warm or as vibrant as he remembered it.

Photographs don't do her justice, he thought.

Before he realized he was doing it, he reached for the phone, and dialed 727-4212.

After the twenty-fifth ring, he let the phone settle back in its cradle, then reached over to slide the pamphlet out of the light of the digital clock.

". . . damn," he whispered, and the night swallowed his words.

Richard stood up from his desk and stretched. "I'm going to lunch. Be back in an hour."

Norman nodded, momentarily startled out of his reverie. When he turned back to his papers, he glanced at the figure that he had been unconsciously doodling on the page. It was a woman posed sitting forward, hand outstretched, eyes downcast.

I can't take this any longer, he thought, and got up from his desk, careful to lock the door to their cubicle on his way out.

Half an hour later he was standing in the museum again, in the same room with her. He waited until one of the interns had finished exchanging one painting for another, then sat on the cushioned seat in front of the sculpture.

Well, now what? he wondered. *What are you going to do, talk to her or something?*

Why not? he decided.

"I miss you," he said, tentative at first, his whispered voice sounding harsh and loud in the room. "I miss talking to you. It was the only thing I had to look forward to when I came home. After a while, it was the only reason for *going* home."

He studied the bronze face, but there was no reaction.

Don't be stupid, he thought. *What did you expect?*

He forced himself to continue. "You were the only one who ever made me feel I was wanted. That I wasn't just some jerk. And now—"

He stopped abruptly as two other patrons browsed through the room. When they left after only a cursory inspection, he wondered if they had heard him, and decided that he didn't care.

"Don't you *understand?*" he said. "I used to feel I was nothing. That I had nothing. And then—then there was you. And everything changed. And I thought: my God, I'm in love. For the first time in my life I am honestly and truly in love. And then it all just . . . went away."

He looked away from her. "Without you, there's nothing left for me. It's not worth it. I'm sorry, Mary Ann, but I just—can't go on like this."

He looked up again.

The sculpture was crying.

A thin line of moisture flowed down her cheek from the corner of one eye. Stunned, he got to his feet and walked closer. It was there, he wasn't imagining it. He reached out to touch the tear-streaked bronze face—

"Excuse me."

Norman turned to see the museum guard standing behind him.

"I'll have to ask you not to touch the exhibits, sir," he said.

"Of course," Norman said, "of course."

The guard lingered a moment longer, perhaps making sure that Norman had understood him before stepping out of the room.

As soon as he was gone, Norman looked back at the statue. The tear streak was gone, if it had even been there at all.

You're losing your mind, he thought, and headed out of the museum.

Norman awoke to the shrill sound of the phone ringing in his ear. He pulled himself to the edge of the bed, fumbling for the receiver. The clock read 3:45 A.M. He found the phone and snatched it up on the third ring, and managed to figure out which end went to his ear. "Hello?"

". . . Norman?" Her voice was distant, as though she were calling from a tremendous distance. "Oh, Norman, it was so hard to call you—it took—almost everything I had. It's dark here, so *dark*— I don't know how much longer I can talk."

The line blurred with a rush of static for a moment, then cleared. "I heard what you said—about not going on. It scares me. It's what I said when—" And now she was crying, her voice heavy with hurt. "He left me, Norman. He left me and my life fell apart. There was nothing left, nothing else—mattered. I was so lonely and hurt and I couldn't make the pain go away, it just stayed with me so long and so hard and I couldn't take it anymore and I had to do something I—oh, please, Norman, please say you didn't mean it, please."

He struggled with his words, wanting to say the right thing, not knowing what it was. Then, finally, "I love you, Mary Ann."

"No, please—"

"I do, and I'm sorry, I didn't think it would happen, I didn't expect it, ever, but—I can't help it. I love you."

The static returned again, like the sound of a wave

crashing on a distant shore, and then he heard her, so soft he could barely make out the words. "Come to me, Norman. Come to me now, tonight."

"But the museum—it'll be closed."

"Don't worry. I'll take care of it. But come, now, before I change my mind. Hurry!"

The line cut off, leaving only a dial tone in its wake. Norman racked the phone and threw off the sheets, stepping out into the chill night that filled the room.

Norman walked up the sidewalk in front of the museum, looking nervously over his shoulder. In three hours it would be light, and crowded with people. But now there was only the night, and the cold, and the museum. Lit by floodlamps on all sides, it was the brightest thing on the street.

He made his way around back, searching until he found a metal fire door. He pulled at the handle, but it refused to budge, locked from inside. Spotting another door down the length of the building, he started toward it—

—when there was a *click* at the door he had just tried.

He walked back to the door and tried the handle. It swung freely open. With a final glance around, he stepped inside.

He felt his way through the rooms, trying to get his bearings in the dark. Some part of his mind realized that the door would be discovered unlocked sooner or later, that museums had security guards just like banks did, but for the moment none of that mattered. He had to find her. That was what was important.

He managed to work his way up into the main hall. From there it was a matter of going straight down to the end, trying not to knock anything over, then left—

And he was inside the room. The dim light from the hall stopped at the door. The room was pitch-black inside, and *different,* somehow. He felt it instantly, the way it felt when he stepped out of an airplane; a difference in pressure. And something else. A sense of movement in the darkness.

"Mary Ann?"

The darkness answered. "I'm here."

And a hand touched his face.

Somewhere, down the hall, he heard a door open and close, a transistor radio briefly audible, then silenced. The guard would be making his patrols. Surely he would find them here, together. But it didn't matter. Nothing mattered.

"Tell me you love me, Norman," she said. "Oh, God, it's been so long since anyone's told me they loved me."

"I love you."

"Then stay with me. Please. I don't want to be alone anymore."

Footsteps down the hall, coming closer. The distant glare of a flashlight, reflected off portraits, growing near.

Norman hesitated. "I—"

"Please."

He nodded, quickly, furtively, in the darkness. Then he felt her holding him, cold, but tightly, as though she would never let go. . . .

The guard came to the end of the hall and swept the adjacent room with the flashlight beam. There had been a noise, of that he was certain. And the rear door had been unlocked.

But so far, there was nothing out of the ordinary.

He let the glow from the flashlight linger just a moment on the sculpture at the end of the room. It was an impressive piece of work, even in the semidark. A man and a woman, locked in an embrace, faces inches apart, gazing into one another's eyes. His hand was on her face, as though lovingly, delicately touching her cheek.

He would have to come back and look at it again, the guard decided, and moved away down the hall.

* * *

On display, a very special exhibit, carved from stone and loneliness; a tender symmetry of line and form suggestive of love finally found . . . in the Twilight Zone.

Introduction to
Acts of Terror

There are two stories behind this particular tale. One funny, one not. I'll tell you the funny one first.

The Twilight Zone was filmed in Toronto, Ontario, Canada. Now, I've been to Toronto. I like Toronto. I was even nominated there once for a Gemini Award for Best Writing in a Dramatic Series (the Canadian equivalent of an Emmy, from the Canadian Academy of Cinema and Television). I like the people who live there.

But Toronto was also the setting for the Great Twilight Zone Animal Wars and Part-time Insurrection.

About half a dozen scripts required animals. Cats, mostly. My script for "The Call" required a cat. An episode just before mine, written by someone else, also required a cat. So one day the telephone rang at my office on the TZ lot. "We've already used the cat in the other episode," the caller from Toronto informed me.

The cat?

As I soon discovered, there are apparently only two actor-cats (or stunt cats, or whatever they're called) in Canada. Two cats. And the other cat, I was told, was under the weather. Looking a mite peaked. I was, to say the least, put out. A country that is from east to west the size of the United States, and they've only got TWO CATS?

The cat became a parakeet.

Then came "The Wall," and the necessary llamas, horses, sheep . . . and a water buffalo.

I don't even want to talk about the water buffalo. So don't bother asking. Maybe in a few years. We'll see.

"The Mind of Simon Foster" required a cockroach that would fall off a cabinet and into Simon's soup on cue. For this task, they came up with six—count 'em, six —stunt roaches. And a roach wrangler. Because it was one of my favorite scripts, I even flew up to Toronto to be on set during the shoot.

And we all learned a remarkable thing.

A cockroach, once set on a cabinet, in spite of being vertical and blinded by bright lights, will not let go regardless of anything you do or say or threaten to do or say. He will cling resolutely and determinedly in the face of every possible form of intimidation.

They tried knocking it off by tapping the cabinet. That didn't work.

They tried blowing it off with little puffs of air. That didn't work.

I think they would've tried boring it to sleep, but a) there wasn't time and b) I suspect they were afraid it would cling even more strongly in sleep.

At one point, one of the stagehands turned to me and asked if we could make it a fly instead. "A fly we can deal with," he said. "You just stick 'em in the fridge until they get reasonable. With a cockroach you've got to beat it over the head with a crowbar until it's knocked senseless."

Finally, they resorted to a compressed-air machine and managed to blow the cockroach off with that. As a technique, it proved reasonably successful . . . except that if you watch the episode very closely, you'll notice that the cockroach doesn't exactly fall. Rather it seems a sirocco suddenly springs to life in the middle of Simon Foster's apartment, whirling the cockroach off the cabinet and into its own eight-legged Oz somewhere over the rainbow.

And then there was "Acts of Terror."

And the Doberman.

We needed a Doberman that could be incredibly fierce on command. In the process of writing "Acts of

Terror," I figured this would not be a problem. I've never seen a Doberman that *wasn't* looking forward to the prospect of ripping my arm off for a late afternoon snack.

We were told that a pair of Canadian Dobermans had been found and were ready to go.

Then the dailies started to come in.

Apparently it was hot that week in Toronto. And being Canadian dogs, they were somewhat loathe to do much acting when it got warm. More precisely, they seemed to be looking for a handy wall to lean up against. At one point, the producer asked, "Do you think it's possible to convince the dogs not to pant so much when they're supposed to be fighting?"

The phone calls from Canada became increasingly dark. Ominous prospects were muttered if anyone dared to write another script with an animal in it.

Finally, on a Thursday morning, I came into the studio office to find Mary Ann Barton, our West Coast casting director, sitting slumped at her desk, a cup of coffee dangling beneath her chin from two fingers. She fixed me with a bloodshot, dark-rimmed stare.

"Because of *you*," she said, speaking in italics, as she was sometimes wont to do, "because of *you* I was up until three in the morning at Los Angeles International Airport with a very large man and a Doberman."

I explained that her sex life was really none of my concern, and she should really keep such matters to herself.

That I am still alive today is stark testimony to the woman's Job-like patience.

It turned out that the *only* way to save the episode was to find a Los Angeles-based Doberman, a *proper* Doberman, and ship it and its owner to Toronto on the red-eye. "It's the Laurence Olivier of dogs," the producer pronounced long-distance the next day, pleased and relieved.

Pleased in part because he'd forgotten that in two weeks we'd be shooting a little thing called "Cat and Mouse" by Christy Marx, requiring a cat capable of running, jumping, method acting, and transforming into a man on cue.

But that's another story.

And I'd promised you a different one for now.

For reasons unknown, I've chanced to know many, *many* women who have been the victims of violent abuse. Mostly by husbands or boyfriends, and sometimes by fathers. I've listened to them, held them, helped them, cried with them, and raged with them. I've done what I could when I could, but most times there's nothing much you really *can* do unless the woman is willing to get out. To take responsibility.

To get mad.

These were women with low self-esteem, who refused to see any other fault than their own slowness or culpability; women who were sure, deep in their hearts, that their husbands/boyfriends really did love them, bruises and broken bones notwithstanding. They were, most of all, women afraid of their own rage, and unwilling to confront it.

For the record: there is *nothing* lower than a wife beater. Nothing. It is a sickness that preys on vulnerability and manipulates emotion, that relishes in the power of the fist or the belt or the stick.

A wife beater is someone too damn cowardly to take on somebody who can fight back.

It's a topic that has been burning inside me for over ten years, looking for a means of expression. So when the opportunity presented by *The Twilight Zone* came along, it became the avenue for expressing the rage I, too, had felt for so long.

Two stories emerged. The first, "Acts of Terror," was produced in spite of several nervous studio executives who were sure such things didn't go on anymore. (And here I'd thought *I* was living in the Twilight Zone.) The second, "Say Hello, Mister Quigley," a story of incest and the supernatural, never got near a soundstage. That one made *everyone* nervous.

But perhaps someday, that story will also be told. Until then, "Acts of Terror" stands alone. As of this writing, the episode has already been included in therapy sessions held by some psychologists for victims of spouse abuse.

Maybe it'll do some good.

I hope so.

God, but I hope so.

"Acts of Terror," production #87011, was directed by Brad Turner, and starred Melanie Mayron (Louise Simonton), Kenneth Welsh (Jack Simonton), Kate Lynch (Claire), Lee J. Campbell (Phil), Trevor Bain (Policeman), and James Barron (Postman). Production began on August 8, 1988, and the episode was originally aired on December 4, 1988.

ACTS OF TERROR

Saturday

Louise Simonton stepped down off the porch, heading to where the mailman was coming up the sidewalk. He noted her with a nod and a smile as he slipped envelopes into the mailbox. "Morning, Mrs. Simonton," he said.

She returned the smile, quickly, furtively. "Good morning."

He riffled through the rest of the mail, putting it in her hand. "You can always tell when it's Saturday. Supermarket sales, fliers, bills, all the junk mail seems to pile up."

"I'm sure it must be very heavy."

"You get used to it after a while," he said. "That should do it. Oh, yeah, I almost forgot. There's this." He reached into his bag and pulled out a cardboard box with her name printed on it in familiar script. "Here you go."

Mail in one hand, she reached for the package, and as she did, the shoulder of her dress slipped just enough to reveal the bruise it had been concealing. Dark and flecked with red, it stood out starkly against her pale skin.

The postman frowned as he handed her the package, and his eyes met hers. "Looks painful."

She glanced at the bruise, and hurriedly slipped the strap back into place. "It's nothing, really. I was cleaning out the upper cabinets in the kitchen and I stood up —rammed right into an open door. Silly of me, I guess."

She risked a glance back at him, saw the doubt in his face, and looked away again.

"Happens to us all, Mrs. Simonton. But—" Again the frown, an expression of things better left unsaid. "Do try to be a little more careful."

"I will. Thank you."

As the postman crossed the street, Louise turned her attention to the package in her hands. She started back up the sidewalk toward the house, a tentative smile appearing as she gently shook the package, wondering what could be inside.

To look at Louise Simonton you might be surprised to learn that she was considered quite pretty, once, not long ago—before the arguments and the years and the stick took it out of her. Louise Simonton, like so many broken on the wheel. With one subtle difference. This wheel has a name.

"Jack?" she called as she stepped up onto the porch and into the house.

The living room was surprisingly dark coming in from the brightness outside. She found Jack bathed in the flickering light from the television. He was watching football, his expression distracted.

"Jack?" she said again, setting the mail down on the sofa beside her as she sat. "Got something from my sister." She began to unwrap the package. It was bound tightly with the kind of clear tape that was almost impossible to rip. "I wonder what it—"

Then from the chair: "No."

She flinched instinctively, even though he'd said it quietly. He had spoken without looking at her, as though trying to avoid being distracted from his game. "But I wasn't going to—I just wanted to see what it was, that's all. It's just that it's my sister and it's been so long."

His eyes never wandering from the television, he spoke to her as to a child. "It's one-oh-five. One o'clock is lunch, Louise. Lunch. One o'clock. Go in and fix lunch. Now."

Biting her lip, she set the unopened package down on the sofa with the rest of the mail and started for the kitchen.

"Any *decent* mail?" he called back to her.

"Just a bill from the electric company. They say they'll turn off the power if we don't take care of it. If we could just send them a little—"

He turned, and for the first time, looked at her. Fixed on her. There was something darkly feral in those eyes, something that seemed to relish the imminence of possible violence.

She had intruded on his consciousness. It was the last thing she had wanted to do.

"Are you saying I'm not doing my job, Louise? You saying I'm not a good husband? I don't take care of you the way you'd like?"

"No, Jack, no, I'm not. I didn't mean that. No, I didn't."

"I mean, it's easy to complain when I'm out there working all day and you just sit around here and do nothing."

She stiffened, just a little. "I do—"

But the sentence died at a look from him. *That* look, the one she had come to know so well. The look she'd seen just before . . .

Just before.

"You do what, Louise?"

She lowered her eyes. "Nothing, Jack."

At the sound of crowds roaring from the television, he turned away. "Now you see? You've made me miss something."

"I'm sorry."

If he heard her, he gave no sign, his attention back on the tube. It was as though she was barely in the room. "Go on. It's one-ten, Louise. Ten minutes past one o'clock. You know what one o'clock is, don't you?"

"One o'clock is lunch," she said, and wiping her hands on her apron, she stepped into the kitchen.

* * *

They ate in silence. Soup, sandwich—a BLT, the bacon crisp the way he liked it—a beer for him and an orange juice for her. As she ate, she glanced furtively past Jack to the living room, to the package that sat, unopened, on the sofa.

He looked up, catching her before she could turn away. "What are you looking at?"

"Hmm?" She tried to appear interested in her food.

"You keep glancing up every five minutes, so I figured there must be something real interesting."

"No, it's—I was just wondering if I could open the package now. It might be—I don't know—perishable or something. You know how Lynn is, always sending cookies and things."

Her words trailed off into silence.

She cleared her throat. "Can I open the package now?"

He grunted an affirmative and returned to his lunch.

Leaving the unfinished sandwich, she crossed to the living room, expectation once again bringing a smile to her face. She sat down and unwrapped the package with careful, precise movements, prolonging the pleasure of anticipation.

"Cookies," he called to her as she unwrapped. "Like she thinks we need cookies. If they *are* cookies, you're sending them right back, you hear me? We can feed ourselves just fine."

She dug through Styrofoam peanuts and felt something cool and hard. She pulled it out, brushing aside pieces of packing to reveal the tiny figurine. It was a porcelain dog, a slender Doberman with wide eyes, exquisitely detailed and painted and gleaming with the late afternoon light. She turned it in her hands, a tiny sigh of delight escaping from her lips. "Oh, Lynn—you remembered!"

"Remembered what?"

She turned to see Jack standing in the doorway.

Instinctively, she clutched the dog closer. "It was— well, it was my birthday Friday."

"Ummm." He stepped closer, reached for the figurine. "Let me see it."

She hesitated. "It's nothing, really, just a little dog, she sent it to me, please—"

"Did I say I was gonna do anything to it?" he snapped at her. "Now let me see it or I'll give you something to be afraid of."

She handed him the figurine. He turned it casually in his hand, looked at its face. "Woof-woof," he said, and laughed, as though expecting it to bark back. "Woof!"

She wanted to take it back, but she knew if she did she would startle him, and if she startled him he'd break it, and it would be her fault.

It was always her fault.

So she sat and waited and did nothing until, finally, he handed the figurine carelessly back to her and returned to the kitchen to finish his lunch.

She cradled the figurine against her cheek, its polished porcelain cool to her skin. It was hers now.

Hers.

Sunday

Her face hurt.

Louise could hear him outside, in the cool predawn twilight, loading the pickup with fishing gear. He was whistling a tune she didn't recognize.

She knelt on the floor and continued picking up the pieces of broken plates, careful not to cut herself on the slivers of glass and china. Afterward she would have to go over the floor with a mop to catch all the bits and pieces of uneaten breakfast. It wouldn't do to miss something and have ants all over the place. Jack hated ants.

The screen door behind the kitchen rattled open, and Jack stepped inside. She didn't look at him, only continued to pick up the pieces. "I'm going," he said.

She nodded.

He stepped closer. "Let me see."

She stood and turned just enough for the light to fall on her cheek, where by now the bruise was purpling. She could feel the swelling pressing against the bottom of her eye, as though something were caught in the bottom lid. She tried not to blink too often. It made her eyes water. They were watering now.

"Ah, it's nothing," Jack said. "Don't make such a big deal about it. Such a little crybaby."

Louise looked away. "I'm sorry I burned the eggs."

"Well, it won't happen again, will it?" he said. "Now I've gotta get going. Those fish won't wait all day." She hesitated. "Come on, give me a kiss."

She lifted her face to his and kissed him, though it made her cheek hurt to do so. That done, he turned and headed for the door.

"When will you be back?" she called after him.

He stood in the doorway, shrugged. "When I get back. What am I supposed to do, punch a clock?" With a sound of disgust, he stepped outside, the screen door closing with a bang and a clatter. She could hear his boots crunching on the gravel driveway as he headed toward the pickup.

Pushing the hair out of her face, she went to the sink where she had deposited the bigger of the broken pieces. One plate had broken neatly in two, leading her to hope that perhaps it could be fixed. She tried to fit the two halves together, but they shifted in her hands, grinding grittily against each other. She pushed harder, as though she might force them to fit, but they kept slipping, more bits and pieces slivering off into the sink, and she was crying, and it wouldn't fit, and her face hurt, and nothing fit anymore, nothing worked anymore, and she was sobbing, great heaving sobs that wracked her lungs as she smashed the halves in the sink, picked up the new pieces and smashed them again, over and over until there was nothing left to smash and she knelt on the floor, her forehead against the cool tile of the sink.

She ran the back of her hand against her eyes, and when she opened them, the first thing she saw was the porcelain dog she had set on the kitchen counter when she'd come in to fix breakfast.

She hadn't remembered turning it so it faced the sink, and her. She reached for it and cradled it in her lap as she rocked back and forth on the floor.

"Damn him," she whispered, quietly, as though afraid to hear herself saying it, "*damn* him."

Outside, in the dark, the car refused to start.

Jack turned the key in the ignition. It caught, sputtered out, caught and sputtered out again.

What the hell? he thought.

Then, out of the corner of his eye: movement. Something black against black, at the edge of the woods behind the house. There and not there. He tried to find it, but there was only the dark.

He tried the engine again. It sputtered—

And suddenly the pickup rocked as the Doberman slammed into it. Big and black and half-mad, its lips curled back in fury, it bit and snapped at the air, at him, clawing at the glass window, howling and barking and rushing the door again and again, out of control. He shouted at it, yelled incomprehensible things at it, but it only launched itself at the door that much harder, eyes burning with anger, with hate and rage, trying to claw its way in, in where he was.

Jack hit the car horn, held it down. Somebody had to come. Somebody had to hear.

The porch light went on. He turned to where the door started to open.

"Louise!"

The night was suddenly silent.

She stood in the doorway, clutching her robe as she looked out at him. "What is it?"

He glanced around.

The dog was gone.

Cautious, in case it was still there, hiding somewhere in the dark, he popped the driver's door. "Jesus, did—did you *see* that thing?"

"What?"

"What do you mean, what? A dog. It was right here. Thought it was gonna tear right into the car."

"I don't see anything."

"Thing must've run off," he said, trying not to sound too relieved. "Probably scared off by the horn. Good thing, too. Man if I'd had my gun." He shook his head, stepped back into the cab. "You get back inside. First thing Monday you're calling the cops, the ASPCA, find out who's got a dog loose around here."

"All right," she said, and stood in the doorway, watching as he drove away. As he passed, he glanced back, and though he couldn't be sure, it looked as though she were cradling something in her hands.

"And it was just the most beautiful dress I've ever seen," Louise said. "I wish you could've been there, you would have loved it. The color was perfect."

Claire sipped at her coffee. "I'm sure it would go just right with the new color on your face."

Louise looked away, turning her attention to cutting out a piece of brownie. Claire was probably her best friend, had been for nearly three years. But some things were supposed to be off limits. Things that had remained unspoken for a long time, and would have remained so except for Claire's insistence on bringing it up again. "I don't want to talk about it."

"I know, I know—but you can't keep letting him *do* this to you."

"It's not his fault, not really. It's me. I do things wrong, I'm too slow. I try not to, but sometimes I just get him mad."

"That's garbage and you know it. There's no excuse for the things he does to you. And how about you? Don't you ever get mad? Don't you ever get angry at what he does?"

Louise stopped as she put the brownie down on the plate.

Don't you ever get mad?

She nodded. "Sometimes. Sometimes, like this morning, I get so mad at him—I could feel it burning inside me, like my whole body was about to explode in fire and smoke and I *hate* myself when I feel like that."

"So instead you bury it. For God's sake, Louise, let it out. It's okay."

Louise smiled. "That's not how my mother raised me," she said, and absently petted the porcelain dog on the counter, "or my sister. And though I don't know about her, there are times I'm afraid."

"Afraid of what? Him?"

"No," Louise said, and returned to the table. "Afraid of what all that anger might do if I ever let it out."

Tuesday

Louise put the finishing touches to the dining room table. Four place settings. The best china. Cloth napkins. A fresh floral arrangement in the middle of the table, just like the one she'd seen in a magazine. She was just lighting the candles when she heard the front door open and close again.

"I'm home."

"Back here," she called.

He stood in the doorway, still clutching his thermos. "What's with the extra place settings?"

"Phil and Claire are coming over for dinner. We set it up last week—remember?"

From the look on his face, he didn't. "Yeah, sure. How come all the fancy stuff?"

"Well, I just thought it would be—nice, I guess. Doesn't it look pretty? I found some of this stuff in the attic. We haven't used it in years. I just thought maybe you might like something nice. You work so hard. Maybe a nice dinner would help you relax a little."

The doorbell rang behind Jack. "That must be them now." With a final glance at the table, she moved past Jack into the living room. She could just see them through the window.

"Right on time," Louise said.

"As always," Claire said, holding a large salad bowl. "Where can I put this?"

"The kitchen's fine. Here, let me get some spoons for that."

Behind them, Jack closed the door behind Phil.

"How you doing, Jack?"

"Fine, fine—listen, can I see you in the garage a minute? Got something I want to show you."

"Sure."

"Don't be too long," Claire called to them as they headed toward the garage. "I think Louise has outdone herself here."

"Do you approve?" Louise said, nodding toward the table as she searched for the appropriate salad spoons.

"Very nice. Is this an Occasion?"

"No, I just thought from now on, maybe if I tried a little harder, Jack would—you know."

Claire nodded. She knew. She smiled, but it seemed to Louise a smile of resignation and care and dismay. She opened her arms and, to Louise's surprise, hugged her. "You're a sweet, forgiving fool, and he doesn't deserve you."

Louise turned away to continue the search for the spoons, embarrassed but somehow feeling very good about herself just now. One more check of the cutlery drawer revealed the spoons hiding behind the silverware tray. "Here you go," she said, and handed them to Claire.

"Thanks."

Louise checked her watch. "The roast's about ready. I'd better get Jack. You know how those two are once they get talking."

She headed down the hallway that connected to the garage, pausing just outside the door. She could hear them talking inside. Phil sounded upset about something, and for a moment, she hesitated, not sure she should interrupt.

"Look, Jack," she could hear Phil say, "what you do on your own time is your own business, but don't drag me into it, okay?"

"Will you give me a break? It's not like I'm asking something big here."

I shouldn't be doing this, she thought, but went ahead and pushed the door open just a crack. Phil was standing beneath the garage light as Jack absently put his power tools into their racks, talking all the while.

"All you have to do is say Frank called you Saturday to go fishing Sunday," Jack said, "and you couldn't make it because you had work or something, so I had to go with him. That's all."

"That's all. Just lie for you."

"Hell, Phil, it might not even come up. I just want us to be clear on this in case it does, okay?"

Phil shook his head in disbelief. "All right, all right. Jesus. How long do you think you can keep doing this? It's only a matter of time before she finds out."

"She won't find out anything. You got to realize she's not real bright, Phil. She believes what you tell her. You tell her the sun shines at night, and she'll go out at midnight with her sunglasses on. As a woman—hell, as a human being—she's not worth the powder to blow her up."

"And Denise is?"

Louise leaned against the wall, distantly aware of the fact that her hands were trembling. She let go of the doorknob, afraid the shaking might give her away.

Although she couldn't see his face, she could hear the smile in Jack's voice. "Phil, she's got legs up to here. And what's between 'em—oh, man, if you only knew."

The world kicked slantwise beneath her, and for a moment she thought she was going to be sick. As from a great distance, she heard her own thoughts. *Close the door, remember to close the door or they'll know you've been listening.* She did it, or thought she did, as if it mattered, as if anything mattered anymore, and walked numbly back down the hall toward the kitchen.

Oh, God, she thought. *Oh, God, oh, God, oh, God.*

She walked automatically to the sink, to the fresh carrots that needed slicing, the carrots she'd picked so carefully that afternoon at the grocery store, and she knew they were there for a reason, but she couldn't seem to remember what it was.

"Louise?" Claire appeared at her elbow. "Louise? You okay?"

Louise nodded. "I'm—I'm fine."

"You sure? You look—"

"I said I'm fine, all right?" She grabbed one of the carrots and began cutting, slicing it into neat, precise one-quarter-inch-thin slices, just like she'd been taught.

Phil came into the room behind her and said something to Claire. It might have been about Jack coming in, in a second, but she barely heard it, because she was busy slicing carrots, because that's what was important right now, nothing else, she couldn't think of anything else, didn't want to deal with anything else, just slice them the way she was supposed to because she always did what she was told, she took care of the house just the way she was told and she made the eggs just the way she was told.

Oh God Christ in heaven I hate him how could he do this to me he was hitting me and going to her putting his hands all over her the same hands he used to hit me and hit me and hit me and I hate him how could he

Inside the garage, Jack was hanging up the last of the power tools when he became aware of the sound. A deep, rumbling, low-pitched growl from somewhere behind him. He turned, slowly, knowing immediately that it was back.

The Doberman stood against the far wall, not moving, just watching him, chest vibrating with the growl that seemed to come from a place impossibly deep inside it. Watching him with a hatred that was terrible to see. Lips curled in fury.

It stepped forward.

Jack backpedaled along the worktable, not taking his eyes off it, fumbling for the rack he knew was there, the shotgun that was hanging on the wall, damn it, it had to be there somewhere.

* * *

Chopping. Chopping and carving and cutting and slicing.

A hand on her arm. "Louise?"

Chopping

The Doberman was halfway across the garage when his hand brushed the cartridges. He thought at any moment it would rush him. But it moved forward slowly, deliberately, one step at a time, never taking its eyes off him, slow and confident and inevitable.

He raised the shotgun to his shoulder.

and slicing and slashing and

"Louise?"

A hand took hers, more insistently this time. It took the knife out of her hands and turned her around. After a moment she managed to focus on Claire. "Are you okay? You're white as a sheet."

Only distantly aware of doing it, Louise nodded. Claire was looking at her *that way* again, with a mix of concern and pity—and in that moment the rage passed, and there was nothing left but a great, gaping numbness in the middle of her soul that chilled her to the marrow.

and *fired*.

Jack winced at the muzzle flash. He'd pulled both triggers and the kick had nearly knocked him over. He blinked to clear away the cordite in his eyes, and looked to where the Doberman had been, where it was supposed to be.

Except it wasn't there.

There was only a huge hole in the gun rack he'd started to build last summer. As he heard the others running down the hall toward the garage, calling his name, asking if he was okay, he broke the shotgun and pulled out the shells. There was no way it could've gotten past him that fast.

But it had been there. He *had* seen it, damn it.

* * *

The two policemen who came to the door a few minutes after the shotgun blast looked unconvinced. "I wish we could be of more help, Mr. Simonton, but we talked to your neighbors and they say they haven't seen a dog matching the description you gave us, and as far as we can determine, none of them owns a dog like that."

"Then it's from outside the neighborhood," Jack said, "maybe it got loose from some kennel, maybe it's got rabies, who knows? I'm just telling you I saw it twice already, and you people better do something about it. That thing could kill somebody. I mean, what the hell am I paying taxes for?"

One of the policemen, the taller of the two, looked to Louise. "Ma'am? You're sure you didn't see it?"

Louise straightened in her chair. "No, I'm sorry, I didn't."

"Then I'm afraid there's really nothing we can do until it turns up again. We've put the word out. If you or anyone sees it, just let us know. Meanwhile, Mr. Simonton, I would remind you of the laws about the use of firearms within city limits. Next time you fire that thing, I suggest you be more certain what you're aiming at."

With that, they left. Claire and Phil made their good-byes a few minutes later. Nobody felt much like dinner now. Whether they sensed what Louise was feeling, she didn't know and barely cared. With an uncharacteristic lack of interest, she watched them leave, cradling the porcelain dog in her lap.

Jack started up as soon as they were out the door. "You were a fat lot of help," he said. "Why can't you back me up once in a while? Why can't you *do* something besides play with that damned piece of junk all the time?"

She left it in her lap. "I didn't see it, Jack. I can't lie, you know that."

"Great. One more thing you can't do."

He went across the room to switch on the television. She set the porcelain figurine down on the coffee table. "Jack?"

"Hmm?"

"How was the fishing Sunday? You never did tell me how it went."

He shrugged, didn't look back at her. "It was fine. You know Frank, talk, talk, talk. Scares away every fish in the county. Surprised he caught anything at all."

"And you didn't catch anything, all day."

"That's right," he said, swiveling around to face her. "What is this, the third degree or something?"

She said nothing.

He stood. "You know, I don't think I like the tone in your voice. Always suspicious, aren't you? So now you're saying I can't even go out fishing with a friend?"

"No, Jack, I was just—"

He moved toward her, his face darkening. She got to her feet quickly, backing up. "You said no, Louise. You know I don't like it when you say no. You got a problem?"

"Jack—"

"You got a problem? Huh? I'll give you a problem!"

Then she was shrieking at him, the voice hardly recognizable as her own. *"I heard you, Jack! I heard you with Phil! I heard you damn it!"*

He paused. For the first time, she'd given him pause. Then he started forward again.

And he was smiling.

"So what?"

"Jack—"

Advancing toward her. "So what're you gonna do about it?"

"No, Jack, please!"

And her head rang with the force of a slap that caught her across the face, and then another, and she held up her hands to fend off the blows but he was too strong, he was always too strong, and another slap knocked her head against the wall, and now she was screaming, "Stop it, Jack! *Stop it, stop it, STOP IT!*"

He stopped. Suddenly, abruptly, he stopped, and through her upraised arms she saw it.

A shimmering in the air between them. A twisting

and a swirling and then the Doberman was there, just there, snarling and snapping, lips skinned back in feral rage. It lunged for his leg, teeth closing on air as Jack cried out and jumped backward, nearly falling over the coffee table in his hurry to get away.

It started toward him.

"Don't just stand there!" he yelled. "Do something!"

She didn't move. She stood with her back to the wall, hands pressed to her mouth. She knew she should cry out, or run, or call for help.

She did nothing.

The Doberman advanced.

Jack bolted for the door, threw it open.

The Doberman was outside, on the porch.

He slammed the door.

It was back inside. With him.

"Christ," he said, and ran for the kitchen, anywhere that was away from the Doberman.

She waited for it to run after him.

It didn't.

It paused, and turned, and looked at her.

She met its gaze. For only a moment.

But long enough for her to recognize the rage in its eyes.

"Oh my God," she whispered, and looked to the porcelain dog, the porcelain Doberman she had held and cradled and wept over. "Oh, God, no, it can't be."

The Doberman turned and ran into the kitchen, after Jack, howling and snarling, snapping at the air. "No!" she called, and snatched up the porcelain figure, running after it. "Stop! I don't want you to do it!"

Jack was already at the back door, throwing it open.

The Doberman was outside.

No way out.

He ran back into the living room, pulling her with him. "Come on! We've got to get out of here! Goddamn thing's not normal—some kind of *thing*, I don't know—"

She fought his grip. "No! Jack, I'm sorry, but I can't

make it stop it just came out I didn't know and now I can't stop it I *can't stop it!*"

He grabbed her, shook her hard. "What are you talking about?"

"*It's me, damn it, it's me!* Don't you understand? It's here because I wanted you to stop hitting me and now it won't go away!"

He grabbed her by the shoulders.

A low, threatening growl came from behind him.

He spun around.

Too late.

It leapt, slamming into him. They fell to the floor, a tangle of limbs and teeth snapping at him, trying for wrists, face, throat, anything that was soft and vulnerable and Jack. He cried out, pushing it away, trying to get a grip on it, but it twisted in his hands, all teeth and fur and fury, and it was like trying to grab a handful of razors.

She wanted to stop it.

She didn't want to stop it.

God, it had hurt so much.

Blood appeared on his arms, through his shirt.

"No," she said, and she thought it sounded as though it were coming from someone else. "No."

The Doberman hesitated.

Jack lurched to his feet and stumbled down the hall, toward the garage.

She looked to where the Doberman was—but it wasn't.

She hurried to catch up with him.

"Where is it?" Jack was shrieking now. He looked at her in the doorway. "The shotgun!" The rack was empty beside him. "Where the hell's the shotgun?"

A growl behind him.

He turned, slowly, to face it.

The Doberman stood in the middle of the garage, straddling what remained of the shotgun.

He reached under the counter, came up with a crowbar and held it in front of him. "All right," he said, "all *right*. You want a piece of me? You come and get it. Come on—COME ON!"

The Doberman launched itself at Jack, and they went down in a tumble, lashing out at each other, trying for the soft places.

The Doberman found it first.

Its teeth closed on his arm, and held on. He screamed and heaved his arm until the dog fell off, taking a piece of his flesh with it. It tumbled to the ground and came up snarling.

Jack held the crowbar in his good arm, no longer convinced of the good it would do.

The Doberman advanced.

"Louise," he said, "please, for God's sake—call it off! *Make it stop!*"

She held out the figurine, her hands trembling. "I can't, Jack! Don't you see? Maybe I could've, once. When I still loved you. But I—God help me, Jack, I don't love you anymore! And now—now there's nothing I can do! I can't stop it!"

Jack licked his lips, edging around as the dog came closer. "Look," he said, and she recognized the voice as the one he used when he was thinking fast, on his face a look of sudden realization, "just call it off and—and I promise it'll be different. Just give me a chance, okay? Just a—*chance!*"

And he lunged.

Not at the dog. At her.

At the figurine in her hands.

He caught it with the crowbar and knocked it clear across the garage. It struck with the crunch of shattering porcelain.

But the Doberman was still there, now positioned between him and the crowbar.

Louise didn't notice. She walked past him, toward the glittering debris at the far end of the garage.

The Doberman advanced.

He scuttled away from it, came up against the wall. "It didn't work," he said, his voice a mix of surprise and fear. "It didn't—Louise? Louise, get—get it AWAY from me!"

She stood over the shattered porcelain figure, and it was as though the man in the garage with her was a complete stranger.

The Doberman stopped. Waiting.

"You broke it," she said, crying. "You broke it and it was the only thing that was really mine and you *broke it* and I *hate you! I HATE YOU!* I wish you were *dead!*"

As though it had been only awaiting that final word, that last permission, the Doberman leapt at Jack in a killing frenzy, teeth snapping at his throat, its roar a nightmare sound, revealed finally in the totality of its madness and rage and pain, and she wanted it to hurt him, she wanted it to hurt him, she wanted—

She pressed her hands to her ears to shut out the sound of his screaming.

Snarling. Tearing. Just another second and it would all be over.

She closed her eyes.

"No," she said, her voice barely a whisper. "Stop it. Stop it! STOP IT!"

The garage vibrated with her scream.

The Doberman stopped, turned, looked at her.

Jack, crying out, but low, afraid to get its attention again, pushed back from it as far as he could.

Louise shook her head, sobbing. "I can't. I just—can't." She looked down at the broken porcelain figure, then at the Doberman. "I can't. But it's broken. I don't know where to send you, where to—"

She stopped.

She knew.

Though she had not wanted to admit it, she had always known.

She bent down on one knee and held out her arms to the Doberman. "Come," she said. "Come on. Come —home."

The Doberman padded softly toward her, and as it drew nearer, she thought it began to shimmer, to become less substantial. A foot away from her, she found she could just see through it to the far wall.

She reached out further. She wanted to touch it. Just once, before it disappeared, she wanted to touch it.

But it was gone.

When she came back the next morning to pick up her things, she had hoped not to find him there, hoped that he would be off somewhere with Diane or Debbie or whatever her name was.

And though he had not been there when she arrived, the sound of his pickup pulling into the driveway came as she was filling the last suitcase. He was getting out just as she crossed the driveway to the car she'd rented that morning. His face was bruised, and his arm hung painfully at his side where the doctor had bandaged it. Apparently he had had time to plan things out, because when she saw him, she recognized the look in his face.

She had had her pound of flesh. Now he would want his.

He came up alongside the car as she threw the suitcase into the trunk. "Where the hell do you think *you're* going?"

She slammed it shut. "Away, Jack. Away from you."

"That so? You think I'm just going to let you leave after what you did to me? You sent your little friend away, remember? And now I've got a score to settle with you, little lady."

She didn't answer, only kept on moving toward the driver's side door.

He put his hand on the door to block her way. "You leave, and I'll just have to come after you."

She met his gaze without flinching. "No. You. Won't."

And from inside the car . . . a growling.

Inside, the Doberman sat on the passenger seat, watching him warily with eyes like smoldering coals.

Jack took his hand off the car door and stood well out of the way as she got into the car, started the engine, and backed out of the driveway onto the main road, heading for any place that was not this place.

Never looking back.

Louise Simonton, driven by pain into the desperate regions of the human heart—only to discover the pre-eminence of her own personal power. An act of recognition that reverberates in, and out, of the Twilight Zone.

Introduction to Special Service

A curious thing has been happening to the American public over the last decade.

If you look at documentary or news footage from the sixties and early seventies, you'll notice that the average guy on the street, upon having a microphone and television camera stuck in his face, got a trifle nervous. He stiffened, his eyes got just the tiniest bit twitchoid, he leaned too close to the microphone, and he always looked hot and fidgety under the portable klieg lights.

Now, turn on the local news tonight and watch for the man on the street interviews. You'll find, on the whole, that they're cooler, more controlled, they look into the camera, they smile pleasantly, stand straight, and usually seem quite at home.

Switch channels.

A reporter does a live remote from a crime scene. In the background, kids and adults crowd around just inside camera range, waving, shouting, and generally carrying on, utterly heedless of the five-car pileup in the background.

Go to the local shopping mall, where camera stores have set up sample video cameras, and watch the passersby smile into the lens, wave, pose. Go to the little studio, like the one in New Orleans, just off Bourbon Street, where for twenty bucks you can star in your own music video, lip-syncing to your favorite song.

Television cameras on rooftops, in airports, banks, supermarkets, and convenience stores, at weddings and picnics and graduations . . . shockproof black and white Minicams for sale as gifts for kids . . . video-camera backups for household security.

Everywhere you turn, there is the Eye.

We are no longer merely the Media Generation.

We *are* the media.

Toss in the sudden increase in so-called "reality programming," and it kinda makes you wonder if we're being set up for something, doesn't it?

Hence, a tale of a very special service, coming to a cable system near you soon.

"Special Service," production #87042, starred David Naughton (John Selig), Keith Knight (Archie), Susan Roman (Leslie), Elias Zarou (Spence), Marlon McGann (Receptionist), Tedd Dillon (Large Man), and Barbara Von Radicki (Pretty Woman). It began filming on December 5, 1988, under the direction of Randy Bradshaw. First broadcast April 9, 1989.

SPECIAL SERVICE

The clock radio chimed at 8:30 A.M., then switched to the preset station. The usually pleasant disc jockey played the usual Vivaldi. John Selig stretched, then sat up in bed. Leslie was already up and fixing breakfast downstairs. The smell of bacon and coffee drifted up the stairs and into the bedroom.

Another day, another one hundred and twenty dollars and fifty cents, John thought, and staggered into the hall bathroom.

"One egg or two?" Leslie called upstairs.

"Two."

He'd risk the cholesterol. He was feeling particularly good this morning. His presentation was finished, the color copies had come out perfectly, the ad campaign was solid . . . everything inside told him that this was going to be a very good day.

Introduction to Mr. John Selig, a reasonably average man who goes through life with both eyes open and both hands firmly on the wheel. Mr. John Selig, practical and steady—who is about to be blindsided by the Twilight Zone.

As he began to shave, John noticed that the mirror was slightly askew. He frowned. He'd installed the mirror himself, as the one on the medicine cabinet wasn't quite the right height. He didn't like it when things he'd done himself started acting up. Somehow, it was easier if it was someone else's fault.

He nudged the mirror back into place, square with the floor and ceiling. It stayed for a moment, then slipped back. He nudged it up again, trying to get it to catch on the nail that was back there, he *knew* it was back there, he'd hammered it in himself.

It wouldn't catch. He tried to force it up again— and abruptly it slipped off its hanger and crashed to the floor. He jumped back, away from the spray of glass.

Concern over getting a shard of glass in his foot was, he would decide much later, the reason it took a full moment for the fact that there was a huge hole behind the mirror to register on his brain.

And another moment for him to recognize the object that was inside the hole behind the mirror: a television camera.

It was during that moment that a small red light suddenly began winking on and off, on and off, and he thought there was a curious buzzing noise coming from within the hole that wasn't there earlier.

"What the hell?" he said aloud, stepping closer to inspect it. Yes, it was definitely a television camera. And yes, that was definitely a worrisome red light. And yes, that was a most curious buzzing noise. He reached down and carefully picked up one of the pieces of the broken mirror. The mirrored side still reflected his face. But the other side of the glass was transparent. He could see right through it—as, obviously, the camera had also been able to do.

"What the hell?" he said again, deciding not to abandon a perfectly good question until it returned with an equally good answer.

From downstairs, he heard the front door open and slam shut again. "Les?" he called. "Leslie? C'mere!"

He could hear footsteps pounding up the stairs toward the bathroom. He turned, but it wasn't Leslie who stood breathlessly in the doorway. It was a repairman, dressed in overalls, carrying a toolbox, wearing a cap and a very businesslike expression.

"That's all right, sir," he said, brushing past John and heading for the mirror. "Don't you worry about a thing. Be fixed in a jiffy." He spoke with a pleasant English accent.

Moving quickly, he started to replace the broken mirror.

"Absolutely scandalous, just shoddy workmanship, pure and simple. Terribly sorry about all this, but that's just the way it is these days, isn't it? Always rush, rush, rush, nobody giving a fig for quality, not like the old days—"

The repairman hammered the new mirror into place. The entire job took only a few seconds. He was a very good repairman.

The only problem that was gradually dawning on John was that 1) he hadn't called a repairman and 2) no repairman could've gotten here that quickly even if he *had* called for one.

"Wait a minute," John said. "What do you think you're doing?"

"Fixing your mirror, what's it look like?"

"But there's a camera back there!"

The repairman looked around, seeming quite astonished by this bit of intelligence. "Where? I don't see a camera."

"Of course not! That's because you just covered it up!"

"Did I? Well, that's one job done, then. Good day."

With a tip of his hat, the repairman hustled out of the bathroom. John looked from the departing figure, to the mirror, and back again. "Hey!" he called. *"Hey!* Come back here!"

John took off down the stairs at a dead run, charging ahead of the repairman and barely managing to block the doorway in time. "Where the hell do you think you're going?"

"Back to work," the repairman said, "and I suggest you do the same. It's nearly nine o'clock, and you know how Mr. Fetheringall gets when—" He caught himself and shook his head. "Never mind. Ignore that bit. Never said a thing. Good-day."

He tried for the doorknob. John put himself in the way. "Oh, no, not until I—wait a minute! How do you know my boss's name?"

"I don't."

"Yes, you do! You just said it!"

"No, I didn't. Must have me mistaken for somebody else. Good-day."

He tried for the door. John refused to move.

"Look, are you going to stand there all day?" the repairman said.

"Yes! Look, I want to know what you were doing up there!"

"Up where?"

"UPSTAIRS! THE MIRROR! THE TV CAMERA! REMEMBER?"

The repairman looked vacantly at John for a moment, then nodded, quite calmly John thought, as though remembering at last where he'd left his keys. "Ah, yes. That. Nothing whatsoever. Just a little routine maintenance."

"That's a TV CAMERA! You've been spying on me!"

The repairman—John noticed the name tag on his shirt read *Archie,* written in script under the anonymous letters JSTV—looked greatly offended at this. "I have *not* been spying on you. It's just part of the job, that's all. You do your work, and I do mine, and now why don't you be a good fellow and let me get back to it?"

"No. I'm going to call the police."

"Oh, you wouldn't want to do that, no, I don't think so."

"Why not?"

"False complaint. Show me where fixing a camera is against the law."

John opened his mouth to reply, but nothing came out. He was quite right, actually, nothing illegal about fixing a camera—

What are you talking about? his brain screamed at him, and he came up out of his reverie just in time to block Archie's hand as he reached for the doorknob.

"That's not the point! I DIDN'T PUT THAT CAMERA THERE IN THE FIRST PLACE! IT'S NOT MY CAMERA! I DON'T EVEN KNOW HOW IT GOT THERE!"

Archie appraised him with a look of utter calm and sudden comprehension. "Ah, well then, you want Installation. Sorry, but that's not my department. Have a nice day."

He grabbed again at the doorknob, barely managing to get a piece of it before John slammed the door shut. "You know, you're really not as pleasant in person as you are on TV," Archie said.

"That's it. I'm calling the police."

He grabbed Archie by the arm and started marching him toward the phone. Archie twisted in his grip, but John wasn't about to let go.

"See here," Archie complained, "there's really no need for this, I—" He looked around nervously, then lowered his voice. "Listen, John—can I call you John?— I'd rather not we made a big scene over this, it makes everything so—complicated. I'd tell you, really I would, but—"

He looked around again, nervously. John wondered if this was a habit with him. "Look, all right, I'll tell you —but we have to stand right—in there."

John looked to where he was pointing.

He was pointing at the hall closet.

"You're mad," John said.

"That's the only place."

"In the *closet?* Why there?"

"It's outside camera range," Archie said, drawing him toward the closet.

"But the camera's in the bathroom."

"No, no, the *other* cameras."

John was still processing this when Archie jumped ahead and stepped into the closet. *"What* other cameras?" No answer. "Get out of my closet!"

From inside: "No!"

"I'm not going in there."

"Then you'll never find out what this is all about."

John sighed. Waited a moment, then sighed again. Under the circumstances, it seemed the right thing to do. *I must be completely out of my mind,* he thought, and stepped into the closet, drawing the door closed after him.

It was dark inside. He reached for the string for the overhead light and pulled it. Nothing. He'd forgotten that the bulb had burned out last week. Fumbling around in the dark, narrow space, he tried to get hold of the flashlight.

He grabbed hold of something.

"That's not the flashlight," said the other voice in the darkness.

"Shut up," John said, and finally found the flashlight. He flicked it on. He thought that the light, beneath their faces, gave Archie a singularly sinister aspect. He hoped it did the same for him.

"You know, you really should have that bulb replaced," Archie said.

"Forget the bulb. Talk."

Archie hesitated. "I want you to know I'm risking my job just telling you this. You're not supposed to know, you see. I mean, it takes all the fun out of it, doesn't it?"

"Takes all the fun out of *what?*"

Archie sighed. "Look at my chest."

"Excuse me?"

He pointed to the name tag on his chest. "Here. See those letters? JSTV written in big, friendly letters?"

"Yeah, so? What about it?"

"Stands for John Selig Television. You're—well, you're on TV."

John blinked. "I am?"

"Yes. Twenty-four hours a day. You've got quite a following. Did you know you've got people who tune in, in the middle of the night just to watch you sleep? Extraordinary. Absolutely extraordinary."

John nodded, suddenly feeling as though his head had become somehow disconnected from the rest of his body and was frantically dialing directory information to get hold of it, only to find it had an unlisted number. "Who's—who's watching?"

"Oh, everyone! Well, everyone who subscribes, at least. It's a special cable channel, just started, oh, I guess five years ago. I hear the ratings are excellent, especially right here in this area. Only natural, I guess, you being a local and all."

"Everybody?" John said. "You mean—the neighbors—all the people I know—they—"

"They were quite helpful, yes. Helped us put cameras all over the place for maximum coverage. Your job, your car, the office, living room, den, bathroom—well, that one was less than perfect, wasn't it—bedroom—"

"My *bedroom?*"

Archie looked momentarily sheepish. "Well, it IS a cable service, adults only, that sort of thing. Well, now you know, so if you'll excuse me—"

With another tip of his hat, Archie plunged out of the closet and back into the hall.

"I don't believe you," John said, following him out. "How could something like this happen without someone telling me?"

"Shhhh!" Archie whispered, looking around. "That's the whole point! If you knew you were on TV, you'd act differently. It'd take all the fun out of it, like I said. So everyone on the service signs a contract specifying they won't spill the beans. Besides, it gives all the folks you know a chance to be on TV, and in my business I've learned that most people'll do *any*thing to be on TV. They'll—"

He stopped as a beeper on his belt suddenly chirruped. He switched it off and took hold of the doorknob. "Sorry. Have to go. Be a good fellow and don't tell anyone I told you, all right?"

Then he was out the door and halfway to his van before John had sufficiently pulled himself together to even consider stopping him. He started out the door, but by that time the van was already backing up, Archie in it. The repairman waved as he turned around in the street and drove away.

As it disappeared, John noticed that the letters JSTV were painted in bright red colors on the rear of the van.

He stepped back inside, closing the door behind him.

I'm losing my mind, he thought, and walked down the hall toward the kitchen.

Leslie bustled toward him from the kitchen, dressed for work. "Breakfast's on the table, better eat it before it gets cold." She kissed him on the cheek, then drew back, smiling. "And you better finish shaving before you leave."

"Where have you been?" he asked.

"Fixing breakfast," she said, quite sensibly, he thought.

"But . . . didn't you see that man?"

"What man?"

"He came right into the bathroom. I just spent ten minutes with him in the closet."

She frowned, looked into his face more closely. "Did you sleep all right last night?"

"I slept fine. It's this morning I'm having a slight problem with."

She shook her head. "Sorry, but I have no idea what you're talking about. Then again, it's not the first time." She checked her watch, and her mouth formed a small *O*. "Oh, jeez, it's later than I thought. Got to go."

She hugged him. "You have a nice day, dear," she said.

Then, still holding him, she lowered her voice and whispered into his ear, *"Don't blow it for us! The ratings are terrific!"*

With a quick kiss on the cheek she hurried past him and out the door.

For a full thirty seconds, John Selig did not move, sure that at any moment the ground would open up and swallow him into some mad, shrieking void.

The ground did not open up.

He did not go mad.

He stepped numbly into the front room, and with wide eyes, began looking at everything as though seeing it for the first time.

No, no, Archie had said, *the* other *cameras.*

He stepped over to the wall and carefully lifted the painting to look behind it. Nothing. Trying to look casual, he wandered over to the sofa, lifted one of the cushions. Nothing.

Of course not, he thought. One really good fat person, and any camera would be history.

"Well," he said, suddenly aware of the sound of his own voice, and hoping he didn't sound too artificial, "let's see. Gee, I think I left my car keys around here somewhere. I think I'll look for them."

Which is more or less exactly what he began to do.

In every single room in the house.

By a little before noon, John finally decided to call the office and tell them he wouldn't be coming in today. He wasn't feeling well, he explained. Which wasn't exactly the truth, but it wasn't entirely a lie, either.

He racked the phone and looked at the huge pile of cameras he had collected from hiding places throughout the house. Big cameras, small cameras, cameras with microphones and cameras without (presumably providing coverage for other sound cameras in the room).

Cameras in the bedroom, behind the bureau mirror.

Cameras in the front room, in a corner of the bookcase.

Cameras in the garage, the workroom, the second bedroom, the bathroom, the *other* bathroom . . . minicameras in the dashboard of his car, the trunk, buried along the front sidewalk. . . .

He picked up one of the smaller cameras. It was jet black and without markings as far as he could tell. He

tarted to pry open the back panel, in search of a serial
number, when the phone rang.

"Yes?"

A woman's voice came on the line. "This is to inform you that destruction of company property is to be
avoided at all costs. Please inform maintenance and do
not touch the equipment again. Thank you."

Click and disconnect.

He looked around. Apparently, he'd missed one.
Or two.

"Try and stop me!" he said, and slammed down the
phone.

He picked up the camera again and threw it against
the wall. It shattered with a particularly satisfying clatter of broken glass and crunched transistors.

The phone rang again.

He picked it up. "Hello?"

The same voice. "You were warned."

Click and disconnect.

John had no sooner racked the phone when the
doorbell rang.

Now what? he thought, and opened the door.

Outside stood two very large men. John decided
that they didn't look overly happy.

"Mr. Selig?" the first one said.

"Yes?"

"You're to come with us, sir."

They each took an arm and led him out of the
house. The second large man closed the door behind
them and locked it.

"Wait a minute! Let me go!" John started to struggle, but the look in their eyes said that it would not be a
terribly wise thing to do. "Where are you taking me?"

They said nothing, only continued to march him
toward a long stretch limousine parked at the curb. He
could see the letters JSTV emblazoned on the side door.

"Look," John said, "I don't know who you are, but
you can't do this to me!"

The two large men stopped beside the car and
looked to one another with apparent surprise. "You

should have told us sooner," the larger of the two said, and shoved him into the back of the limo.

Archie was already there, looking not at all pleased to be riding in the back of an otherwise splendid limousine. "Well, now you've gone and done it, haven't you?"

The engine roared to life, and the limo shot forward. "Done what? Where are we going?"

"Into quite a bit of trouble, I'd say. Yes, quite a bit of very serious trouble indeed." He pointed to the back of the front seat. "Smile for the birdy, Mr. Selig."

Naturally, there was a camera there.

The car finally came to a stop at a security gate outside a tall, glass-and-steel office building. As they pulled into the driveway, John noticed two things.

First, the truly extraordinary number of extremely attractive, nubile young women crowding the gate and mobbing the car as they drove through.

Second, the logo bannered in wrought iron over the security gate: JSTV.

The women elbowed one another aside, trying to get near enough to peer in the smoked-glass windows of the limo, pointing and shouting and generally carrying on. It was the sort of reaction he'd come to expect for rock groups and movie stars.

"Who're they?" John asked.

Archie seemed barely aware of them, staring glumly ahead at the office building with all the enthusiasm characteristic of a trip to the dentist for major gum surgery. "Fans," he said.

"I can see that. Whose fans?"

"Yours. Now that the secret's out, they can finally come out of the woodwork." He looked out at the pressing bodies, the tangle of hair and lipstick and polished nails, and shook his head. "All those hormones, repressed for five years—disgusting, isn't it? Probably rip the clothes right off you in a second. Just like that."

John glanced at the women. Part of him found the idea rather intriguing. "Do you really think so?"

Archie didn't answer, his sullen funk growing as

they passed the crowd and entered the JSTV Studios main lot.

Just jealous, John thought, and waved back at the women as the car pulled away.

He was reasonably sure he saw one of them faint.

It was a *big* room.

Soft grey walls, maroon piping along the corners, a black granite desk with just one telephone on it and nothing else, and a receptionist who smiled quite brightly at him as he and Archie stepped into the room.

Correction: as he was nudged from behind, and the door slammed shut behind him.

Accuracy was important in these things.

"Mr. Selig? Mr. Spence will be with you momentarily. Please, make yourself comfortable."

Archie took the first seat at hand, near a television set. John thought he was getting downright sullen.

"Thank you," John said, adding, "is there a restroom around here?"

"Right in through there."

She indicated a door recessed into one wall. He smiled at her, and stepped through.

He was halfway across the bathroom floor when *it* occurred to him. He stopped in midstride, turned around, stepped back into the waiting room, and sat down next to Archie, who was fiddling with the remote control.

"What's wrong?" Archie said.

"Afraid there might be cameras in there, too."

"Ah."

It was then that John noticed what was on the television screen.

Himself. In the waiting room. Looking at the television. At himself.

Archie flicked through channels, and the same image was on every one. "Typical, isn't it?" Archie said. "All these channels, and nothing interesting on."

John was in the middle of deciding if it was worth his time to hit Archie when the receptionist's phone beeped at her. She lifted the receiver, listened quietly, said something he didn't catch, then hung up. She stood and smiled across at him. "If you please—right this way, Mr. Selig."

He followed her to the doorway at the other end of the office and let her open it for him, closing it again as he stepped inside.

The next room was just like the first—except that it was larger, the desk longer, and instead of a television, rows of books lined the walls. A slightly overweight, greying man sat behind the desk, dressed quite conservatively in a dark blue suit and what was probably an old school tie. Somehow, he reminded John of his grandfather.

Which was, he supposed, probably the intent.

"Sit down, Mr. Selig," he said. "Please, make yourself comfortable."

"Thank you." John sat in the nearest of the highbacked, leather chairs, sinking nearly an inch into the seat.

"Would you like a cigar?" Spence said. "Something to drink?"

"No. Thank you."

"Ah. Comfy, then?"

"Yes. Thank you."

"Good, good," Spence said, sitting back in his chair and staring up at the ceiling. "Now then, Mr. Selig . . . *what the hell are you trying to do to us?*"

The suddenness nearly knocked John out of his chair. He recovered quickly, however. "What do you *mean*, what am I trying to do to you? What are *you* doing to *me?*"

"To you? My dear Mr. Selig, look around. This is a multimillion dollar business. When we—when *you* first went on the air five years ago, we could barely get a hundred dollars for a thirty-second commercial. Now we're right up there getting a hundred thousand dollars for a thirty-second spot. We got here through long and careful work. We were just starting to break even, clear out our deficits—and now you pull this."

"So you're the one who decided to do all this?" John said.

"No. It wasn't me."

"Then who?"

Spence shrugged. "Who decided you have to pay taxes? Who decided you have to get up for work at eight instead of ten? Who decided what money you use, what fashions you wear?"

"I don't know."

Another shrug. "Same guy."

"This isn't the same thing," John said. "You can't just put my life on television! I have rights!"

"Yeah?" Spence reached into a desk drawer and pulled out a heavy book. "Here. The U.S. Constitution and the Bill of Rights. You show me where it says in here that we can't put you on TV."

"That's a technicality."

"Whole empires have been built on technicalities," Spence said. "Like this one." He took a long breath, let it out slowly. "Mr. Selig, I have no wish to argue with you, so let me come straight to the heart of the matter. Over the last five years you have become an institution in American television. People like you. I like you. Hell, I watch you every Friday night, playing bridge with the Clearsons. Oh, and by the way—he cheats. We've got a better view of his hand than you do."

"I thought as much," John said, "he's always—"

What are you saying?

"Look, I just don't understand. Why put me on television? What could possibly be interesting about me?"

"You know Marilyn Carstairs," Spence said, "the woman on all those game shows, black hair, rhinestone glasses? What's the last thing she actually did that made her famous?"

John started to answer, realized he didn't have the slightest idea, and let his mouth close again.

"Can't come up with a thing, can you? Well, don't feel bad, neither can anyone else. But she's on TV. Some people are famous just for being famous. You put their faces on TV long enough, next thing you know, they're celebrities. We took the same chance on you. And it paid off. Things got slow once in a while, but you have to expect that. Like when you lost your job, two years ago. At first, the ratings went up. People were wondering what would happen next. You stayed out of work. The ratings went down. So we stepped in and arranged for that new job at InfoTech."

"*You* did that?"

"Of course. Mr. Selig," he said in a voice of infinite patience, "do you really think things happen by accident in this world? Haven't you ever noticed how sometimes things just—seem to go your way? Out of the blue, something'll happen, and you'll think, 'Well, isn't that strange? Isn't that lucky?'. That would be us, Mr. Selig. We have a whole department in charge of happy coincidences. How do you think you met Leslie?"

"My *wife?*"

"Hired by us, yes. We auditioned over a hundred women before we found someone right for the part. Though I suppose now we'll have to find her a new spot —if you persist in making a federal case out of all this."

Spence rose and went to the window, pointing to the parking lot below, at the people filing in and out of the building. "Thousands of jobs and millions of dollars of income are riding on you, Mr. Selig. Is your so-called privacy really worth more than that? Can't you just— forget it all happened? Go back, live out your life the way you did before?"

"No," John said, feeling, despite himself, a little less resolute than he had earlier. He hadn't realized that so much was involved, so many jobs dependent on him, so many—

Wait a minute.

"That's not fair," John said. "I didn't start this, and you've no right to make me feel guilty. I want my privacy back, and that's final."

Spence sighed. "As you wish, Mr. Selig. I'll have a car brought round to take you home."

He pushed a button on his desk and headed for the

door, pausing just long enough to glance back at John and shake his head. "You could've been our biggest star, Mr. Selig."

Then he was gone.

Is that it? he thought. *That quick? That simple?* Somehow it felt anticlimactic. He'd expected a struggle,

tap, tap

a fight over who owned his life, a—

tap, tap

A tapping?

He looked to the source of the sound. A woman—a very *attractive* woman, part of his brain noted—stood on the window ledge. A considerable wind ruffled her hair, and she seemed quite adamant about getting inside.

Perhaps, John thought, it had something to do with the fact that they were six stories up.

He went to the window and opened it, helping her inside. As she turned to him, it occurred to John that she was one of the women he'd seen outside, as they'd driven onto the JSTV lot.

"It's you, isn't it?" she said. "Mr. Selig, oh, I'm your biggest fan, I watch you all the time, oh, I think you're just wonderful."

"Well, thank you very much, but I—"

She pulled a small book out of her purse. "Can I have your autograph?"

"No, I—" He stopped. Why not? "I suppose it couldn't hurt. It's all over now anyway."

As he signed his name, she leaned in closer to him. "I want to have your baby," she whispered.

"I beg your pardon?"

"Then a lock of your hair. A jacket."

"No!"

"Anything!"

"*No!*"

"Please!" She clutched at his arm, dragging him toward the floor. "Oh, Mr. Selig, I came all this way. PLEASE!"

He pushed her off him. "I said no. Now I'm sorry, but you're going to have to leave."

Taking her by the elbow and ignoring her protests, he led her to the door Spence had used a moment earlier, opened it—and there stood the rest of the women he'd seen downstairs.

"There he is!" they screamed as one, and lunged for the door.

John slammed it shut, locking it from inside. The door shook with the pounding on the other side.

Across the room, the other door banged open. John turned, relieved to see that it was only Archie.

"I'm supposed to take you home," Archie said.

The woman beside John pouted and pressed a sheet of paper into his hands. "Call me," she said, and headed for the window. "I'll let myself out."

She even blew him a kiss as she stepped back out onto the ledge.

"Amazing," John said. "Absolutely amazing."

Archie seemed not at all impressed. "Well, you'd best come along, now. I want you to know I've been sacked because of all this. Two weeks' notice, and out, cold as you please."

"I'm sorry," John said, truly meaning it. It seemed they'd been through so much together, and he'd only been doing his job. "I didn't mean to get you in trouble. I wish there was something I could do."

Archie glanced down at the sheet of paper with the phone number in John's hand and snatched it away, putting it in his own pocket and patting it through the cloth. "You just did."

The drive home in Archie's compact wasn't nearly as exciting.

Three days later, when the last of the repairmen had left, John took a quick tour of the house. All the damage done by his removal of the cameras had been seamlessly repaired, all paid for by JSTV.

He wandered back into the living room, to the sacks of mail that had been deposited there. He'd barely worked his way through a third of it, and more was coming everyday. He had plenty of time to read now that Leslie was gone (he'd gotten a telegram saying thanks for all the exposure, and inviting him to see her in summer stock in San Diego over the summer), and since Infotech had given him the week off (he wondered how much longer he'd have the job—apparently they'd gotten plenty of free advertising through him, and now that was gone).

He picked one of the letters at random. *Dear John,* it began, *I just wanted to say that I'm one of your biggest fans, and I think you're one of the nicest men I've ever seen, on or off television. I'm terribly depressed about your show, though. I'm sure it must be quite a blow.*

He was considering how to answer that one when the doorbell rang. He opened the door to find Archie standing on the porch.

"Oh, hi," John said. "Come on in. I was just going over the fan mail. I had no idea so much had been collected. And the gifts—offers of marriage—it's amazing."

"Hmm," Archie said, unimpressed. John wondered if he'd practiced that *hmm* until he'd gotten it exactly right. "I just came to drop this by. Finishing off old responsibilities before moving on, all that sort of stuff."

John took the offered envelope, began ripping it open.

"It's a check," Archie said. "Back pay for the last five years. Oh, yes, they always intended to pay you. They just kept it in a trust fund until you either found out or the show got canceled."

John looked at the figure in front of the decimals.

He'd never seen that many zeros in one place before. "This," he started, then worked his voice down into a slightly more natural register, "this is a *lot* of money."

"Hmm." There it was again. "Yes, I suppose it is."

He then went to the corner of the living room,

where all the cameras had been stored for pickup, and began gathering them up.

"Um, what are you doing?" John asked, trying to sound casual.

"Company equipment. Not needed here anymore, now is it? Show's been canceled. Now that you know, it's not much fun anymore, now is it?"

"No, I suppose not," John said, unable to take his eyes off all those zeros. "But the money—the women—all this!"

"Sorry," Archie said. "Not my department."

"Then—it's really over? Just like that?"

Tucking the cables and equipment under one arm, Archie turned, looked at him. "You wanted your life back, just the way it was, right? Well, that's what you've got. And I hope you're satisfied."

With that, he started toward the door.

"I'm sorry about your job," John said. "Really, I am."

"Yeah, well, that's the way it goes. Thanks for the thought, though. Guess that makes two of us."

"Yeah. Funny thing is, I was—I was just getting used to it."

Archie nodded, balancing back and forth from foot to foot. "Well, nothing to be done about it, I suppose."

"No, I suppose not."

Archie glanced over at him and, perhaps reading the feelings John suspected were evident there, set down the cameras and walked past him into the living room. "Here. Come here."

"Where?"

"Into the closet."

John followed him inside, closing the door after them. He switched on the flashlight.

Archie indicated the bulb above them. "Still haven't got that fixed yet, eh?"

"I've been busy."

Archie nodded, then dropped his voice. "Look, you didn't hear it from me, but you know, I was thinking. If you were the guy in charge, and I were you, what would you do? Maybe you really *would* take me off the air, just like they said."

He leaned in closer, looking ghastly in the glow of the flashlight. "Or, on the other hand, maybe you'd just *tell* me I was off the air, so I'd think I was, but in reality I'm back on television again without knowing it. This way I'd go back to acting normal, which is what everyone wants in the first place, isn't it?"

With that, he clapped John on the shoulder and opened the closet door. "Good luck," he called back. "Break a leg."

Then he gathered up the cameras and stepped out of the house, closing the door behind him.

John stepped very slowly out of the closet.

And stood in the middle of the living room.

And looked around.

At *everything.*

It all looked just as it had before.

Perfectly normal.

As though there weren't any television cameras around him.

Which didn't mean there weren't.

Which didn't mean there were, either.

He could look, he supposed, but if there weren't any, he'd just feel silly.

And if there were—

He looked at the piles of fan mail, the check, the note from Leslie.

And cleared his throat.

"My," he said, his voice sounding unnaturally loud in the empty room, "but isn't it a wonderful day?"

Silence.

Didn't mean there was.

Didn't mean there wasn't, either.

The first rule of show business, John thought, *is never, ever bore your audience* . . . and segued, quite professionally, he thought, into an a cappella rendition of "Me and My Shadow."

And step *two, three, four* . . .

And *smile* for the birdy.

* * *

The next time you think people are talking about you behind your back, or a happy coincidence seems just a little too good to be true—check behind the bathroom mirror, and see if there are any channels missing from your TV. It just might be that John Selig's ratings have dropped—and you've become a star—in the phosphor-dot world of the Twilight Zone.

Introduction to
The Wall

Every so often, I'll be halfway through a script, or a story, or a book, and only then, at that curious midpoint, will I discover that what I'm writing about isn't what I'd *thought* I was writing about. The story pops its head up and tells me what it's *really* about.

"The Wall" was one such story.

The premise for the story came out of a request from the producer to try and limit some of the episodes to only a few sets. The goal was to try and bring down the budget a little, so we'd have more to spend on episodes where they'd be most needed. All of which was fine by me—I like enclosed shows. Usually it's me trying to convince the producer to go for such a story, rather than the other way around. So when the opportunity came along, I grabbed it.

Consequently, "The Wall" began not so much with a particular character or situation, as with a location. I knew that I would have to keep most, if not all of the first act in one locale, preferably in one room. The rest of the script would cover another locale, but only one or two places in that locale, and should return on occasion to the first location so that the set budget wouldn't be wasted on only one act.

I knew that the first location would have to be very important. Something would have to have happened there, something vital enough to draw in our characters. The second location, I realized, would have to be connected to the first in some way. So the idea of a journey of sorts grew out of this as a logical extension of the setup.

As the story began to reveal itself, I realized that it would only function with a military cast. Which was also fine by me, since we hadn't had one thus far.

With the basic structure ironed out, I began to write about a most extraordinary journey.

And was brought to an abrupt halt midway through by the realization that I wasn't, in fact, writing about a journey at all.

I was writing about the man *taking* the journey.

It wasn't about where he was going, as interesting as I wanted to make it.

It was about *who he was*. And *why* he was. And *what* he was, and wasn't, and could possibly be.

And I realized that "The Wall" wasn't the one he encountered in that strange and lonely room.

It was the wall he encountered within himself.

And that, for me, is what makes "The Wall" a far more personal story than I had first anticipated. I can only hope that if I should ever find myself face-to-face with the same wall, that I will act as well and as honorably as did Major Alexander McKay.

"The Wall," production #87037, was filmed from September 26 through September 30, 1988, in studio and on location. Directed by Atom Egoyan, and starring John Beck (Alexander McKay), Patricia Collins (Berenn), George R. Robertson (Gregory Phillips), Steven Atkinson (first Military Advisor), Sharon Corder (Technician), Jack Bloom (second Advisor), Eugene Clark (Kincaid), and Robert Collins (Perez). First broadcast on February 12, 1989.

THE WALL

1

The corridor smelled strongly of wet paint, motor oil, burned rubber, and freshly poured concrete. There were no windows. At two hundred feet beneath the surface, there was no day, no night, no season, no movement of stars or sun to track. The only sounds were his own muffled footsteps, and those of the guards on either side of him. They looked straight ahead, their uniforms crisp and starched. They had said nothing more than "This way, sir," since he'd shown them his identification. *Major Alexander McKay, AF117B59, Clearance Level Blue-5, Date of Issue: 7/17/92, Date of Expiration: 7/17/93.*

At every corner, they passed another checkpoint and went through the same routine (ID card, retina scan, phone check with the office upstairs) before continuing. Conversation was kept to a dead minimum. He'd seen tight security before, but rarely anything like this.

Something was up.

They reached the final checkpoint, set before a massive steel door that reminded him of a bank vault. The guards, once again, put him through the routine. He watched the reflectorized scanner as his face was probed for retinal and profile verification. It was a face no longer as young as he still saw it in his dreams, showing lines from sun and space. The red light of the sensors brought out the flecks of white in his hair. There were more of them every day, it seemed.

The scanner beeped once and glowed green. One of the guards removed a magnetic disk on a chain from beneath his shirt and slipped it into a slot in the vault door. With the sigh of pneumatics and escaping air, the door opened and the guards who had accompanied him this far preceded him into a room filled with computers, monitors, and whole banks of equipment he didn't recognize and couldn't begin to put a name to. They hummed and clicked and beeped at him from three sides, a constant undercurrent of the sort of noise machines make when they think. Cables and power cords ribboned away in every direction, the equipment looking hastily installed.

The fourth wall, dead ahead, was the only one not lined with equipment. It was either very thick glass or some kind of heavy-gauge polymer, at least three inches thick. Just on the other side of the glass, also running the length of the room, was a solid steel wall. There were still holes in the walls on either side, places where the brickwork had been crudely sawed away to make room for the glass-and-steel barrier. *This was all done very quickly,* Alex thought. *They must've had to move fast. But why?*

It took him a moment to notice Gregory Phillips, seated at one of the consoles. It was only when Greg got up and started toward him that the movement caught his eye. His first impression was that Gregory hadn't been sleeping well, or much, lately. His eyes were red and tired, his grey hair matted in the back from where he'd probably been resting when Alex had entered. He extended a hand with a look of weariness and relief at the sight of a friendly face. "Alex."

"General."

Gregory looked pained, as he always did when reminded of the difference between the two of them. Though Gregory was the older of the two, they'd come up through the ranks of the Air Force together, before taking separate roads to where they wanted to go. "Ranks later, all right?"

Alex nodded, and as he released the handshake, he noticed Gregory's face fall slightly, as though it had required great effort to maintain even this much of a sense of normalcy, and having done so, now returned to its worried, distracted expression.

"So what's the job?" Alex said. "With all the secrecy around here you'd think we were back in the Manhattan Project."

Gregory started to answer, then gestured to the two guards still inside the door. They saluted smartly and headed out into the corridor. The vault door sighed shut behind them.

Gregory stuck a cigarette in his mouth and lit it. As he spoke, he paced the room, indicating the equipment surrounding them. "Two months ago, this was a research lab. Government contract, particle physics, that sort of thing. Nothing special about it. Then something happened. Either something very right, or something very, very wrong."

He paused in front of the glass wall, gazing at the steel on the other side and, Alex thought, actually *through* it, to whatever was on the other side. "But I'm getting ahead of myself," he continued. "Just before everything happened, the research team was running a new experiment on wormholes, theoretical subspace corridors, like black holes, that let you go anywhere in the galaxy in a second. Somewhere along the line, things got—out of hand, shall we say. There was an explosion. And when they cleared the rubble, they found what's on the other side of this wall."

He stepped away from it and picked two pairs of dark goggles off the nearest console, handing one to Alex. They were heavy, the smoked glass unusually thick. "Better put these on," he said. "They'll help, a little. But don't look directly into it."

When the goggles were secured, Gregory toggled a switch. With a sudden sharp *clang* and the sound of gears grinding under a tremendous load, the steel panel behind the glass began to rise up, receding into a troth in the ceiling.

The room was instantly filled with a brilliant white light that bled through the widening gap between the steel wall and the floor. Even through the goggles, it was painful to look at. It was a terrible, bone-white light that bleached everything it touched but, curiously, seemed cool where it struck his skin. With the additional barrier down, he also became aware of the sound —a relentless roar and rush of wind that buffeted the glass wall like a winter storm. A whirl of smoke and fog curled in the room beyond the glass, and as his eyes slowly, painfully adjusted to the brilliant light, he could distinguish its source.

The room extended another ten feet beyond the barrier, ending at a brick wall at the far side.

The light and sound and wind were pouring in through a seven-foot-wide hole in the far wall. All of which would have been unusual enough on its own— Alex had never seen a light like that before, not from any natural source—except. . . .

Except that the wall, like the rest of the lab, was at least two hundred feet beneath the ground.

So where was that light and that wind coming from?

"My God," Alex said.

Gregory nodded. "My reaction precisely. Once we saw it, we brought in scientists from all over the place. Cornell, NASA, JPL, they've poked, prodded, scanned —the high-IQ types from CalTech said terminology is irrelevant. Something about phenomenology exceeding the limits of language. I called it a gate. They didn't argue."

"Where does it go?"

"We don't know. The data from the experiment was wiped out in the explosion. All we know for sure is that, somehow, the equipment here is generating it. We might be able to figure it out in time, but until then we haven't the vaguest idea how it's doing it. It's as if we've unlocked a door, but we can't remember the combination, so if we close it, we may not be able to open it again."

He shook his head, crushed out the cigarette. "We *have* to know what's on the other side, Alex. That's why we called you. The brass wants you—to go *in there*."

Major Alexander McKay. Former test pilot with a paper-trail of commendations and a closetful of broken records. A man for whom the unknown is to be faced, not feared; conquered, not surrendered to. Alexander McKay, who is about to face yet another unknown—but this one is unlike all the others. For this one burns at the very heart of . . . the Twilight Zone.

Alex rubbed at his eyes. Even though the wall had been lowered back into position, when he closed his eyes he could still see the hole, and the terrible light that streamed through it. "How," he started, his mouth dry, "how can you be sure it's a gate?"

"We weren't sure," Gregory said. "Not at first. Then we found there was a wind coming through from the other side. That's why we put up the wall. No telling what kind of bacteria might be coming across. Then, after a while we—well, we started sending things through."

"*What?*"

Gregory stepped across the room to a file cabinet and pulled out a thick folder. He dropped it on the table in front of Alex. "Background's all in there. We started off with just a rock. One point three ounces. Tossed it into the heart of—that. It disappeared instantly."

"Vaporized?"

"We thought about that. So we sent through a homing beacon, about a foot around. We maintained contact with the beacon for just under a minute. Then it went silent. Same for a video camera on a motorized dolly. Maybe it was destroyed once it reached the other side, or couldn't find its way back. Maybe the signals can't reach back, we don't know. But without question there is *something* there, on the other side. And we have to know what it is."

Alex nodded. "So why me?"

Gregory flipped open the folder. Inside, clipped to sheets of computer readouts and transcripts and memos marked CONFIDENTIAL were five photographs. "You weren't the first name on our list, Alex," Gregory said, flipping through them. "They went before you. Colonel Jeff Massie, Second Lieutenant Emilio Perez, two sergeants—Ed Marks and Len Sinclair—and a captain. Henry Kincaid. They all volunteered. They all took with them the best equipment we could give them. And then they all went *in there*. None of them have come back."

"No contact at all?"

By way of reply, Gregory walked over to a tape recorder built into one of the consoles, and hit PLAY. At once the room was filled with static, coming from concealed speakers. Then, faintly, a voice: *I'm through, do you read me, Com-Con? It's—there's something here—can't quite—my, God—can you see it? Can—*

Then the voice was swallowed by static. Gregory let the white noise rush over the room for a moment before shutting it off. "That was Kincaid. Maximum contact time: ten seconds. Then—static. Five men, Alex. Five good men. State Department wants to close us down, pull the plug and make it all go away, just forget it ever happened. Pentagon's pushing on grounds of national security. They wanted one more chance. As for me, if there's any way to rescue those five men, assuming they're still alive—"

Alex nodded. "Understood."

Gregory studied him for a moment, his lips thin. "It's only fair to tell you that I didn't want you for this, Alex. You've paid your dues, and then some. But the brass decided we needed someone with your experience. Even so, you don't have to go. Just say the word."

Alex stood and wandered over toward the glass wall. He could see Gregory's reflection in its surface. "Don't know if they told you," he said, "but I got the word last week—seems I'm getting a little too old to be a rocket jockey. They're putting me behind a desk, Greg. I can't live with that. Given the choice . . ." He glanced over his shoulder at Gregory. "Be a hell of a way to go out, wouldn't it?"

"You'll come back. If anyone can, you can. You're a good soldier, Alex."

Alex looked back at the wall. "Yeah. That's what Sarah said the day she left me. Good soldier, always ready to follow orders, do his duty."

If Gregory heard, he said nothing. Only waited.

Finally, Alex turned, smiled. "So, where do I suit up?"

2

Twenty-four hours later, as a phalanx of technicians escorted Alex down the corridor to the lab, he was reminded of the scenes of crewmembers boarding the space shuttle. Video cameras winked at him from both sides, recording every moment as he maneuvered through the narrow doorway. "A complete record is kept of every attempt," the technician had explained as they were sealing him up into his pressure suit.

"Let's hope this'll be the last one," Alex had said. The technician had smiled back at him, but hadn't looked convinced.

The outfit they'd stuck him in was only a little slimmer than a full space suit, with digital readouts and telemetry that would be relayed back to the lab constantly—or for as long as he was in contact, at any rate.

Ten seconds, he thought. *The record so far is ten seconds.*

A lot can happen in ten seconds.

The lab, previously empty, was now a hive of activity. A dozen technicians manned consoles, tested telemetry, ran checks and counted backwards to zero. He caught snatches of conversation, little of it making much sense.

Gregory hovered over it all, looking nervous. He

found Alex and moved toward him, stepping around cables and wires. The others began to take note of Alex's presence, and he could see them looking at him nervously before turning their attention back to their consoles. It was a look he'd learned to recognize the first time he took off in a jet that needed testing, a jet that nobody was sure could do what it was supposed to do.

It was a look that said, *He's not coming back.*

It disturbed him less than he had thought it might, after all this time, to finally see the same expression on Gregory's face, too. "Almost time," Gregory said, glancing back at the wall. The steel barrier was still locked down. "Just in case—I mean, *just* in case—is there anyone you want me to—"

Alex shook his head, saving Gregory the pain of finishing the sentence. He held out his hand. Gregory took it. His grip was firm, even through the thick glove.

"See you soon," Alex said.

He stepped toward the only access to the other side of the room—a pair of thick glass doors that served as an air lock. He bent low to allow one of the technicians to slip the helmet over his head, then fasten it tight. There was a *click* from somewhere at his back, and a flow of cool oxygen began whispering into the helmet.

Gregory's voice came into his ears, filtered and tinny sounding. "You receiving, Alex?"

"Loud and clear."

"Proceed."

Alex stepped into the air lock, and a moment later the door closed behind him. In an instant, all sounds from the lab were lost. He felt, for a moment, as though he were underwater. Then the door on the opposite side hissed open, and the silence was gone, replaced by a roar of wind. He staggered momentarily as the wind buffeted him, then leaned into it as he moved into the other half of the room. Behind him, the steel wall rose into the ceiling, and he could see the technicians watching him.

Closer now, he could make out details of the earlier *incident* that had opened the hole. Consoles showed scoring and black marks where an explosion had melted circuits and blown out controls, merging everything into a new and thus far unknown configuration. There was blood on one of the computers.

And always, in the middle of it all, that terrible brilliance. It cut through even the helmet's filtered visor.

He pulled out the tie-line that fed out through the side of the suit and looped it onto a hook on the floor, then stood and gave Gregory a thumbs-up.

Gregory nodded, then looked around to the rest of the technicians. "Are we recording?"

A technician nodded, said something the microphone in the other room didn't pick up.

"All right, Alex," Gregory said. "We're clear to proceed. Remember—no heroics. Strictly threat analysis. Get in, take a fast look around, and get out of there. Do you copy?"

"Affirmative, General. Entering the gate—now."

He moved toward the pulsating center of light. Curiously, the closer he came, the less resistance there was from the winds. He seemed almost to be pulled toward it. *Gravity effect?* he wondered.

Then it had him.

It was like being grabbed in a giant's fist and slammed against a wall. The wind was knocked out of him, the light blurred, and the only sound audible over the sudden roar was a voice, already broken up by static, that filtered into his helmet. Gregory's voice.

"God go with you, Alex," he said.

Light. Wind. *Sound.*

Alex tried to force words out. *Come on, damn it, talk!* He was disoriented. He felt he was falling, but wasn't sure if he was falling up or down. The force of movement pressed him against the back of his suit. *(Acceleration?)*

". . . moving, moving fast," Alex managed, his teeth rattling so that he thought they might fall out of his mouth, "feels like it's—like it's shaking me apart.

Acceleration. Tremendous. Can't see anything—just white—just—"

White.

And the sudden blackness that appeared behind his eyes.

Fight it, damn you! Don't black out on me! Don't black out! Don't—

The last thing he heard, or thought he heard, was Gregory, calling his name, over and over, from someplace that sounded impossibly far away.

And then the white went away.

And so did Alex.

3

My nose itches.

His arms felt strangely heavy as, eyes closed, he tried to scratch his nose. But for some reason he couldn't get to it.

He opened his eyes. There was glass between his face and his hand.

Helmet.

Then he focused past his hand, to a vaguely purple sky that pinwheeled above his head.

Damn, he thought, and sat up, *damn, damn, damn!*

He toggled the SEND switch. "McKay to Com-Con. Do you read, Com-Con? I repeat: This is McKay. Do you copy, Com-Con?"

Silence.

How long was I out?

Fighting the heavy suit, he levered himself to his feet. He was on a grassy clearing. Leaves, green shot through with delicate white veins, clung to his suit. He brushed them away. Trees lined the clearing on all sides. If he didn't look too closely, they could be the same as trees he'd seen all his life. But even from here he could see the white, pulsing veins that ran through the thick trunks, the unnaturally straight branches reaching toward a foreign sky.

He gained his footing and caught himself before

falling over in the opposite direction. *Gravity difference*, he decided. He felt more than a few pounds lighter than he had moments earlier. He felt behind him for the tie-line and found it had been severed cleanly. The end looked almost cauterized.

He looked around again, and it was then that he saw the glove lying on the ground a few feet in front of him. He picked it up, careful not to let the top-heavy suit throw him over again, and checked it against his own glove.

They matched.

He toggled the SEND button again. He could feel the tiny recorder in his chest console begin to whirr, preserving it all for posterity. If he could find one. "Don't know if you're getting this or not, Com-Con, but I'm going to keep recording anyway. If someone else finds this record, maybe they can get it back. I've found evidence of one of the pressure suits. Your men made it, General, at least one of them. Looks like it might have been abandoned. Don't see any sign of a struggle."

He twisted around to read the atmosphere sensor. It showed a slightly higher oxygen mix than Earth-normal, and a few trace elements the sensor couldn't identify. "Atmosphere and environment appear similar to our own. I'm going to try it. If it's livable, I'll switch to that. If not—well, I've got about half-an-hour's worth of air left in the suit."

Gingerly, he popped the helmet. Air rushed out past his face. He held his breath a moment, then sniffed at the new air that filled his helmet. It was good, clean air, full of the smell of leaves and pollen. "Oxygen atmosphere, all right," he said for the benefit of the recorder. "Sweet, cool, crisp air."

He looked around. There was nothing out of the ordinary in his surroundings. "Don't see any sign of the gate on this side. Perhaps it's not in the visible spectrum here. . . ."

Or he had rolled or fallen from his original location.

Or he had been moved.

And wasn't *that* a comforting thought?

"Moving on. Will continue log entries at five-minute intervals."

4

It was fully half an hour later when Alex topped the last rise and stood looking down at the village.

You're dreaming, he thought.

It was like something out of a Brueghel painting.

Even from here, there was a feeling of serenity about the place. Men and women—also Earth-normal, as far as he could tell—carried earthen jars and gathered grain. Children were playing with sticks, rolling a rounded stone ahead of them and laughing as they fought to determine which way it would go. Animals grazed near a series of thatched huts ringing a communal building of sorts—

"Welcome, Major," a voice behind him said.

Alex spun around, hand instinctively reaching for the gun that rode his belt.

A woman stood ten feet from him, wearing a long peasant skirt, her face all but hidden beneath a wide-brimmed hat. But the voice had not come from her; it had come from the man beside her. The uniform he wore was standard Air Force issue, identical to the one that Alex wore beneath his pressure suit. The man's face was equally familiar, and it took Alex only a moment before realizing that he had seen it in the folder Gregory had given him to study.

"Kincaid? Captain Henry Kincaid?"

He saluted smartly, smiling broadly. "Present and accounted for. We've been waiting for you. Well, not you in particular, but someone like you. Have to say that I'm happy with the selection, though. I can't think of a better choice, for their needs—and ours."

Alex wasn't quite ready to drop the gun yet. "Excuse me?"

This time the woman answered. She lifted her head a little, so that he could see her. Her face was plain, but not unattractive. At first glance, she looked a few years older than Alex, and when she smiled, Alex thought that it was the purest, least self-conscious smile he had ever seen. "Everything will be explained in time, Major," she said, her voice soft and vaguely lilting. "In the meantime, please, if you will come with us."

They started off down the hill toward the village. Alex didn't move.

"Come with you where? What is this place?"

Kincaid glanced back over his shoulder at Alex and laughed. "Call it—heaven," he said, and continued toward the largest of the huts.

Alex hesitated, then followed them down. At a discreet distance.

For the moment, at least, there was nowhere else to go.

5

"Still no communication, General."

Gregory paced the lab, looking at his watch. It had been five hours since they'd lost contact with Alex. "Boost the signal."

"We've tried. We're still not getting anything."

Then boost it some more!

He walked to the glass wall, peering through slitted eyes at the too-white hole in the wall. Had it eaten him, too, like the others? He touched his palm to the glass. It vibrated under his touch.

"C'mon, Alex," he whispered. "Where the hell are you? Talk to me!"

6

"Please try and calm yourself, Major," Berenn said. That, he'd learned, was the name of the woman who'd met him alongside Kincaid.

"I will," Alex said, "just as soon as somebody gives me a straight answer to a simple question. Where are we? What is this place?"

He looked, one at a time, to the faces surrounding

him at the table. They were all here—Massie, Perez, Marks, Sinclair, and, of course, Kincaid. They sat at the big table in the middle of the communal building. There was straw on the floor, and bowls of strangely textured fruits on the hand-hewn table.

Glances were exchanged at his question, and Perez sat forward. "Lieutenant Perez here, sir. Navigational specialist. I've been here for about a week, and the stars —well, Major, the stars are all wrong. I don't know where we are, but it's not Earth. Frankly, I don't think we're even in the same neighborhood anymore."

"Why haven't you tried to get back?"

This time Kincaid spoke up. The others seemed willing to defer to him. "Stone-cold truth is, we can't go back. We've surveyed the area, and as far as we can tell, the gate doesn't exist on this side. It only works one way, from there to here. Like it or not, we're stuck here, Major. Permanently."

Alex felt as though a cold fist had seized hold of his stomach and given it a sharp twist. He looked to the rest, but they avoided his glance, possibly not wanting to replay their own feelings at the discovery, perhaps—

Don't get paranoid, there's no cause—so far.

"Is it such a terrible fate, Major?" Berenn asked.

He turned in his seat to look at her. She sat on the outer perimeter of the circle they had formed, watching them as a teacher might watch a particularly interesting class.

"That's not the point," Alex said. "A lot of this still doesn't track, in my opinion. Like you. This place. How can you know my language?"

"Funny as it may sound," Kincaid said, "it's a matter of economics. Seems each of the communities around here has its own language or dialect. Since they operate on a barter economy, they select the one with the greatest facility for language to be in charge."

"Then why not let her speak for herself?" Alex said.

"It is as you have been told," Berenn said. "Ours is a simple existence. What we do not need we trade in exchange for that which is required. Which is very little.

We are quite self-sufficient here. But we believe in maintaining the peace, and there is no peace without communication. That is my task."

"She's good at it, too," Sinclair piped in. "She was speaking pretty fluent English within a week. She only had to hear a word once to memorize it and know how to use it properly. The rest are a little slower, but most of them are picking up on it now."

"As for the similarity to Earth-normal," Massie said, "we're as much in the dark as you. If I had to make a guess, I'd say that maybe the experiment they were running had some correlation to a search for livable planets. If that part of the program was in memory when everything blew, then that may have had something to do with it. Otherwise—chalk it up to blind, dumb luck, the way a drunk manages somehow to drive home without wrapping himself around a tree."

Alex looked back at Berenn. She returned his gaze calmly and with, he thought, a hint of amusement at his instinctive distrust of the situation. "And you just welcome everybody. Just like that."

"It is my prerogative, as leader of this community. We are a peaceful people, not suspicious. Of supplies we have plenty, more than enough to share. If we have become an unintentional prison for you, please be assured that we will exert every effort to make it a pleasant one. There is much we have to offer."

She studied his face for a moment, and her expression became more serious. "They have told me about the world you come from. A place of such *hate,* that at first I could not believe it existed. A terrible, dark place where more and more struggle for less and less. Here, Major, we have no wars. What would we fight over? No one lacks for food, or shelter, or company. We have no possessions to steal; no religion save for the sanctity of life; no law but one: be kind to one another. That's why we were pleased to see it was you who was sent. They say you are a man of honor. There will always be a place among us for such as you."

"It's the kind of place we've all dreamed about, Major," Massie said.

"I think I'll reserve judgment on that until I've checked things out for myself," Alex said. "Meanwhile, I hope you won't mind if I poke around and see for myself whether or not there's a way home."

"Not at all," Berenn said. "We encourage you to explore. We will give you all the help we can, as we did for the others. Let me show you our world, Major. In time, I think you will come to like it."

And again, that look, as though she were hoping that if she studied him just so, at just the right angle, she might be able to see right into him. "I sense in you a man who has searched for peace a long time, without finding it. Here, in this place, you will."

She said it so earnestly, that for the barest flicker of a moment, he almost believed her. But he knew it would pass.

It always did.

7

The lab was empty. Dark. The hole, with its swirling white madness, was safely tucked behind the steel retainer. Gregory could almost pretend that it wasn't there at all, wasn't still thrashing around in some kind of electronic storm, wasn't still holding his friend in a place he couldn't reach, an unknown place of infinite white.

I never should have listened to them, he thought. *Anyone but Alex, I should have told them. He's too old. Let him retire while he can still walk away from the last one.*

Then: *Get on with it.*

He clicked the dictating machine back on. The cassette whirred softly in its casing. "It has now been three days twelve hours since Alexander McKay entered the gate. In another twenty-four hours, we will consider him lost in action."

He leaned across the desk to pick up a file folder

One more folder. One more name. "I've recommended we shut down operations, and send no more men through the gate without a more detailed analysis. The brass wants to try a few more times. 'We lose more men in training exercises,' they told me. They've already picked the next volunteer. He comes highly recommended."

He flipped open the folder and gazed at the photo inside. A serious, thoughtful face. Someone's son. Someone's lover. "I don't know him. Thank God for small favors."

He switched off the recorder and left the room, turning off the lights behind him.

8

The sun, despite being smaller and whiter than the one he was used to, shone down warmly on Alex's face. A dozen yards away, just down the hill from where he was sitting, children were playing. Their laughter had the same curious lilt he had come to associate with all those who lived here, and the words they called out to one another were foreign but needed no translation. He smiled as he watched them, and he was surprised at how easily the smile came.

He felt relaxed. More relaxed than he had felt in a long time. Perhaps it was the lighter gravity, the richer oxygen mix.

Or perhaps it was just that for the first time, he didn't have to report anywhere, didn't have to do anything but sit here in the sun.

His attitude surprised him, but it was something he'd come to accept over the last five days.

He'd accepted a lot of things in that time.

But he still wore his pistol.

But he also accepted that, in time, that too would probably change.

"Good morning, Major."

He looked across to where Berenn came out of one of the huts and, waving to him, climbed up the modest slope to where he sat. He never ceased noticing the grace with which she moved, her total and complete ease with him and everyone around him.

She glanced over her shoulder at the children chasing a hoop in the clearing. "You do not play, Major." It was less a question than a statement.

He shrugged, pulling at the high grass in front of him. "Too old, I guess."

"That will change. You're not quite as old as you think." She smiled and joined him in watching the children for a moment before looking back at him. "Have you had any luck trying to find the way back?"

"None. You were right. From dawn to dusk we've searched every square inch of the area I came through. Nothing. Funny thing is, the more time I spend here, the less I begin to worry about it."

"Really." It, too, was less question than statement.

He nodded. "See, I've been a soldier all my life. And my father, and his father before him. They always said you have to fight for what you believe—but they never told me what to believe. They told me you have to follow orders—but they never told me why. If you stay busy enough, though, I guess you don't have time to think about it. Maybe that's what I've been doing all these years."

He laughed. "Friend of mine calls that *water skiing*. I didn't know what the hell he was talking about. He said it's when you keep moving as fast as you can, never slowing down, because you know that what you're standing on isn't enough to support you if you stop moving."

"The others said you were a—a test pilot?" She said the word as though she were trying it on for the first time, and seeing if it fit. She nodded to herself, deciding that it did. "Is that dangerous?"

"I suppose. That's pretty much what I was getting at. When you're in the cockpit, there's no time for questions. You're caught between the blue and the black, with death always just over your shoulder. It made me feel alive—and disappointed, when I landed. I sometimes thought about how I'd like to go, in a blaze of fire and glory, doing what nobody else could ever do, just once. But it never happened, and now I'm wondering if maybe all this time I've been trying to find something worth dying for without having anything worth living for."

She sat quietly for a moment, then asked, "Do you have a family?"

He looked away. It wasn't something he liked to talk about a lot. "Not really. My wife walked out a year ago. Said she didn't believe in bigamy. Took me a while to realize it, but she was right. How do you compete with honor, and duty, and orders, and all the rest of it? It's just—"

He tried to find the words, but found that he had run out of steam. The pain wasn't there anymore. Just a sadness, at all the words he had never said, the words he *had* said, and now regretted. He felt tired, but it was the kind of tired that comes after finally dropping a great weight, and realizing at last that he was no longer burdened by it all.

He glanced up to find her studying his face with great gentleness. She put her hand on his and tightened it. "I'm glad you're here with us, Alex. Very glad."

He smiled. It was the first time she'd called him Alex.

9

It was well after dusk when Alex returned to the center of the village. Earlier, he'd walked nearly a mile into the woods before stopping, when he was sure he would be alone. He needed to sit, and to think—about this place, about home, about their inability to find the gate from this side.

Kincaid had been right. This was heaven, of a sort, and if there indeed wasn't any way back, as now seemed to be the case, then perhaps he should begin thinking about his other options.

He wanted to find Berenn.

They would have much to discuss if he were to try and make a place for himself here until help came.

If it came.

And if he wanted it to come.

He entered the communal building, passing Perez, who was on his way out.

" 'Evening, Major," he said.

Alex clapped him on the shoulder. "I think Alex will do for now. Have you seen Berenn around?"

"I saw her go out a little while ago with Kincaid to draw some water. She'll probably be back in a few minutes."

Alex nodded and continued into the large hall. It was empty, everyone else having either retired to their own huts or enjoying the night air. He wandered over to the corner where they had let him store his equipment with the others' gear. When he'd been told that they didn't have locks, he'd been concerned about having his equipment stolen. But it remained just as he'd left it five days ago.

He looked at the pressure suit in the smoky light cast by the oil lamps that hung from the walls. It seemed to him now a foreign thing, a curious artifact that had nothing to do with him or this place.

Some of the other suits were nearby. The name tag on the closest read KINCAID. In a niche on the chestplate was a tape recorder, similar to his own. He picked it up. It felt unusually light.

Alex popped the EJECT button. Nothing came out. The cassette had already been removed.

He checked another recorder, on the suit marked MASSIE.

The cassette on that one was gone as well.

A quick check showed all five cassettes missing.

He frowned. *Who would have removed them? And why?*

He rummaged through the corner, pushing aside the piles and tangles of gear. As long as they were here somewhere, perhaps put away quickly, without antici-

pating a thorough search, he should be able to find them
eventually.

He did.

10

There were footsteps approaching the communal
hut. Footsteps, and the sound of laughter. It was loud,
against the night, but not loud enough to drown out
Kincaid's voice on the recorder.

*. . . this place is Paradise. We can't go back. We
know that now. We've told Berenn of our decision and
asked her to keep the children away from the area of the
gate at night, to make sure none of them accidentally
wanders in. They say they'll set up a watch, keep an eye
out for anyone else who might come through . . .*

It was much the same as the information on the
other four cassettes.

The door opened, and Berenn stepped inside, Kincaid following her.

"There you are!" Berenn said as she drew near. "I
was wondering where you'd gotten off to. We were
just—"

They stopped at the sound of the recording.

Alex switched off the speaker and held up the other
four cassettes. "You lied to me."

Berenn paled. "Alex, please, we can explain—"

He threw the cassettes to the dirt floor and they
clattered away. "No! You *lied* to me! You told me there
was no way back! But there is! The gate's there, all right.
But because of the refraction, the way the light bends
and gets sucked into it, you can only see it at night."

He glared at Kincaid. "That's why you would only
take me there during the day. You knew I wouldn't find
anything. 'Stone-cold truth is we can't go back.' No,
Captain. The stone-cold truth is that you *decided* to stay
here—and make sure no one else went back."

"We told you the truth," Kincaid said, "the best
way we could. Look, Major, if we went back and reported what we found, pretty soon this place would be

swarming with troops and experts and God knows what else. They'd ruin it."

"That's garbage."

"Is it? You know how the military thinks. What do *you* think would happen if they got hold of it?"

Alex paused at this for a moment, then shook his head. "You could have left out some of the facts."

Kincaid snorted. "Wouldn't work. They'd just keep asking more and more questions, and eventually they'd find out all of it. There are ways of making any of us talk. Truth serum, you name it.

"We didn't want to lie to you. Given a choice, we wouldn't have. And eventually we would have told you the truth. But until then, we couldn't let you go back— not until you'd discovered for yourself what this world was like. Perfection is a fragile thing, Major. It doesn't survive the microscope. So once we saw what kind of place this was, we took a vote. The decision was unanimous. We're not going back. We're happy here, for the first time in our lives. This is Eden, Major. Would you want to be the one to bring the snake into the garden?"

"You're forgetting something," Alex said. "I didn't vote. Now, you're young, so maybe you can forget your duty, and your responsibilities, but I can't. And I'm going back."

He moved for the door. Kincaid stepped in his way.

"I'm afraid we can't allow that, Major."

"I don't recall giving you a choice, *Captain.*"

For the first time since he'd arrived, Alex's gun was off his belt and in his hand. It was ironic—he'd come tonight to turn the gun over to Berenn as a gesture of his trust. Now he was glad he hadn't.

Kincaid gazed down at the gun without moving out of Alex's way. "You see how easy it is, Major? The first solution of the angry man. How many other guns do you want to turn loose here?"

"I don't want to hurt you, Kincaid. But I'm ordering you to get out of my way."

"Then you'll have to kill me, Alex."

Alex studied his face. He had no doubt that Kincaid meant exactly what he was saying.

He lowered the gun—then brought it up quickly, cracking Kincaid under the chin. He went down hard, and Alex ran past him toward the door.

"Alex!" Berenn cried out. "No!"

He hit the ground running, heading across the clearing toward the path he had searched so many times before, always by daylight. He knew it well enough now to follow it even in the dark. Behind him he could hear Berenn calling after him, calling to the others.

"Help! Please, someone stop him!"

She was running after him, and a quick glance behind showed others coming out of their huts, running into the woods after him.

He ran.

(to what?)

Lungs pounding, not daring again to look behind him, he ran

(where?)

toward where he knew it was waiting, where he knew he had to go, no matter what.

(why?)

Because I've got orders, damn you!

Down the next hill, over the rocks, and finally he saw it—a five-foot-wide rectangle suspended in the night air just above the ground. It glowed dully, and he noticed as he worked his way toward it that it was visible only from the front.

He hurried toward the gate, hearing them behind him. Almost there—

"Alex! Wait! Please!"

He stopped, just a foot short of the gate. Even from here he could feel the force pulling at him. He risked a glance to where Berenn came up the path toward him.

"Please," she said, "don't go!"

"I'm sorry—but I have to."

"*Why?* You told me yourself, there's nothing back there for you."

(why?)

"Because I'm a Good Soldier," he said, hearing the bitterness in his own voice. "It's all I've ever been. Maybe it's all I'll ever be. If you take that away, then what's left? You said I was a man of honor. Please, leave me that. It's—it's all I have.

"Good-bye, Berenn."

And then, even as she reached for him, he dived into the gate.

And the white took him.

11

"So you're convinced they're a totally agrarian society?"

Alex nodded. "Judging from everything I saw—yes."

The others exchanged glances. As soon as he'd come back through the gate, to the sound of alarms and Gregory's surprised, pleased face, calls had been put through to a half-dozen government agencies. The rest would be showing up soon. He didn't know the names of the men talking to him across the table, and he knew he wouldn't be told even if he inquired.

They asked. He answered. That was the game, and he knew it by heart. They had been at it now for over two hours.

"What's your estimation of any potential threat they might pose to national security?"

"Nil. They have no offensive capability whatsoever."

"No weapons? No technology?"

"Not that I saw, no, sir."

"What about their defenses?"

"Same thing."

They exchanged a look, and Alex thought he didn't much like what he saw in their eyes. "Thank you, Major. If you'll just give us a moment."

Alex stood, saluted, and moved to the other end of the lab. Gregory was there, chain-smoking but pleased.

He knew that the men at the table were from about as high up as you could go without hitting the Oval Office, and that their presence signaled a massive escalation in the importance of the operation. There was no telling how big things would get, but Gregory intended to be a part of it all the way.

"Comments?" said one of the men at the table, and the rest huddled into conference with him. Their voices were low, but still carried in the small lab.

"I think we're in a perfect position," one of them said. "The press isn't aware of the situation—it's a whole new frontier."

"What about trade? We could set up a barter situation. Technology, advisors, maybe even weapons to support their system of government—whatever it is."

There was a short laugh from one of the others. "I think we'll keep the guns in our own hands—for the time being. I kind of like the symmetry of that."

Gregory gestured for Alex to come closer, then clapped him on the shoulder. "Good job, Alex."

He shook his head. "I stink."

"No. Sure, it was hard. But you did what you had to. You followed orders."

"Yeah," Alex said, without enthusiasm. "Yeah, I did that, didn't I?" He looked behind them, to where the advisors were locked in discussion. "Tell me, Greg— would you have let the snake into the Garden of Eden?"

Gregory shrugged, lit another cigarette. "Fortunately for me, it wasn't a decision I had to make."

From across the room, one of the advisors signaled to Gregory. "Be right back," he said, and went to join them.

There was a whispered exchange between Gregory and the top advisor, while the others continued their analysis.

"I think you're overlooking the strategic value of all this," the first one continued. "What if we can open more gates from that world to anyplace on earth? We could use it as a transfer point for troops and materiel."

"Agreed. The first-strike potential is enormous!

There's nowhere on Earth we couldn't hit with troops or tactical nukes in a hot second. Hell, we could store the stuff up there and the Russians would never be able to take it out with a first strike."

Alex reached up and carefully removed the major's cluster from his epaulet and placed it on the console in front of him.

No one noticed.

"Except what happens if the Russians get their hands on the same technology?"

He stepped back across the room, past the MP, to stand in front of the air lock that led into the other side of the room. He brushed his fingers along the cool metal.

No one noticed.

"It's a chance we'll have to take. Which is why we have to get in now, so we can call the shots. The Pentagon—"

He was through before they could stop him.

Red lights flashed, and he could hear alarms shrieking all around him. He yanked a metal pipe out of the damaged wall and jammed it into the air lock, ignoring the pounding from the other side.

Don't stop, he thought. *Don't stop or you'll never go through with it.*

Water skiing.

He was through the second door, into the main chamber, as the steel barrier started to rise into the ceiling. Behind it, through the glass, he could see all of them. Some were pointing at him, some cursing, one was shouting into a phone. *Probably calling security.* He could hear none of it through the soundproof glass.

He found another damaged pipe loosely hanging from the wall and yanked it out as Gregory finally found the intercom switch.

". . . the hell do you think you're doing?"

Another MP was coming at the glass wall, a fire ax in hand.

It would take them at least a minute to break through all that glass.

Time enough.

Alex toggled the intercom switch on his side of the room. "Listen! General! I have a message for you! Tell the brass—tell them that perfection is a fragile thing! Tell them that I did my job! And tell them . . . *tell them I retire!*"

And with that, Alex brought the heavy lead pipe down on the nearest console. It struck with a flash of sparks and the clatter of shattering gauges and instruments. He slammed it down again and again, no longer hearing the protests from the other side, keeping one eye on the gate, watching, watching—

—as it flickered, then suddenly looked tenuous, like a bulb, about to burn out.

Now! he thought, and with a final blow to the console, he leapt into the gate.

As the white took him, he could hear, but not see, the explosion that ripped the last of the consoles apart.

He hoped only that the gate would finish carrying him to his destination before finally winking out of existence.

12

They stopped beside one of the trees that reached toward the sky with too-straight limbs. Far below, they could just barely see the village. They had walked all morning to get here. The view was every bit as glorious as she had promised.

After a moment, Berenn gazed over at him. Even before she spoke, he knew what she would ask; knew that she had waited until enough time had passed without further arrivals that they could be certain that the gate had truly been destroyed. "Are you sure they won't be able to build another one?"

He nodded. "It was a freak combination in the first place. If the gate were still there for them to study, maybe they could duplicate it in time. But it's gone. Permanently."

She smiled and took his hand. "So what do you do now?"

"For the moment," he said, gazing out at the fresh world that stretched before him, "absolutely nothing."

Major Alexander McKay, retired, who learned that there is a better world than this one—and that sometimes heaven is a place better left untouched by human hands. There may be one more commendation yet to come for the major—one that says "For services rendered . . . in the Twilight Zone."

Introduction to
The Trance

When I sat down to write the writers' bible for the new *Twilight Zone*, one of the items to be included was a list of topics we wanted to cover while working on the series. *Loss of Identity . . . The Homeless . . . Terrorism . . . Alcoholism . . .*, the list went on and on. One of the items I added was *Trance Channeling*.

It was, at the time, all the rage.

It continues to gain in popularity.

It was, and is, in my view, utterly and completely bogus, a form of latter-day table-tapping. When the subject was first mentioned, producer Mark Shelmerdine wasn't sure what trance channeling was.

I described one of the popular practitioners working in the field, who, I explained, channeled "a ten-thousand-year-old warrior."

He nodded and frowned, and eventually I discovered that he'd thought I'd said "a ten-thousand-year-old *worrier.*"

It remains one of the funniest images I've heard, conjuring up visions of an ancient wise man puzzling over a toaster, *"What do I know, maybe it'll blow up, don't plug it in, don't touch it, you don't know where it's been, who understands these things?"*

Trance channeling moved quickly to the top of the list—and that line ended up in the story.

"The Trance" became one of the earliest episodes that we decided to produce.

The task of producing "The Trance" was at once simple and mind-bogglingly complex. In terms of sets and effects, the show was minimalistic. But it required an actor of rare and extraordinary ability, and demanded that he play, essentially, *three* roles in the same episode: the role of Leonard Randall himself, the Delos persona, and the Voice persona. Leonard had to be rendered convincingly, without falling into caricature. Delos had to be equally convincing, so that even the viewer would be initially fooled. It was also a point of logic. Practitioners of trance channeling are very good at what they do. For Delos to be anything less than convincing would be to diminish the reality of what's out there, and the intelligence of the other characters in believing in him.

And the Voice . . . well, that had to be the most convincing of all.

The actor would have to bounce back and forth between the three personas, in some scenes moving from one to the other in sequences separated by no more than a single sentence. In that brief pause, his entire attitude would have to change—his body language, voice, inflection, intonation, pronunciation, facial expressions . . . and all would have to be consistent throughout the episode.

Without question it was the most difficult acting job in the entire batch of thirty scripts.

And Peter Scolari was the absolutely perfect choice. His performance, for those who have not yet seen it, is stellar and totally convincing. Known predominantly for his work on the *Newhart* series, Peter Scolari gave what should be an award-winning performance, if there is a God.

And if there is . . . does he know how to work a toaster?

"The Trance," production #87007, was directed by Randy Bradshaw, and featured Peter Scolari (Leonard Randall), Ted Simonett (Gerry), Neil Munro (Don), Hrant Alianak (Dr. Greenberg), Jeannie Becker (Kilgore), Glynis Davies (Believer #1), and Mona Matteo (Believer #2). Written by Jeff Stuart and J. Michael Straczynski. Production on the episode began on August 11, 1988, and it was originally aired on November 27, 1988.

THE TRANCE

(with Jeff Stuart)

They filled the tiers of seats on all four sides of the room—the faithful, the curious, those who believed, and those who wished to believe. They spoke quietly among themselves, in hushed tones, every so often glancing toward the door at the far end of the soft-lit and soundproofed room. Waiting.

Promptly at seven P.M.—although there were no clocks in the room they knew he would be on time, he was *always* on time—the door opened, and the vessel stepped into the room. His eyes downcast, nervous, a shy man made nervous by their sudden and complete attention, he stepped up onto a small stage in the center of the room. The stage was bare except for a lone chair.

Leonard Randall, who looked no more than thirty or thirty-five, hesitated beside the chair and looked around at the assembled. "I'll need complete silence," he said, his voice almost inaudible.

That done, he sat in the cushioned chair, closed his eyes, and exhaled slowly, slowly. . . .

The change was beginning.

Lights, a crowd, the proper atmosphere, and the common coin of desperate belief—commodities necessary to the life and times of Leonard Randall, who may or may not be someone else as well.

* * *

From the first row they could see his knuckles whiten on the armrests. From the third row they could see the veins tense in his neck, hear the shiver of breath that came in increasingly irregular intervals. From the fifth row they could see his head jerk upward until it was balanced almost imperially on his neck. His eyes still closed, he raised one foot, moved it forward until it was precisely flush with the floor, and dropped it again with a *thump* that seemed unnaturally loud in the otherwise silent room. The other foot followed suit.

His breaths came in shuddering gasps, exhaled like a man in bitter cold, in and out, slowly, in and out—

And then he stopped.

His head tilted, as though listening to some strange music that they could not quite hear. He turned his head further from side to side, slowly, as if looking out at them even through lidded eyes.

Then, abruptly, his eyes snapped open . . . and the fortunate few brought to witness the miracle gasped as one voice.

"I am Delos," he said, seeming to look at every single one of them in turn. "And I am here."

He pushed himself away from the chair and stood. Where the man who had walked onto the stage was quiet, almost painfully shy, the one who inhabited his body now stalked the stage with supreme, almost regal confidence.

Every eye on him, he spoke again, his voice tinged with an accent they couldn't place—because it was one that had long ago ceased to exist.

"Ten thousand years ago was I born, and nine thousand five hundred years ago did I die. I have walked the cobbled streets of that place which men call Atlantis, but which we called Shumma Zamoria. I have seen the fragile glory that was Greece. My master in wisdom was Eli Ben-Zamoran, who studied at the feet of the Undying One himself, whose name my lips are not worthy to speak. From them to me to you I bring what little I can offer against the darkness."

He paused, and once again looked about him at

those who had come to see, and to speak, and to ask. "I —am Delos. And I am among you. Speak, and you shall be heard."

One by one, the hands went up around him.

And Delos smiled.

The woman in the third row stumbled quickly through her question, knowing they were almost out of time, knowing who she was addressing, knowing that this opportunity might never come again. "—so David is a nice man, and I think he may be a soul mate, but I'm not sure, and I don't want to get married again unless I've found that soul mate." She smiled, a pale, nervous flicker of a smile. "I'm getting pretty desperate."

Delos paced for a moment, and when he spoke, there was a faint trace of amusement in his voice—not amusement at her dilemma, but the amusement of a father at a daughter who asks the most obvious question in the world.

"My child—in Shumma Zamoria there was a rare breed of butterfly, with wings as golden as the morning sun, and very very fast. If you tried to catch it, so!—" He made a grab at the empty air before him. "—You would never possess it. And the more you would try, the angrier and more desperate you would become, you would open your hand and find there only air. Sometimes the children would watch strangers trying to do this very thing, and laugh, and finally say, 'Watch.'

"And they would lay down and empty their thoughts and be calm. And soon enough the golden-winged butterfly of Shumma Zamoria would land just *so.*" He closed his eyes and gently touched the tip of his nose.

And he smiled.

And they all smiled with him.

He opened one eye, and then the other, and he looked at her with infinite patience. "Do you understand?"

"Yes, I do. Thank you, Delos," she said, and bowed before sitting.

Delos returned the gesture and turned his attention back to the rest of the assembled. Only a few hands remained raised. "This vessel is growing weary. We must not tax the good will of our host. I may answer one final question." He pointed to a woman in the second row. "You."

She stood, smoothing her dress, and bowed. "Thank you, Delos. A question, but not for my own benefit. You've been silent for so long—why have you come back now?"

He turned and walked back toward the center of the room, his fingers templed at his lips. "You ask two questions. I come through the one called Leonard because he has been—chosen to receive wisdom. The universe has selected him, and through this he shall gain great wisdom. As for the second question . . ."

He turned to look back at her, and in his face was a concern and a seriousness that even the regulars had never before seen. "Ten thousand years ago, I was born on the heels of a great—*change*. A thing happened of which I may speak some other time, a thing which changed the world. For good, and for ill.

"Five thousand years ago, another change came, and Shumma Zamoria was destroyed, cast down beneath the waves, a victim of its own decay. And now the cycle turns again. A third change is nearly upon us. It may bring great good, or great evil—and you, all of you, will tilt the balance."

He stood before the chair, turning to look out upon them one last time. "My time here is ended. He whose body I inhabit has reached its limit, and I must go. Remember all that I have said here today, and seek the light within each of you. I am Delos. And I wish you well."

Then, slowly, fatigue finally taking him, he sat. All remained quiet in the room as they witnessed the change reversing itself, until finally, the shuddering and shivering gone, an exhausted and sweating Leonard Randall opened his eyes, blinking against the bright light. He looked out at them with nervous anticipation. "Did—did Delos come?"

They answered his question with applause.

Under the applause, Don Huntley, Randall's aide, came in from the main entrance. He moved quickly to Leonard, putting a protective arm around his shoulders and gently waving away the attentions of the assembled.

"Thank you all for coming," Don said, "but I'm afraid Leonard will have to rest for a while. We invite you to come back next week. And remember, an audio cassette of tonight's session will be available in the front lobby in about an hour."

On their way out, some of them paused to touch Leonard's hands.

He smiled. Shyly.

But permitted the touch.

By the time Don was finished with the concession receipts, there were only a few stragglers waiting in the reception area for a final glimpse of Leonard. Their faces fell when they saw that it was only him passing through. "I'm sorry," he said, "but as much as Leonard appreciates the attention, he must have his rest in the meditation chamber. The act of channeling Delos is very tiring. Thank you."

He waited to watch them leave, just in case. When the last of them was gone, he straightened his tie, turned on his heel, and headed for the large double doors at the end of the long hall marked MEDITATION CHAMBER.

The room inside was spare, the lines clean. A modular sofa ran along the circular wall, broken only by the door at one end and a full-length mirror at the other. The only other object in the room was the round, marble desk that had been flown in from India at great expense. The light, dim and properly atmospheric, came from recessed lamps and track lighting positioned for greatest effect. The meditation chamber was Leonard's retreat, and only a special few were ever admitted. And because they *were* special, ready to lend their financial and spiritual support in exchange for private sessions, the atmosphere of the room had to be kept suitably metaphysical.

Leonard was sitting at the desk, the chair swiveled so that it faced away from the door. Don could barely see the back of Leonard's head—inclined as though in deep meditation.

"They're gone," he said. No response. "Leonard?"

After a moment, the chair swiveled around to reveal Leonard earplugged into his Sony Watchman, grinning broadly. "Can you believe it? The Clippers are actually winning for a change."

"We live in an age of miracles."

Leonard popped out the earplugs and set the Watchman down on the table. "So how was the take?"

"The usual. Up from yesterday, which was up from the day before."

Leonard grinned. At times like this he was like a little kid counting his nickels and seeing how high he could pile them without knocking them all over the carpet. "Give me numbers."

Don pulled out his notebook and glanced down the long line of receipts. Leonard liked accurate figures. "We're booked solid on the three-day retreat; crystals, tapes, and amulets are up five percent, book sales up by ten but holding. We've got the printer standing by for another run after the TV show tomorrow. Oh, which reminds me, don't forget you've got the pre-interview this afternoon at three."

"Got it," Leonard said. "Should be quite a reaction when Delos goes coast to coast."

"Big time tee-vee. Once we break through there, there's nothing we can't do. Just a hop, skip, and a jump until we have a show of our own."

Leonard held up a cautionary finger. "One step at a time. As our good friend Delos might say—" he suddenly frowned, puffing out his chest and putting on the Delos attitude—"never take anything for granted in the prophet biz."

Then Leonard looked away, and in a slightly different voice, added, *"Words far truer than he suspects."*

"Hey, good one," Don said.

"Hmm?" Leonard seemed to rouse a little. "Oh, thanks, yeah it is a good line. So listen, before the show I want you to get me everything you can on Kilgore. The more I know going in, the better I'll be able to tailor Delos."

Don closed the notebook and stuck it back into his vest pocket. "Will do. Shall I also send her a bio on you?"

"I suppose," Leonard said. "But nothing spectacular, just indicate that I'm a humble tool of the great Delos."

Then he looked away again. *"But a worthy tool can be made from even the basest of metals."*

"Right." Don chuckled, and headed out of the meditation chamber. That Leonard. Always in performance mode.

The TV studio was cold and busy, full of the sound of hammering and mike checks. Stagehands moved props from one set to another, stepping with practiced ease around what looked to Don like several miles worth of cable and power lines and wires. Five different shows were taped at the studio, including a cooking show and a health series, but only the Ann Kilgore talk show was a real, bona fide hit in the syndicated TV market.

With Leonard at his elbow, looking appropriately overwhelmed, they followed the production assistant across the maze of cables and TV cameras toward the rear of the studio. "This is just a formality," Gerry said. "Ms. Kilgore likes first-time guests to come by, get a feel for the place, let us know what kinds of things you'd like to talk about. Right through here, please."

They stepped through the door into a small but thankfully warmer office. Posters of Ann Kilgore dominated both walls, punctuated by photos of guests who had previously appeared on the show. "Have a seat," Gerry said, and pulled a tape recorder out of a desk drawer, setting it on the table between them. "Hope you don't mind. It saves me the trouble of making notes. After we're done, I'll give this to the secretary, and she can put together the questions Ms. Kilgore will ask you later."

"I'm sure that'll be fine."

"Good," Gerry said, and switched on the tape recorder before turning his attention to Leonard. "So, Mr. Randall, I understand you're a mind reader."

"Not exactly," Don said, jumping in. Leonard much preferred it for him to make the explanations in situations like this. "Mr. Randall is a trance channeler. A spirit guide named Delos speaks through him."

Leonard picked up his cue and glanced modestly away.

"Got it," Gerry said. "Now, is there anything in particular you'd like to mention while you're on the show?"

Leonard opened his mouth to answer—and suddenly hesitated, staring off into the distance.

What the hell? Don thought.

Then Leonard sat forward, meeting Gerry's gaze with interest. *"I would mention only that the true meaning in life is that which we choose to give it—for the universe is not without mercy, and not so jealous that it cannot allow a multitude of visions. All truths are correct, all creeds valid, and the only secret—is that there is no secret."*

He sat back, blinked. "And we're having a rally at the Pacific Arts Stadium on the 14th."

Gerry dropped his pencil, looked to Don.

Don shrugged.

Leonard looked from one to the other and cleared his throat. "Well, I just thought it might be worth mentioning, it's going to be a big event for us. So Ms. Kilgore might want to get into that."

"Which part?"

"Excuse me?"

"You'll have to excuse Mr. Randall," Don said, smiling. If Leonard were pulling some sort of stunt without clearing it with him first, Don would have his hide made into a seat cushion. "He's been working very hard—sometimes it's hard to keep it all straight."

Leonard shook his head. Sat straighter. *"I have no difficulty seeing things as they are. That is, indeed, my curse. I see this television as the single greatest time-waster in the history of mankind."*

He looked to Gerry, and his face was somber, his voice deeper and more compelling than even a moment earlier. *"You make sport of people's pain and exploit people in order to sell trinkets to those who cannot afford them, all to increase your own wealth. Yes, I see things quite well indeed. And I see that the woman in whose employ you labor—is an adulteress, a user of chemicals—"*

Abruptly, Gerry stood, red-faced. He snapped off the tape recorder. "I think that'll be enough. If you'll excuse me."

He stormed out of the room, slamming the door behind him.

Don wheeled on Leonard. "What the hell is wrong with you?"

"What?" He looked around. "Where's the guy?"

"Gone. And I wouldn't blame him if he had Kilgore cancel the appearance, after what you said."

"After I—Don, I didn't say anything!"

"Don't kid with me, Leonard."

"I'm not! I swear!"

"No?" Don turned the tape recorder around. "Listen." He punched PLAY, and the voice that sounded so unnaturally different from Leonard's usual voice filled the room. Leonard listened, shaking his head.

"Who's that?" Leonard asked.

"It's you. Leonard, *it's you.*"

Don told the receptionist to hold all calls, then headed toward the meditation chamber. A few discreet inquiries had yielded the name he needed. The only hard part would be talking Leonard into it. But he'd find a way.

Leonard stood up as he entered the chamber. "Did you talk to the producer?"

Don nodded.

"So . . . what's the situation?"

"It took a lot of talking, Leonard. A lot of favors called in. But we're still due to go on the air."

Leonard rubbed at his face, relieved. "Well, that's good, at least."

"Maybe so, Leonard, but we can't keep going on like this. You're going to have to do something before we go on the show. You have to get control of that—that voice, whatever it is."

"Well, it can't be Delos. There's no such *thing* as Delos. For chrissakes, Don, we made him up. Remember, the first time I suggested it, I said 'A ten-thousand-year-old warrior,' and you thought I said a 'ten-thousand-year-old worrier?' Hell, I thought you'd never stop laughing."

"Yeah. Only it's not funny anymore, Leonard. The money, and the good times, it all comes to a stop unless you can get this under control." He reached into his pocket for the slip of paper he'd put there earlier. "Which is why I've made an appointment with someone for you. A specialist. I think he can help."

Leonard glanced at it without taking it. His lips thinned angrily. "A *psychiatrist?* No way. Not a chance."

"Leonard, I don't know what's going on here, and neither do you. All I know is everything's riding on this show tomorrow. Mess up, and we're finished."

"I said no. N. O. I can handle it."

Don studied his face. "Leonard," he said, very slowly, "do you remember Atlanta? Do you remember what it was *like*, going from one tent to another, pulling nickels and dimes out of the dirt, hustling Bibles and—"

Leonard snatched the paper from his hand. "All right. I'll go." He turned his back to Don, reaching for his coat, and paused.

Straightened.

Ah, crap, Don thought, and when Leonard turned

to glance back at him over his shoulder, the smile he saw there wasn't Leonard's. *"It should be—most enlightening."*

Don groaned.

Leonard started, looked up. "It happened again?"

"It happened again."

"See if you can move that appointment up a few hours," Leonard said, and headed for the door.

Frowning, Dr. Greenberg reached for another cigarette. "I'm sorry," he said, "look, can we backtrack a moment? I think there's something I'm not getting here."

"Sure," said the man sitting on his couch. It had been a hurried appointment, and five minutes into Leonard's explanation, he was sure he'd missed something.

"You say you hear voices?"

"No, not exactly. I'm probably the only one who *doesn't* hear it, for some reason. But everybody else does. I just sort of go blank, and this voice comes out of me, and says things I have no control over."

"That's what I thought." He checked the notes on his clipboard. "You're a trance channeler, aren't you?"

"Yes."

"Not to be judgmental, but—you're *supposed* to hear voices, yes?"

"Yes."

"Then what's the problem?"

"Well, it's . . . you have to understand, Dr. Greenberg, I'm *really* getting this voice, and I've got to go on TV tomorrow, so unless—"

"Ah, television," Greenberg said, nodding. "Now I start to get the picture. So to speak." He extinguished the cigarette and reached for another. "Mr. Randall, I've worked as a psychotherapist for twenty years. I pride myself on my record. If it's all the same to you, I would rather not be the subject of this little publicity stunt. You can claim to hear as many voices as you wish, Mr. Randall. You may claim to have the entire Mormon

Tabernacle Choir singing Brahms to you in the middle of the night—but do not come to me to add credibility to your little scam."

He lit the cigarette, waiting for the protest that would of course follow. But Leonard said nothing. Then he sat a little straighter in the seat and studied him intensely for a moment before nodding. *"Yes, you are a good man. One of the few I have met recently."*

"That's right, and I—" He leaned back, noting the change in Leonard's tone. He's good, Greenberg decided. Posture, vocal tone, attitude, all had subtly but definitely shifted. "So this is the voice, is it? Very nice. What else do you do?"

"I speak honestly, that's all. It is not unlike what you do, I think."

"I see. And who might you be?" Greenberg asked, sitting back and taking a long drag on the cigarette. "Napoleon? Aristotle?"

"Napoleon is dead. Aristotle is dead. And you do not look well yourself. Why do you do—that—to yourself?"

"What?" Greenberg asked, then saw that Leonard was looking at the cigarette in his hand, and felt a flash of resentment. "I think that will be all for today, Mr. Randall."

"You miss her very much, don't you?"

"I beg your pardon?"

"I see such pain in you. But there was nothing you could do. Even if you had arrived sooner—it was too late." He stood, walked a pace or two toward Greenberg's desk. *"Your wife misses you as much as you miss her—but she would prefer you did not hurry the reunion."*

Greenberg slammed a fist down on his desk. "Get out," he said.

Leonard started at the sound. "What? What did I do?"

"You know very well what you did!" Greenberg said, jabbing the air with his cigarette. "How dare— how *dare* you use my wife to give you some kind of authenticity! Of all the cheap—look, just get out. Forget my fee. Forget the whole thing. Just—go away!"

Leonard quickly backpedaled toward the door, grabbed his coat from the wall hanger, and stepped outside.

Damn him, Greenberg thought, as the pain came back anew.

Damn him.

He opened the desk drawer where he kept her photograph. She smiled up at him from the faded picture. It was the last one he'd taken of her. She'd always been after him to quit smoking, even when it was only half a pack a day, before it went to two packs and counting, before she—

He closed his eyes. Then, after a moment, he opened them again.

And extinguished the cigarette.

Don came into the makeup room at ten minutes to air. The audience was solid. They'd slipped a few of their own people in to keep the applause properly enthusiastic when Ann Kilgore introduced Leonard. Everything was in place. He hoped.

Still wearing the makeup bib, Leonard was pacing nervously. "How's it look out there?"

"Never mind that. How are *you?*"

"I think it'll be okay. I got one of those voice-activated recorders on my way in yesterday, and left it beside the bed. The—voice, whatever, didn't say a word all night. Maybe it's gone."

"Let's hope so," Don said, and glanced back at a knock at the door.

Gerry, holding a clipboard and wearing a headset, stuck his head into the room just long enough to say, "Three minutes, Mr. Randall." Then he was gone again.

Don pulled the bib from Leonard's collar and helped him on with his coat. "Just keep telling yourself —get through this, make Delos a star, and we're set up for life." He let out a deep breath, checked for stray makeup, then clapped Leonard on the shoulder. "Ready?"

"Ready."

The stage was minimal, just a few overstuffed chairs ringed in a half circle facing the three cameras. Don paced behind the cameras, watching the monitor as the standard opening for the *Ann Kilgore Show!* went out live to seventy-five affiliate East Coast stations. A heavy-duty three-quarter-inch videotape machine recorded the images for later rebroadcast on the West Coast.

Ms. Kilgore did her usual teaser first: letters from viewers, and then a quick profile of tonight's lineup before breaking for a commercial.

After what seemed like an eternity, the floor director held up a hand for silence, then three fingers, two fingers, one finger, then pointed to Ann Kilgore as the red light atop camera one lit up.

Here goes, Don thought.

"Well, we're back," Kilgore said, smiling for the viewers. "Our next guest has been making quite a splash these days, and we're very pleased to have him on the show. He's a 'trance channeler,' a fascinating subject that we'll explore in a moment—but first I'd like to personally welcome him on this, his first television appearance, Mr. Leonard Randall."

Leonard came out on stage, smiling shyly. He shook hands and took his assigned place on the stage-right chair.

"Well, Leonard," she said, "why don't you start by telling us what all this trance channeling is about? I mean, how would you describe what you do?"

Leonard considered the question, opened his mouth to speak—and paused.

And sat a little straighter.

Don instinctively covered his face. "Oh, no," he whispered.

It wasn't Leonard anymore.

But having never before spoken to him, Kilgore wouldn't know that, would she?

He braced himself for the worst.

"These are sad times, Ms. Kilgore. All that is mysterious, all that is magic, has been leached away. People who do not see the magic in themselves seek it in someone else. They are so desperate for mystery, for something to believe in, that they accept without question even the most outrageous propositions."

"Such as?"

"Such as the man sitting in this chair."

Don prayed for a lightning strike. A blackout. Anything that would put him out of his misery. But the voice just kept on going.

"And for the honor of being treated like sheep, for the distinction of being treated as gullible children, they are willing to pay, to sacrifice, all they have. Money, relationships, love, property—they would give it all for a scent of magic."

Kilgore nodded absently. This wasn't the answer she'd been expecting. "Perhaps, Mr. Randall, you could let us speak to Delos," she said, trying to steer the conversation into more comfortable waters. "That's the ten-thousand-year-old warrior you channel, isn't it?"

"There is no Delos. There never was."

We're dead, Don thought. Even Gerry was now watching openmouthed. He heard the director's voice, soft, spilling out of Gerry's headset. "Jesus! Okay, camera two, ready for close-up. Go two."

Leonard's face filled the television screen, looking out at the audience with beatific calm. *"Consider it an investment in innocence that turned a considerable profit. And now the game is over, the masquerade is ended. To the followers of Delos, I can offer only the sincere apologies of Leonard Randall, and one slightly used piece of wisdom. Do not seek enlightenment in the vain and self-indulgent proclamations of those who insist you must pay for your own soul. Do not seek it in this box, or in the opinions of others. Seek it instead in the quiet turning of your own considered conscience. Thank you."*

With that, he sat back, smiling. Having said what he had to say, what was left?

Not diddly, Don thought, as Ann Kilgore's face reappeared on the monitor. And now she was smiling too. How often do you get a confession on national TV?

"Well folks, you heard it here first," she said. "We'll be back right after these messages."

Leonard walked into the meditation chamber and sat heavily behind the desk. He felt numb, weightless, limbless. He'd watched the replay of the Ann Kilgore show, had heard the words he didn't recognize coming from his own mouth, and had known at that moment that it was all over.

His first reaction had been to go out and get drunk. But as his face filled television screens all over town, in bars and nightclubs, even that escape was closed to him. Not wanting to deal with the phone calls that he knew were even then flooding the mission, he had checked into a hotel room for the night.

And now the mission, headquarters of Delos Incorporated, was empty. Twenty-four hours, and it had gone from busy to dead silent. The five thousand extra copies of *THE BOOK OF DELOS* sat gathering dust in the conference room. He hadn't even bothered picking up the three-inch-high stack of messages with his name scrawled on them at the front desk.

It was over.

And it had been such a great idea, he thought.

When the door opened, he half expected to see the police there. But it was only Don, who looked as though he hadn't slept much more than Leonard—which was not at all.

"I'm almost afraid to ask," Leonard said.

Don approached, dropped a manila folder filled with papers on the desk, and began leafing through them as he spoke, hardly bothering to look at them. "The scandal's killing us. Everyone who's ever given us a dime is asking for it back. We've logged over two hundred angry calls, investors are pulling out left, right, and sideways, the IRS is nosing around—we were on shaky financial footing as it was, but now—if you're lucky, there's enough to get you a hotel somewhere for the night. If not—" He shrugged. The meaning was clear.

"What about you?"

"Me?" Don laughed harshly, tiredly. "Man, I am *out* of here. It's too bad, really. I thought you were sharp. I thought you had it. I was wrong." He gathered up the papers and stuffed them back into the folder. "I've got a gig with a healer down in Panama. Folks say he's the best around. Probably make it big in a few years. With the right lieutenant."

Leonard nodded numbly.

Don leaned forward on the desk, his expression as sincere as Leonard had ever seen it. "Get some serious help, Leonard. And if we ever cross in a hallway somewhere—pretend you never met me. I know I will."

He waited a moment, perhaps waiting for a response. When one failed to come, he looked away, picked up the folder, and headed out of the meditation chamber, closing the door behind him.

Leonard didn't move. He surveyed the room with suddenly old eyes. "Well, Leonard," he said, quietly, "looks like it's over."

Then he heard it.

Quite to the contrary. It is only the beginning.

He jumped to his feet. It was the voice. The same voice he'd heard on the tape recorder, and the videotape. Only now it seemed to be coming from all around him, from *inside* him.

"You," Leonard said. "It's *you!*"

Yes. I'm pleased that you can hear me at last. There was so much in the way between us—that's why I had to get rid of it all, you see. You couldn't hear me.

Leonard stalked the room, tearing up the sofa cushions, looking for a speaker or a microphone or something. When he found nothing, he kicked the sofa, knocking out a wooden leg.

Anger, Mr. Randall? It seems rather pointless,

don't you think? Isn't that what you said, what Delos said? Submerge anger, find the center.

Leonard pounded on the desk, throwing papers in all directions. "WHERE ARE YOU? I'LL KILL YOU, YOU—WHERE *ARE* YOU?"

I am here, Mr. Randall. With you.

"Why are you doing this to me?" he shouted at the walls. "WHY?"

Look over here, Mr. Randall.

He looked to the mirror, and suddenly it seemed to cloud over. It began to swirl with colors that pulsed just beneath the surface. Then, gradually, he began to make out a silhouette; just the barest impression of a face.

I'm here at your urging, Mr. Randall. You said that the universe had chosen you to receive great wisdom. Remember? And you, of all people, should know that sometimes, when you speak to the universe, the universe . . . listens.

This can't be happening, Leonard thought.

You asked for wisdom, and now you will receive it. It will be a long process, but to that end I am willing to be your constant companion—for as long as it takes.

Then, abruptly, the image disappeared, to be replaced by Leonard's own reflection.

He spun about, frantic. "How long?"

Silence.

"HOW LONG IS IT GOING TO TAKE?"

Then he felt his back stiffen, felt his arms relax at his sides, felt his lips curl up into a gentle smile.

And heard himself say, *"Twenty, thirty years. At most."*

Then it was gone.

He clapped his hands over his mouth.

But it was no use. The voice came from all around him.

And now, as you say in your modern world—let's take it from the top.

* * *

Critical reviews received and reluctantly acknowledged by Mr. Leonard Randall, a case study in showmanship who found himself upstaged in the final act—by the Twilight Zone.

Introduction to Rendezvous in a Dark Place

There is, in even the most reasonable and least macabre among us, a terrible curiosity about death. It draws us to horror films and roller coasters, where we can vicariously experience our own deaths; it plucks at our thoughts at funerals, where we see our inevitable future laid out in satin and hardwood; it comes to us in what is known as the Hour of the Wolf—the time, between midnight and dawn, when we lay listening to the tenuous sound of our own heartbeats, and the unfair shortness of our time here weighs most heavily.

Death horrifies us—and fascinates us. Repels us—and draws us. Like a riddle we cannot solve, but which we cannot stop thinking about, it is always there, just over our shoulder, waiting. It is, in a curious sense, the basis of our equilibrium. Ignore the possibility of death, and we become reckless. Living as though we were immortal is the fastest way to embrace our terrible mortality. But to dwell on death leads us into far deeper and infinitely darker waters.

Perhaps it has something to do with the tradition of White Russians, but in my family death has always been a sort of unintentional icon. When I was young, I was taken to funerals for family friends, my grandmother's boarder, and, on occasion, to the funerals of kids who had met with some terrible accident, whose fate was meant to serve as a warning lest I do likewise. My step-grandfather was a grounds keeper at a cemetery, and would often take me on his rounds. Sometimes he would even talk to those beneath the ground. If they were Polish, he spoke to them in Polish. If they were Russian, he would address them in Russian. And so on. I once asked him what he did when he didn't know the language. He shrugged, smiled, and said, in his broken English, "Then I leave more flowers."

I heard again and again how my real grandfather had died drunk, lying in the street. Whenever the phone rang, it was generally expected that it would be some relative or other, telling us of another death in the family, which would always be discussed in great detail, down to the last shuddering gasp.

And my paternal grandmother . . . well, my grandmother had this little habit of going to funerals for people she didn't even know, and then complaining about the food later. I never asked her why she went, or what she found there, but I long suspected it had some-thing to do with ritual and ceremony and a rush of the same kind of emotion you find in airports, where good-byes are tearful and rushed but not usually as perma-nent.

She was dying for twenty years. Her health was decent, no better or worse than most women her age, but she was convinced that she was dying, and would not last out the season (whatever season that happened to be at the moment). For twenty years, death was on her lips all the time. She expected to go at any moment. After a while, death went from a part-time obsession to a full-time occupation. When she finally did pass away, there were more than a few of us who wanted some proof that this time it had actually happened.

But it had. And in the rows of people who came to her funeral, I wondered if among them sat some who did not know her, but were instead possessed by a curi-ous fascination that drew them to the funerals of strang-ers.

These thoughts, and others—too private to be discussed in this forum, dealing with deaths close to me, and a terrible brush with it of my own—brought me to the story you are about to read. It was one of those stories that seemed to write itself. And why not? I had lived with it for twenty years.

When director Rene Bonniere received the script, we met in the studios of Atlantis Films in Toronto to discuss it. He told me he thought it was an important script, one that he wanted very much to do. And he told me something else. "What I love about the story," he said, in a wonderful, thick French accent, "is that it is a romance, is it not?"

I looked across the table at him. "A romance?"

He winked at me. "It is a seduction, yes? The only thing that I have not yet determined is, who is seducing whom?"

It was, I decided, a very good question indeed.

"Rendezvous in a Dark Place," production #87039, was filmed starting November 14, 1988, under the direction of Rene Bonniere, starring Janet Leigh (Barbara), Stephen McHattie (Dark Figure), Todd Duckworth (Trent), Malcom Stewart (Jason), Eric House (Dying Man), Lorne Cossette (Reverend), Lori Waller Benson (Nurse), Michael Millar (Police), and Jeff Grantham (Doctor). First broadcast March 12, 1989.

RENDEZVOUS IN A DARK PLACE

The chapel was small and simple, but filled with flowers and people and the subdued sound of an organ playing somewhere discreetly out of sight. Daylight filtered in through the stained glass windows, throwing patterns of shifting color on the polished surface of the coffin.

The service concluded, they filed past the coffin one at a time, making their silent farewells and then moving on. Some ran their hands along the sleek wood, as though trying to reach through the cool surface for one last embrace. Some could not bring themselves to touch the coffin, but their desperate and solemn love was no less apparent.

Barbara LeMay, at the end of the line, lingered beside the coffin when her time came at last. She ran her gloved hand just over the surface of the coffin, barely an inch from the dark and polished oak. She closed her eyes, and when she opened them again she gazed down at the face that reposed within, her own calm reflecting the quiet tranquility she saw there.

A voice came from beside her. "A great loss."

She turned to find the reverend standing at her elbow, then let her gaze return to the coffin. "Yes, it is."

"Were you a relative?"

"Hmm?" she answered distractedly. "Oh. No, not at all."

"A friend of the family, then?"

She turned to him again, her hand leaving the coffin only reluctantly, as she might release the hand of a lover. "No, I'm afraid not. Actually, I don't know anyone here. They're all strangers to me."

She smiled at him, and rested a gloved hand on his arm. "But it was still a lovely service, Reverend. A very lovely service."

She squeezed his arm gently, then moved past him, to where the others were gathering for the reception. She glanced back just once, burning the scene into her memory.

It was perfect. So terribly, terribly perfect.

Barbara LeMay, the woman in black, out of place in a world of colors and sounds and life; a woman caught on the edge of a knife between fascination and something more profound and less earthly; a special kind of love, found only in the Twilight Zone.

Jason LeMay pulled the three heavy grocery sacks out of his rented car and duck walked up the sidewalk, trying desperately not to break anything else. He fumbled with the key to his mother's house only to find it unlocked, as usual, and despite his repeated warnings.

He pushed through, kicking the door closed before slumping against it. Why was food so heavy? Why was the kitchen always twice as far from the front door whenever he was carrying something heavy? Why was it always so dark in here? And where was his mother?

"Mom?"

From somewhere upstairs she called back. "I'm changing. I'll be right down. Put them in the kitchen."

"Right." His left hand was getting numb where it clutched the third sack, which supported the second sack, which was balanced up against the first sack, which he now noticed was torn along one side. *I'll never make it*, he thought, but charged ahead toward the kitchen anyway.

To his surprise, he made it with the bags intact. Mostly.

When he stepped back into the living room, his arms numb, she was coming down the stairs. As usual, she was dressed in a black dress and black shoes. The light in the room was subdued, contained safely behind thick curtains hung at the front window.

"I fear I must report your dozen eggs have just turned magically into ten." He flexed his arms, feeling the blood gradually starting to return. "I think gravity had something to do with it."

"You look exhausted, Jason," she said. "Go and sit down. I'll unpack."

"An excellent idea," he said, and walked across the room, toward the overstuffed sofa that was the room's centerpiece.

"Thank you for going for me," she called back. "It's been such a busy day."

"No problem." Before collapsing on the couch, he glanced again at the curtained windows. It was dark as a cave in here. A brief search revealed the drawcord. He opened it, letting in the daylight. It filled the room, warming him immediately.

"Would you like something to eat, Jason? You must be starved."

"I'd love something," he called, and sat heavily on the couch. It was remarkable how different the place looked when fully lit. Sunlight glinted off tiny porcelain figures and plates behind glass cabinets, and chased shadows out of the corners where they had claimed homesteaders' rights.

Barbara emerged from the kitchen carrying a tray loaded with a glass of milk and a plate covered with finger sandwiches. "Here you go, dear."

"Thanks."

She circled around the couch, heading back the way she came. As he leaned forward to take one of the sandwiches, the sunlight went away. Darkness descended on the room, and the eager shadows rushed back to reclaim their territory. He glanced back over his shoulder. She had closed the curtains again on her way out.

He briefly considered getting up and opening them again, but he was too tired, she was too determined, and he was hungry. He took a bite, then another. "These are good, Mom."

"Thank you," she called from the kitchen.

"So what did you do today? You said you were busy."

He could catch an occasional glimpse of her in the kitchen, putting away the groceries as she spoke. "Well, first I went by to pay my respects to your father. We have to talk to the grounds keeper again. I found some paper wrappers in the grass. People should be more careful of these things."

"I'll talk to him," he said, then added, more quietly, "again."

She swept back into the room, carrying a carefully folded napkin. "Then on the way in, I stopped off at Forestview. They were having a lovely service."

Not again, Jason thought, and swallowed the last of the sandwich. "Mom, Forestview is at the other end of town. You'd have to go clear around the world for Forestview to be on the way in."

She looked at him in that way of hers that said she wasn't listening. "You're spilling crumbs," she said, and handed him the napkin before heading back into the kitchen.

"As I was saying," she continued, "it was a lovely service. I suppose there must have been a hundred, maybe a hundred and fifty people there. There was a reception afterward. They served the most wonderful finger sandwiches."

Jason stopped in midbite. Looked at the finger sandwich in his hand. *Couldn't be,* he thought. But he put the sandwich down anyway, glancing up as she came back into the room and sat in the chair opposite him. "So who was the service for? I hadn't heard of anyone we know dying."

"I don't know," she said. "Well, I mean, I heard his name a few times, but you know how I am on names."

"You don't—" He took a moment to compose himself. "Mom, I thought we'd settled this a long time ago. You've got to stop going to funerals for people you don't even know."

"Why?"

"Well, it's—*wrong*, that's all."

"They had white roses," she said. "You should have seen them. White roses, tied with tiny red ribbons. Silk, I think they were. One for each year. They had them arranged in this tall vase—I believe it was carnival glass —so that they were lit from behind by the sun. I don't think I've ever seen anything so beautiful. And there was music, and there were such words spoken, such love, such peace in that place."

Her eyes were distant, her thoughts inward. There was a slight, wistful smile on her face as she thought about it. "When I go, I think I would very much like something like that. Would you see to it, dear?"

"Mom—"

"I believe there's a vase in the attic that would be just perfect."

"Mom, will you stop it? You know I don't like to hear you talk like that."

"I know you don't. But we have to be prepared for these things."

"Prepared? Mom, they didn't prepare as much as this for the Allied invasion of Normandy Beach. Besides, I talked to your doctor last week. He says you're healthy as an ox."

She nodded absently. "Did I tell you about Mrs. Rosenbloom? They told her the same thing. Last week, she went to bed and didn't wake up. I think they said it was an aneurysm. These things happen, Jason. We hate to think about them, but—"

"No. That's where we part company, Mom. You *don't* hate to think about them. You *love* to think about them." He stood up, pacing behind the sofa. "Why is it every time I see you, every other word is death? When I invited you out to the Coast to see Margie and the kids, you couldn't. Because you said you couldn't make any long-term plans. How the hell am I supposed to explain

hat to the kids? 'I'm sorry, Gramma can't come for
Thanksgiving because she can't make reservations because she doesn't know if she'll be alive or not?' You
hurt them."

She looked down at her hands. They were so white,
almost translucent. "I'm sorry. Really, I am."

"I know. I just wish you'd stop all this. Wear something other than black. Get outside once in a while for
something other than somebody's funeral. Let some
light in here."

He threw open the curtain again. She winced at the
sudden flash of daylight, but didn't move to stop him.
"This *obsession* of yours, it's not good. It's not healthy.
It's morbid. I love you. And I want you to see your
grandkids grow up."

"I'll try. Really I will."

"What's to *try*, Mom? You just—" He stopped as his
watch beeped at him. He switched it off and looked
across at her as she stood up and approached him.
"Damn. I have to go, Mom. Plane to catch."

"Then go," she said, and touched his face. "And
give my best to Margie and to Ben and Susan. I'll be
fine. Really."

"All right. I just hate the idea of you living out here
in the boondocks. I want you to promise you'll keep the
doors locked around here, okay? It makes me feel a
little better."

"I will."

"I didn't mean to yell," he said, and studied her
face for a moment, then kissed her cheek. "I'll give you
a call as soon as I get in. See you in a few weeks, Mom."

"Good-bye, Jason."

She always said good-bye, he thought as he stepped
out into the cool afternoon air. Never *see you*, or *until
later*. Only *good-bye*.

Let it go, he thought, and climbed into the rented
car to begin the long drive back to the airport.

Halfway there, he thought back, and couldn't remember if he'd heard her lock the front door or not.

* * *

Barbara awoke suddenly to the sound of thunder though she knew it was not the thunder that had awakened her. She sat up on one elbow, peering into the night that filled her bedroom, listening for the other sound that still echoed in her ears. After a moment, it came again—a creak of floorboards, and a muffled drag *thump* from downstairs.

She slid out of bed, finding her slippers and robe on the dresser nearby, and felt her way out of the room to the hall. It was dark downstairs, and she could feel a draft even through her heavy robe.

"Hello?" she said. Silence. She flicked on the light switch at the top of the stairs. Down below, the door was open, a brisk, wet wind ruffling the curtains beside it. Water was pooling on the floor. She edged down the stairs, eyes watchful, until she reached the door and closed it. She reached for the living room lights—

"Don't—don't try it."

She turned, slowly, to the source of the voice. A young man stood in the middle of the room. He braced himself against the sofa, one arm hanging limp at his side. Even from here, in the dim light from the stair well, she could see a dark smear of blood on his shirt. There was a gun in his other hand. He was drenched from the storm, shivering, and in pain.

"All right, lady, don't—don't move, don't call the cops, or," he squinted against the pain, which shivered through his body, "or I swear, I'll kill you, I swear, I'll—"

He never finished the sentence. He swayed, then fell, unconscious, to the floor.

Barbara went to him and gently put a hand on his chest. His breath was ragged, shallow, and when she pulled back her hand it came away covered with blood.

He's dying, she thought, and with that thought came another: *He'll come. He'll come here, tonight.*

In spite of herself, she tried to call an ambulance but when she picked up the receiver she got only static. The storm had knocked out the lines, as they sometimes did. But at least the radio worked, and she turned it to a local news station.

Not wanting to risk moving him up onto the couch, she found a blanket and covered him where he lay on the floor, hoping it would keep the cold away. She grabbed one of the pillows from the couch and set it under his head as gently as she could. A first-aid kit in the closet let her bandage up as much of the wound as she could, but it was bad, and deep, and without doubt fatal. This done, she moved around the room, turning on only a few lights here and there, just enough to see by, never taking her eyes off the young man on the floor. She didn't dare look away. In that moment, she might miss it. Miss him.

She started back when she heard the young man stir. She went to him, knelt down beside him as his eyes fluttered open. For a moment they seemed unable to focus on anything, then they finally found her. He licked his lips, managed, "Who—"

"Shhh," she said. "Don't try to talk. I did what I could, but it's—bad, I think. Very bad. I tried to call the hospital, but the lines are down. It happens sometimes in a big storm. I could try again."

He shook his head. "No. Don't want t'die—in no hospital."

"I didn't say you were dying."

His eyes met hers. "Yes, you did," he said, and glanced away. "Knew it soon's they shot me. Funny, ain't it, how you just—know—"

He stopped as a spasm of pain shot through him. He bit his lip, barely holding on to consciousness. When he opened his eyes again, it took him longer to focus on her. "I *am* dying, ain't I? Just—tell me straight, okay? Nobody—ever tells you nothing straight."

She hesitated just a moment, then nodded. "I'm—I'm not an expert, but—yes, I think you're dying."

He let his gaze linger on her, and she thought she saw a light go out behind them with her statement, as though in spite of everything he had been holding out some small hope that she would say otherwise. With the pronouncement, he let his head loll to one side, away from her.

"While you were unconscious," she said, "I turned on the radio. It mentioned a robbery. Some all-night liquor store."

"Twenty-seven dollars and change," he said. "Ain't that something." He licked his lips again. They were dry, parched.

"I'll get you some water," she said, and started to rise.

But he grabbed for her, getting only air. "Wait—don't go."

She sat back down, resting a hand on his chest. He was cool to her touch, and seemed to take some comfort from the warmth of contact. "Don't worry. I won't leave you alone. I understand. Perhaps better than you know. I'll wait with you. We'll both wait together."

He nodded, his eyes closed, and then went away again.

Barbara did not move.

She would wait with him, as she had promised.

It was half an hour later when she felt the room suddenly go cold around her. At the same moment, the young man's breathing became shallower and less frequent. A breeze brushed the back of her neck, and she turned to see the curtains rustling even though the windows were closed.

She sat up, straining to see in the half light, listening for the slightest sound. A curious hush descended on the room. The sound of the clock ticking on the wall grew muffled, as though wrapped in cloth.

Something had changed in the room.

She was sure of it.

"It's you, isn't it?" she said to the night, her voice low and carefully calm. "You're here, aren't you?"

At first, there was no response. Then something separated from the shadows, a lightless shape deeper than the surrounding night. Its face was obscured, eclipsed by darkness.

"I . . . am here," he said.

She stood, moving slowly, not wanting to startle

him, if that were possible. "Are you surprised?" she asked. "That I can see you?"

"No."

"No, I guess you wouldn't be. We've spent so much time together, you and I. I guess it makes one a little more sensitive than most."

"Yes."

"I was in the hospital once, and the woman in the room next to me died in the night. When it happened, I —*felt* you nearby. I thought, at the time, that it was a dream. But it wasn't."

A sound from the floor distracted her. The young man forced open his eyes, and tried to focus on her, this time failing in the attempt. "Who—who you talkin' to?"

She knelt down beside him. "No one. No one at all. It's all right."

He nodded distantly. ". . . 's cold in here."

She pulled the blanket tighter around him, then stood. "He can't see you."

The darkness before her seemed momentarily to shiver, then reappeared across the room, nearer to the young man. "For him—I will not exist—until his time."

"Where do you take them? To a better place?"

"Sometimes."

"It must be beautiful."

"It is a place, like any other." With that he knelt down—no, she corrected herself, seemed to flow downward—toward the young man.

"Wait," she said.

He did.

"Why don't you take me—instead of him?"

"What is he to you?"

"No one," she said. "Nothing. But he does not see the beauty in you. I do. I've seen it in a million ways. Peace. Freedom. Tranquility. The poignant, fragile beauty of that one final exhalation, the gathering of the soul, the ceremony, and so much more."

"It is his time."

"But he can't appreciate you, as I can. I have no one here, not really. Not since—"

The shimmer again, and now he appeared at the other end of the room. When he spoke, it was in a voice colder than she had ever heard. "No," he said.

"But why? I thought such things were possible."

"I cannot take life—where there is none to take."

He moved slowly, flowing through the room, and though she could not see his eyes, she could feel them on her nonetheless. "I have seen you in so many places," he said, calling to her from the shadows. "You have called my name so many times. You have worshipped at my altar, walked in my shadow, seen my reflection in the faces of others, and still it is not enough. You do not run from my touch, you seek to embrace it—and yet I cannot take you more than I can take this table . . . for neither of you lives."

"I—don't understand."

He flowed toward the young man, and paused, letting the shadow of his hand fall across the face below. For a moment, the shadow seemed to oppress the young man, but then he fought back, struggling against the touch that had not yet come.

The darkness flowed back a little, but only a little. "You see how he resists me, even in sleep? He cherishes life, even in pain. He clings to each second for in each second is the possibility of joy, however often defeated. Even now, this close to me, he is more alive than you.

"I have become the totality of your existence. Your days and nights are full of the thought of me and nothing else. You have made death a lifestyle—and I only come for the living."

And then he did.

He knelt beside the young man and suspended his hand an inch above the sweating, frightened face. "I bring you peace and sleep," he said. "Do not be afraid, for I alone of all will never leave you."

For just the barest moment, the young man's eyes met his, and in that flicker of recognition Barbara saw no fear. There was only peace and resolution, and then the eyes closed one last time, never again to open.

She went to the young man and touched his wrist. No pulse beat beneath the skin.

When she glanced up again, *he* was gone.

"You can't do this," she said, distantly aware that she was crying. "Please, you can't just leave me. We've spent so much time together—it would be rude."

Silence.

"What do you want me to do? Go feed the pigeons in the park? Is that living? I don't have anyone else, don't you understand? My son doesn't need me anymore. Everyone I knew is gone. They're with you. *You took them away from me and now you won't even take me!* What, am I not good enough? Not pretty enough? Is that it?"

The cold in the room began to fade. She grew aware of sounds returning, the night wind outside beating against the house. Her hands flew to her face, and she glanced around frantically, vainly searching the shadows for the darkness that was no longer there. "I'm —I'm sorry I yelled. Please, just stay with me a moment, that's all. Just—a moment."

But the night did not respond, and she was alone.

Barbara watched impassively as the two uniformed officers rolled the stretcher out the front door, only marginally listening to the sergeant sitting beside her on the couch.

He touched the young man. But not me. He would not touch me. He would not touch me.

She looked over at the officer, wondering vaguely what he was talking about, why he was still here. "I have to give you credit for a lot of courage, Mrs. LeMay," he was saying. "Dead phone or not, I think most folks would've been out the door in a second as soon as he fell."

She shrugged. "He was harmless. And he was in pain."

"No, not anymore. That's what they say, isn't it— the only two constants being death and taxes."

She smiled, and in smiling thought her face might

crack in two. "Not always," she said. "He didn't touch me. Not once."

The officer studied her for a long moment before closing his report book and standing up. "You sure you'll be all right, ma'am? Maybe you should have a friend come over—"

"I'll be fine, officer. Thank you."

Though he looked unsure *(he doesn't understand, no, but then none of them would, not in a million years)*, he nodded and headed for the door, reminding her to call if she had any further questions or recollections.

Then she closed the door, and the silence that had been waiting eagerly in the shadows crept out to reclaim its dominion.

Jason was carefully solicitous on the phone. She put his fears to rest, she was perfectly all right, no, nothing was stolen, and she didn't want to bother him with it, knowing how busy he was. And of course there was no need for him to fly out again, plane fare was so expensive these days. Yes, she would be more careful about locking the door. She would talk to him tomorrow.

"Good-b—" she started, and then caught herself. "Good night, Jason," she said, and set the receiver back in its cradle.

She would be fine. Just . . . fine, she thought.

And continued crying.

She emerged from the bedroom, wearing a lie. She went to the mirror to inspect it. The dress was green, and there were flecks of silver sown through the fabric, and it seemed so loud, so out of place. Walking stiffly, as though in costume, she went to the closet and found the box of makeup. The tints and powders were dry from lack of use. She had to moisten them with water from the sink to use them.

She tried the mascara and the rouge and the powder, and now the lie was on her face, and the more she applied the greater the lie became, and it was laughable, and it was pathetic, and she looked like some dime-store mannequin, and her mascara was streaking with tears, the tears she vowed would not come again, and she picked up the box and threw it on the floor, scattering colors and pigments into their component untruths.

She sat on the floor for a long time, crying, before she remembered the medicine cabinet.

The pills were easy enough to find. The date on the prescription wrapper had expired, but that hardly mattered, did it?

Not in the least, she decided, and shut the door.

Barbara sat alone in the living room, watching television with the sound down. Somehow it was better that way. The bottle of pills, still unopened, sat on the table in front of her.

She was sitting in just that same position when—was it hours or only minutes later? she wondered idly—the room grew chill around her, and the image flickering across the television seemed to recede into darkness.

And his voice came to her from the shadows. "I have hurt you."

"No." A lie. "Yes."

From another corner of the room. "It was not—my intention."

"No, it never is."

"How have I hurt you?"

"I've been asking myself the same question a lot, these last few days," she said. "It just seems as though, one by one, everyone I knew went . . . away. They went with you. I suppose, in my way, I got jealous. You took them away, and if I couldn't have them, then I wanted you too. So I started finding out everything I could. About you." She searched the shadows, and for a moment thought she glimpsed movement. "And I began to see why they went with you."

"It was their time."

"Was it?" she asked, and then nodded. "Yes, perhaps it was. But there was more to it than that. I saw it in their faces, after they had seen you. No more pain, no more weariness, no sadness or loss. Only peace. I saw a gift beyond any I could ever hope to offer. I went to hospitals, and I heard the cries of people in pain, people who were crying out for help, crying out—for you. In the end, you're all we have, aren't you?"

He did not answer, and she felt him now in the darkness behind her, moving slowly, so slowly. "My husband always did everything he could to make me happy," she said. "I loved him for that, but I suppose I would have loved him regardless. Then, at the end, he was in such pain, and I could not do the same for him, couldn't make the pain go away. You did that. For him. And for me."

A whisper of movement, a nod in the shadows. "I remember."

"I was so glad for him, so glad that it was finally over, that I—I believe it was then that I began to fall in love with you."

"It is not permitted."

"No, I suspected as much." She glanced at the bottle on the coffee table. "After you left, I—well, there were quite a lot of pain pills in the cabinet, left over from some back problems a while ago. I thought about taking all of them. Whatever you say, even you can't stop me from making it my time, can you?"

Silence.

"I thought as much. But I just couldn't do it. I tell myself that perhaps it would be too—forward. But the truth is that I'm too much of a coward, even for that. It would seem I'm not even very good at dying, am I?"

She looked down at her hands, and the wetness on her cheeks told her that she had again broken her promise to herself. She rubbed it off with the back of her hand, noting as she looked up again that the darkness had drawn closer, and was in front of her now, near enough almost to touch.

His voice was soft and low. "There is a thing I have

heard said among the living. There are always—possibilities."

She gazed up at him, trying to see a face through the shadows. "What kind of—possibilities?"

He moved slowly around her, circling her. "Do you love me?"

"Yes. I wasn't sure before, but—yes. To the heights and depths my soul can reach."

"Then there is—a way."

The darkness shifted and he held out a hand to her. She reached for it, but hesitated before touching his hand.

"Now, at the last, are you afraid of me?" he said.

"No," she said, and took his hand. It was warm to the touch. "I'm not afraid."

Then she looked up, and for the first time saw his face. He was beautiful.

He stepped away, holding her hand.

"Where are we going?" she said.

"Where we are most needed."

And then the world melted away from her.

There was light, all around her, and she was dimly aware of standing, though she could not feel the floor beneath her feet. The first thing she became aware of were the voices.

I'm afraid he doesn't have much time left. Cancer's eaten away virtually everything. Have you checked back with the front desk?

Yes, Doctor.

And there's still no next of kin?

They're still checking. Though it doesn't look like we'll find anyone before it's too late.

Gradually, the bone-bright white gave way to forms and movement. The doctor, shaking his head, moved away from the nurse, who stepped across the room to a bed covered with an oxygen tent. Inside lay a man. She would have guessed he was in his sixties, but somehow she knew he was fifty-two. The cancer had gnawed away at him with terrible efficiency.

The nurse dabbed at his forehead. He was pale, frightened.

He licked his lips. "Is it—is it cold in here?"

"Yes, it is. It's colder in here than it should be. I'll have it checked." She started away from the bed.

He reached for her hand. "No—please, don't—don't leave me. It's all right."

The nurse smiled sadly and looked as though about to reply when the speaker in the ceiling buzzed sharply through the room. *Code Blue, Oncology Ward, Code Blue.*

Her face tightened, and she started to pull away. "I have to go."

"No, please—"

"I'll be right back, I promise."

She touched his hand briefly, then rushed across the room, reaching for her beeper.

"Wait," he called, almost inaudibly, but she was already gone. He closed his eyes, and his breath came in a long, low, ragged sigh. "I want—a drink of water," he said, softly. "Just a drink of water. Please, someone."

He looked up at a warm touch on his arm. "Here you are."

He took the offered paper cup, letting her steady his hand as he drank in small, careful sips.

"Better now?" Barbara said.

He nodded, and then his lower lip started to tremble. He turned his face away from her, so she would not see him cry. "I'm sorry," he said.

"Don't be."

"It's just—I'm afraid. And it hurts—oh, God, it just hurts too much."

"I know. It's all right. I'm here. I won't leave you."

He turned a little, and the tears on his face reflected the harsh light of the overhead fluorescents. She stroked his pale face, gently, soothingly. "I bring you peace and sleep. Do not be afraid, for I alone of all will never leave you."

He looked up into her eyes, and in that instant she knew that he believed.

Then she passed her hand over his face, and Barbara felt him leave, felt his presence pass through her on its way—elsewhere.

What had he said? *A place, like any other.* Perhaps, in time, when she had proven herself further, he would show her.

That would be nice, she thought.

She stepped away from the bed as the nearby monitors and screens started beeping and flashing and buzzing. Doctors and nurses came from down the hall, rushing past her without seeing her, their image in return already growing faint to her eyes, swallowed up into the light that seemed to come from every direction, caressing her, holding her, lifting her away from this place.

Then at last there was only the light, and him.

"Did I do well?" she asked.

He smiled and softly stroked her hair. "You did—fine."

Then he took her hand, and together they moved on through the white, to where they would again be most needed.

Cold winds, and warm hands, together a gift greater than the sum of their parts—a partnership of peace rendered to those in pain. Call it a marriage made in heaven . . . and born in the Twilight Zone.

Introduction to Something in the Walls

I don't care *what* you say, there's something creepy about linoleum. Oh, sure, *you* think it's just a floor covering.

And I'll bet you think the patterns in flocked wallpaper don't look at you whenever you're not looking at them, right?

As I thought.

You're doomed.

Or you're one of *them*.

I probably shouldn't say anything more about this story—in case *they* might be listening—except to observe that this is probably one of the first treatments for television of a little optical oddity that practically everyone has noticed at least once.

You've seen them. Oh, yes, I know you have.

And so do they.

"Something in the Walls," production #87040, was produced the week of October 24, 1988, under the direction of Allan Kroeker, and starred Deborah Raffin (Sharon), Damir Andri (Robert Craig), Lally Cadeau (Becky), Kate Parr (Maid), Douglas Carrigan (Dancer), Janice Green (Dancer), Aaron Foss Fraser (Dancer), Martha Cronyn (Dancer). [A dancer is a mime, of sorts, specializing in movement, used in this case behind a sheet of painted, pliable material to represent those normally visible only out of the corner of the eye, and in the walls.] First broadcast on January 29, 1989.

SOMETHING IN THE WALLS

"That'll be ten dollars."

Dr. Robert Craig riffled through his wallet, coming up with the ten dollars in cab fare. It figured that his car would break down on his first day of work. Wasn't there a scientific principle involved?

He grabbed his attaché case and stepped out of the cab onto the grassy lawn in front of the Oak Park Sanitarium. It was an older building, red brick and whitewashed windows beneath a grey sky. The wind was cool and moist, promising rain. As he stood, taking it all in— his first major position, overseeing a staff of five nurses and an entire wing of patients—he thought he saw a face at one of the upstairs windows. But when he looked again, it was gone.

Probably just the residents getting a look at the new doctor, he decided, and headed for the front door.

We direct your attention to the man with the sleek leather briefcase. His name: Dr. Robert Craig. Occupation: interning psychologist, newly employed by the Oak Park Sanitarium. For the last two weeks, he has been visualizing his first day, looking forward to it with eager anticipation. But somewhere behind those almost painfully cheerful-looking walls is something that nothing in his education has prepared him for.

* * *

The office door was already equipped with a brass nameplate announcing DR. R. CRAIG. He ran his hand along the burnished surface, then entered the office. It was plain, but comfortable: a desk, two chairs, a sofa, built-in bookshelves, and a window which ran along the far wall that looked down onto the front lawn. The boxes he had sent ahead were piled up in the middle of the room, along with the Indian rug that had been a feature of the last four offices he'd occupied.

He set his attaché down on the desk, then turned at the sound of a knock at the door. A nurse, arms heavy with papers and envelopes, stood in the doorway. "Dr. Craig?"

"Yes?"

She stepped inside, extending her hand. "Rebecca Simms. Most everyone calls me Becky. I'm sort of the catch-all Head Nurse, Advisor on Policy, and Tracker Down of Missing Paychecks. Pleased to have you aboard."

"Thank you. Glad to be here. This place has a fine reputation, I hope I can live up to it."

"You'll find we're a low-key, but very supportive group here, Dr. Craig. Our clients are our first concern, and I suspect most of them know that. It's a good place, with good people. And speaking of which, I'll go and get the files on your clients. You'll be taking over Dr. Parnett's group. About six or seven people." She stopped beside the door, and smiled. "I think you'll find them all quite—fascinating."

By five-thirty, when he could hear the afternoon cleaning staff leaving for the day, he was nearly finished with the files on his new caseload. He planned to start in earnest tomorrow, meeting each of them individually and letting them set their own agendas for a while. Changing therapists midprogram could disrupt even the smoothest-running treatments. It was best to move slowly, create a nonthreatening environment in which they could relax with him and accept him.

Most of them could wait the extra day.

Except . . .

He spotted Nurse Simms as she passed his door. "Becky? Can I see you a second?"

She stuck her head in the door. "Sure. What's up?"

He tapped the photo on the file in front of him. She came around the desk to peer over his shoulder. "What can you tell me about this patient?"

"Sharon Miles?"

"Yes. The records indicate that she committed herself."

"That's correct, although Dr. Parnett seemed to think there might have been some family incident, maybe pressure from there to get her in for treatment."

He scanned the file, running down the inventory of notes and prescriptions and therapy sessions. "It says she refused to leave the house, was constantly rearranging furniture in strange ways, and refused to sleep anywhere but in a plain white room."

"Yes, that's right," Becky said. "Since she's been here, she's repainted her room, oh, I guess half a dozen times by now. Dr. Parnett said to let her do it, that it might be good therapy for her. She dresses in only solid colors, and refuses to leave her room for anything except meals or counseling sessions—and that only with difficulty."

He nodded. Parnett had indicated as much in his notes. "I've never heard of anything quite like this before. Is she rational?"

"Eminently. She's quiet, does as she's told, keeps to herself . . . she could probably be released tomorrow on her own recognizance, but she won't go."

"Do you have any idea why?"

"No. The only thing I do know is that any time we've discussed releasing her, she's—well, Doctor, I don't know what it is, but she's desperately, deathly afraid of—something. I've never seen anyone so totally, utterly terrified in my entire life. She covers it pretty well most of the time, but there are moments when it's so plain and painful you think you could touch her, and the fear would come off on your hand. Whatever it is, it's got her scared nearly to death."

"No idea at all what it is?"

"None. Even Dr. Parnett couldn't figure that one out. Is there anything else, Doctor?"

"No, thank you, Becky," he said. With a perfunctory nod, she stepped out of the office and returned to her routine.

Robert glanced down at the photo. Even in the blurry black and white, she looked so vulnerable, so alone.

Perhaps it wouldn't be such a bad idea to get just a *little* jump on his schedule.

Sharon Miles's room was almost uncomfortably spartan. The walls were a solid, nearly overwhelming white and freshly scrubbed. Even the ceiling looked newly painted, its surface absolutely flat. The furnishings were meager, only an undistinguished plain brown chair, a bed with white sheets and solid grey blankets, a whitewashed dresser and side table, and a simple rocking chair, in which she sat, reading, as yet unaware of his presence in the doorway. Her hair was a sandy blonde, above large green eyes. She wore a plain grey sweater and blue pants.

There were no patterns anywhere in the room or in her clothing, no interlacings of color or line. The room was like a page out of a particularly unimaginative child's coloring book; a child armed with only a few primary colors and a determination to keep everything as simple as possible.

He knocked twice, gently, and she looked up from the book she was reading. "Hi. I know it's a little after regular office hours, but I thought I'd pop by and say hello—if you don't mind."

She shut the book and set it down on the dresser beside her. "Not at all. Please, come in, Dr. Craig." She must have noticed his expression, because she smiled, if thinly. "News travels fast around here. Not much to do *except* gossip. And I've never been much good at basket weaving."

"Arts and crafts are pretty much beyond me, too," he said, taking the plain brown chair opposite her. "Ever since junior high. I tried to make a bookcase once in shop—ended up as a napkin holder." He looked around the room. "Very nice. Spartan, but nice."

"Thank you," she said, and let the silence sit between them for a moment before continuing. "I have to say I'm surprised. Your first day doesn't officially start until tomorrow, am I right?"

"Yes. But I was going over the caseload and yours is quite interesting. I noticed that you graduated to voluntary therapy."

"That's right," she said, and he noticed that her tone was much cooler now. "Things were going well, and Dr. Parnett decided not to push matters. If there was something I wanted to talk about, I'd talk about it."

"But you didn't. You haven't been to a therapy session in nearly two months. I'm sure that if you were to try again—"

"No. I don't think that would be a good idea. Not yet. When I'm ready, maybe."

She reached for her book and opened it on her lap to the page she'd been reading when he came in.

Audience concluded.

He stood and headed for the door. "All right. But if you ever should feel like talking, you know where to find me. Good evening." He waited a moment, in case she would respond. But the only sound that came back was the turning of pages.

He stepped back into the hallway, heading toward his office. His first perception of Sharon Miles had done nothing to dispel his curiosity. She seemed perfectly normal, if nervous and a little resistant to discussing her problem, whatever it was.

Well, he would find out the full story over time, he was confident of that much.

He nodded to the last of the housekeeping staff, who were making up rooms for the night as he passed, then noticed Becky coming around the corner a few doors up.

"Ah, good," she said, "there you are. I've been looking all over for you. Before everyone went home for the night, we thought we'd introduce you to the rest of the staff, brief you on the schedule."

"Fine. I'm sure that'll be—"

Sharon's scream echoed down the hall at him.

He rushed back to her room, to find one of the housekeeping staff stumbling out, half-running, half-shoved, followed a moment later by a blanket flung after her.

"Get it out of here!" Sharon screamed from inside the room. *"I told you I don't WANT it! Get it AWAY from me!"*

The maid turned, pleading to Robert. "I told her, we don't *have* any other heavy blankets! It's getting colder, and—"

"I want a plain one, no patterns, don't you understand?" Sharon took a step toward her.

Robert put himself between the two, hands upraised. "Okay, okay—we'll take care of it." He turned to the maid. "Look, it's no big deal, just go back and get two or three light blankets, all right?" He looked back to Sharon. "Will that be good enough?"

She glanced away, biting her lip, then nodded. "As long as they're plain," she said, recovering her composure. "One color. No—no patterns."

"No patterns," Robert said. "I promise." He waved the maid on down the hall. "Go on," he said, "it's all right."

The maid looked resentful, but went to do as instructed. When he turned back again, Sharon was closing the door. He caught only a glimpse of her before the door shut, but it was enough to see her sobbing, one trembling hand pressed to her face.

And afraid. So afraid.

Of what?

* * *

Robert was eating lunch at his desk—ham and Swiss on rye from the deli down the street—when he glanced up at a knock at the door. "Yes?"

Sharon stepped inside, hesitating inside the doorway. She smiled hesitantly, brushing the hair out of her face. "Guess I didn't make the best of all impressions last night."

He shrugged. "It happens."

"I know. But I wanted to thank you for what you did. The staff gets a little impatient with me, at times."

"All forgotten. But it would help me tremendously in the future if I could know your reasons."

"Hey, Doc," she said, too quickly, he thought, "haven't you heard? Nobody in here but us loonies. We don't have to have reasons for what we do."

"I disagree. And for what it's worth, I don't think you *are* a loony. But I would like to talk to you for a while."

She looked down, and for a moment, didn't move. Then, almost imperceptibly, she nodded. "All right," she said, then pointed at the Indian rug that covered the floor near the sofa, "if—at the risk of sounding loony —you could just get rid of that for the time being."

"No problem," Robert said, and began rolling.

". . . which I guess was about a year after I finished college. That's when I met Jeff. We got married about a year later, and we had one boy. Eric. He's five now." She glanced up at him. "And I don't hate my mother or my father, I never wanted to sleep with my brother, and I wasn't frightened by a checkered sheet when I was a little girl."

"But you were frightened the other night, weren't you? I saw you. You were terrified by the bedspread—"

"No. No, not the bedspread. The patterns."

"Why?"

She opened her mouth as though to answer, then closed it again, and looked away from him.

"Don't you want to leave this place?" Robert asked.

"I can't imagine that you'd want to stay. Don't you miss your family?"

"Of course I miss them. What do you think I am?"

"Then why don't you tell me—"

"Because I'm afraid! And you—you leave my family out of this! Can't you see I'm doing this for them? For their protection?"

"Protection from what? From whom?"

She smiled, but it was full of bitterness. "You wouldn't believe me if I told you. You really *would* think I was loony."

"Try me."

She chewed her lip for a moment, and he could almost see the debate raging inside her. Then, finally, she sat a little straighter, as though having reached a decision. When she began to speak, looking up at Robert only in quick, nervous glances, he got the impression that she'd rehearsed this very moment many times over, but never followed through on it—until now.

"Have you ever looked closely at patterns, Doctor? I mean, the kind of patterns you see in wallpaper, in cracks on the ceiling, in linoleum floors, that sort of thing?"

"I suppose so, yes."

"And have you ever seen *faces* in the patterns of floors or wallpaper? The way the cracks and colors come together so that if you look at it just *so,* you could swear you see a face in it?"

Robert smiled. "Of course. There was a linoleum floor in my mother's house. I used to sit there all day, making faces out of the patterns. That's the way the brain works. It tries to find order in chaos. Given the chance, the mind plays a game of connect the dots with whatever it happens to be looking at, at the moment."

She sat forward in her chair, and in her eyes he saw a desperate need to be understood. "Yes, but did you ever wonder why you mainly see faces? Not plants, or animals, or buildings—but *faces?*"

"No. Actually, until you mentioned it, it hadn't occurred to me."

"It didn't occur to me, either," she said. "At least, not at first."

She sat back again and looked away, silent for a moment. Then she began again, her voice low, her eyes fixed at a nowhere point past the window. "It was Sunday, I guess around nine, nine-thirty in the morning. I woke up, and it was warm, and the sun was coming in through the window, and I could smell Jeff cooking bacon and eggs downstairs. I'd slept in a little. If you've had kids, you know how five-year-olds can wear you out.

"I was feeling warm and content, and just lying there, looking up at the ceiling. It was one of those ceilings that are covered with speckles, like little ridges, you know the kind?"

He nodded.

"Anyway, I was looking up at one of those patterns in the ceiling when I—I saw a face in it. And Doctor, I swear to God—*it looked back at me!* It looked right *at* me. I caught it, I guess. Off-guard. Because I got the terrible, horrible feeling that *it knew that I saw it!* Then Eric knocked on my door, and I looked away, just for a second. When I looked back, it was gone."

Robert nodded. "Let me ask you this. Is it possible that you only *thought* the face was looking at you? The way you can look at a painting for too long, and it seems to move after a while?"

"Absolutely not. You know when you're crossing the street, and you make eye contact with the driver the way everybody tells you to, and even when you can't see them clearly you can *feel* when you've met his eyes? You *know* they're looking at you? Well, this—*face* —was looking at me. Just like that. And if it was something physical, why would it suddenly disappear like that?"

"You said yourself that you looked away. In that moment, your mind rearranged the dots into a different pattern, one without a face."

"No," she said, and her voice was cold with determination. "You asked me what I'm afraid of, and I'm telling you the truth. There was something there, Doctor. I saw it. And it saw me."

She hesitated, as though holding back one last piece of information. Then, apparently deciding she'd come too far to back off now, she finally said, "And I think . . . I think it's trying to kill me."

Robert backed up the tape recorder, always kept discreetly out of sight when he was counseling. It saved him from making notes, which sometimes put patients off. Sharon's voice echoed in the now-dark office.

"Something was there, Doctor. I saw it."

She seemed so absolutely sincere.

"Dr. Craig?"

He switched off the recorder and looked up from his notes to where Becky stood in the doorway, buttoning a heavy overcoat. "Yes?"

"Staying late?"

"No, not really. Just about to leave, actually."

"Hope you brought your coat. It's getting on to the rainy season." She glanced at the folder on his desk. "How's the client working out?"

"Very well, I think. Very well indeed."

"Good luck," she said, and with a quick smile, continued down the hall.

When she was gone, he switched the recorder back to PLAY again.

"And I think . . . I think it's trying to kill me."

He listened through the end of the tape, with her promising to return tomorrow for another session. As he switched off the tape, he glanced back at his notes and noticed that during the last few minutes he'd been absently doodling on the desk blotter, unconsciously connecting a coffee stain, and a tiny rip, and two ink blotches.

Without intending to, he had drawn a face.

Sharon showed up nearly a half hour late for their next session. For a while he'd been afraid she wouldn't come, and then having come, she seemed willing to talk about anything but their conversation the day before.

So he nodded and waited, and let her find her own timing. He could wait. Neither of them were going anywhere.

After a while, she picked up the thread where she had left it the day before. With the faces.

"After I saw the first one, I started seeing more of them. Watching me. I don't know why, maybe just the fact that I saw the first one made me more aware of them—the way you don't notice a sound for a long time, then suddenly you're aware of it, and then you can't hear anything else.

"I could see faces in the patterns of cracks on the walls of my house. I tried to paint them over, but they kept coming through. Faces in the pile of leaves next door. Faces in tree trunks, in brick walls—faces in the doodles of my six-year-old son! My clothes—I had to stop wearing patterns. That's why I don't allow patterns in my room. They can hide in any pattern. It lets them inside.

"I tried to pretend it was all just in my mind, but it went on and on regardless, and the more I became aware of them, the more *they* became aware of *me*. Sometimes, I thought I could hear them talking, whispering about me, trying to decide what they were going to do about me."

"You keep saying 'they.' What do you think they are?"

"I don't know," she said, though something in her tone said she had a pretty good idea. "Sometimes, though, I get this feeling like they're looking in from someplace else. Someplace parallel to this, that only intersects this place at certain points. And I kind of get the feeling that they're—old. Very, very old."

She shook her head. "My mother once told me that there's a lot in this life that you can see only out of the corner of your eye. If she only knew how right she was."

"What do you think they would do to you if they finally got you alone?"

"I don't know." Again the sense that she was with-holding something. She smiled thinly. "I try not to think about it. And I'm not going to give them the chance to find out."

"In all this, you haven't mentioned your husband. Didn't you tell him what was happening?"

"No. Not at first. I was going to, but—"

Suddenly she stopped. Caught herself on the edge of saying—what?

"You were saying, Sharon?"

"Nothing."

"Are you sure? Does this have anything to do with your decision to commit yourself?"

She stood, smoothed out her skirt. "I'm awfully tired, Doctor. Could we pick this up tomorrow?"

"Certainly," he said, and walked her to the door. As she stepped out, he put a hand on her shoulder. "To-morrow, will you tell me what happened?"

She looked over her shoulder at him, seemed mo-mentarily to waver, then suddenly shook her head no, fiercely, her eyes welling up. She bolted away from his office, down the hall to her room, her footsteps echoing as she retreated.

It was dark, and she closed her eyes, and she would not think of it.

Didn't you tell him what was happening?

She clung to the darkness that lingered just behind her eyes, inviting her to the sleep of oblivion.

No. Not at first. I was going to, but—

She would not think of it.

But what?

Because to think of it was to relive it, and that above all she could not permit.

The voice on the phone, so distant in the dark of the bedroom, her bedroom, her house, her life, so far away now.

"I'll be home by about three tomorrow, Shar. Plane comes in at noon."

Silence in the night, the familiar hesitation.

"Good. There's—something I have to talk to you about. But not over the phone. When you come back."

Then the good-nights, and the promises, and the prayers for safe flights.

And then the darkness, suddenly deeper as the lights go out, moonlight spearing through the window, splashing on the wall, the wall with its complex patterns coming through the paint, touched now by shadows thrown by branches and window, shadows and patterns merging and flowing and entwining into new shapes that seemed to breathe beneath the paint, beneath the paper, lines like veins and capillaries taking on flesh, rearranging themselves into coherent shapes.

She stood, and there was a sound in the room, a rustle and a slide, a whisper behind the walls like the rustle of dry leaves on concrete, all dryness and death. It moved through the room like a living thing and she somehow in its belly. And everywhere the moonlight like a pale stain on old paper covered with writing she could almost but not quite recognize.

She neared the wall, the murmuring low and brittle, and this time, as so many times before, there was no mistaking the face that turned in the light and looked up at her, eyeless but seeing. Then, abruptly, it thrust itself forward, as though straining against the fabric of the wall to snatch at her hand, at her own face so near its own. She jumped back instinctively, her hands at her mouth as she watched it move slowly from side to side, as if familiarizing itself with its momentary freedom—

And then it slid beneath the surface of the wall, sliding like oil on water, fast, down along the wall to the corner, then up and over the corner, further and further toward the door, rustling as it went.

When it hit the doorway, she feared for a moment it would somehow leap the distance and appear before her, no longer fettered by its whitewashed prison. But instead it vanished from view. She listened, but heard nothing.

It had seemed so determined, so direct in its movements, toward the door and—what?

Then she remembered. Around the door. Down the corner. Past the flocked wallpaper, and then left.

To Eric's room.

"Eric!"

She ran, mindless and heedless of the faces around her, ran blindly down the hall to Eric's room, to the open door of his room. He lay sleeping, breathing normally in the still night beside the wall they had so lovingly papered with clouds and airplanes and stars and planets.

She stepped into the room.

And suddenly she could hear them tearing at the wall. Tearing at the wall from inside.

She rushed to Eric, held him in his sleep, keeping his head turned away as the jagged lines appeared in the wallpaper over his head, lines forming words, each slash coming with a sound like whips but sharper and more deliberate. Angry gashes like open wounds illuminated by an inner light that spilled into Eric's room, spelling out

TELL NO ONE

And a line extended out from the last letter, tracing a jagged path down the wall, down and down and down to where Eric slept—then stopped.

"No," she said, not knowing if they could hear her, there behind the wall, or if it would make any difference. "No, no, no, no. . . ."

NO!

Robert was halfway to bed when the phone rang for the third time in two hours. The storm that rattled and shook his windows was wreaking havoc with the phone lines. Each time he picked it up only to hear static and a mutter of distant voices.

This time, though, the connection was solid. He recognized Sharon's voice immediately. "I wanted to let you know," she said, "I've changed my mind. I can't go on like this anymore. Someone has to know. Tomorrow—tomorrow I'll tell you everything."

"I'm glad to hear that, Sharon."

She hesitated. "And Doctor . . . I lied to you. I think I know what they are, and what they're trying to do. Not only to me, but to everyone. I promised them I'd be quiet, but the more I think about it, the more I think I can't trust them. I shouldn't trust them."

"Please," she said, "if anything should happen to me, I want you to look after them. Jeff and Eric. Promise me you'll do it."

"All right," Robert said, "I promise."

Then there was the click of the phone being hung up, replaced a moment later by the dial tone. He racked the receiver and wandered over to the window. Rain washed down the glass panes in sheets, and he could feel the cold wind forcing its way in through the window jamb.

Tomorrow. Tomorrow he would know it all. And then, finally, he could begin helping her.

Robert pulled off his raincoat and stuck it on a hook on the door to dry. The office was absolutely arctic, the windows fogged and moist. He was about to investigate the dripping noise behind his desk when Becky appeared in the doorway.

"Good morning, Doctor," she said, and pointed to the half-filled bucket behind his desk, which was catching the occasional drop from a stain in the ceiling. "You'll have to pardon the bucket. We had the roof fixed last winter, but it still leaks here and there. We've got buckets all over the place."

He moved his chair to one side, deciding to work around it. "Quite a storm last night, wasn't it?"

"Oh, yes," she said, and smiled ruefully. "Caused us quite a night all right. A storm always agitates the patients, and last night's was a doozy. Around midnight we finally had them all quieted down, and then—well, let's say it had quite an effect on your favorite patient."

Robert looked up. "Sharon? How?"

"She just started screaming, right in the middle of the night. Screaming at the top of her lungs, and pounding on her door, trying to get out. Kept saying she wanted another room, that she had to get out."

He headed out of the office and into the hall, Becky keeping pace beside him. "Did she say why?"

"Nothing I could make any sense of. She was hysterical. We might have given her another room, but you know how crowded we are, there wasn't anyplace else for us to put her. She was too disturbed to let her wander around, so we had to lock her room. Called for a nurse to help sedate her. She really fought us, too."

He walked more quickly, feeling a sudden, terrible sense of urgency. "Why didn't you call me?"

"We would have, but she finally quieted down around two this morning. We didn't want to bother you."

He was running now, Becky falling behind.

They should have called him, damn it. If something had caused her to regress—

He turned the corner and put out a hand to the wall to keep from running into Sharon, who was coming around the other side. She smiled at him. "Good morning, Doctor. I was just coming to see you."

"Were you?" he said, catching his breath. He smiled. "I hear you gave our nurses quite a night."

"Yes, well, I was being quite silly, and I realize that now. Storms frighten me. Actually, thanks to you, I realize now that I've been silly about a lot of things."

"Such as?"

"Such as being here. Committing myself, practically abandoning my son and my husband just because of some perfectly irrational fears. It's silly. And it's wrong. And I can see that now. In large part, thanks to you. I guess all I really needed was someone to talk to. That was you. And I appreciate it more than I can say."

"And I suspect . . ."

He stopped. Having caught his breath, and recovering from the surprise of running into her, for the first time he actually *looked* at her.

Looked at her clothes.

She was wearing a print blouse, an intricate inter-weaving of colors and patterns, lines and shadows. Over it she wore a silk scarf with complementary patterns.

"Yes, Doctor?" she said, still smiling.

"I suspect you give me far too much credit." He reached over to touch the scarf at her neck. "That's a very pretty outfit. Very intricate patterns. I thought—"

"Just one more sign that all is well. I called the front office and had it unpacked. I've signed the paperwork, and with luck, I'll be leaving this afternoon. Isn't it wonderful?"

Leaving? "Well, yes, but I thought we could at least finish our sessions."

"We did," she said, with sudden firmness. Then the smile returned. "You've done me a world of good, Doctor. Thank you again."

With a polite nod, she turned and headed down the hall toward her room.

Robert watched her leave, then walked back the way he'd come. If she wanted to discharge herself, it was her option. She'd committed herself in the first place. And hadn't he wanted her to get well? Hadn't he wanted her to return to her home, and her family, free of the irrational fears that obsessed her?

Of course.

Absolutely.

So why, then, did he feel a cold knot in the pit of his stomach?

Sharon was packing the last of her suitcases when Robert rapped lightly on the door. Her room, like his office, was equipped with two buckets that caught the leaking rainwater. When she turned, she smiled again. It was, he decided, a very precise smile.

"Your cab's here," he said. "Thought I'd give you a hand with your bags. Besides, I couldn't just let you go without saying good-bye, could I?"

"No, of course not," she said, and latched the final

suitcase closed. She indicated the handle. "Please, all help is quite appreciated."

Taking one of the smaller bags, she stepped out of the room. Robert grabbed the two remaining bags and was about to follow suit when he stopped in the doorway.

Listening.

For a moment, he'd thought he'd heard something. A voice, calling to him.

Must've been the wind, he decided, and took another step.

Help me—please, someone—help me—

He stopped again. Looked around, more closely this time. He seemed to hear the voice more in his head than in his ears. But there was no one in the room, and nowhere to hide. Just the bed, bookcase, dresser, mirror, and an open closet.

And the buckets.

He let his gaze wander up the walls, to the ceiling. Pristine and plain white the day before, it was now stained in places by leaking rainfall, the watermarks forming concentric circles within circles where it had seeped through during the night.

Patterns.

And in one of them: two dark circles, like eyes, and a smear for a nose that looped around into a mouth.

He looked at it.

And suddenly it looked back at him.

That's not me! Please, God, you've got to do something—it's not me—don't you understand—IT'S ONE OF THEM!

Sharon's face.

Sharon's voice.

"Coming, Doctor?"

He turned to see Sharon

one of them

standing in the doorway, smiling patiently.

He looked up to the ceiling again, but the stain was now only a stain, and nothing more. "Yes, of course," he said, and picked up the bags.

All the way to the cab, he noticed his hands were trembling.

It would be a long, long time before they ever stopped.

Next time you're alone, look quickly at the wallpaper and the ceiling and the cracks on the sidewalk. Look for the patterns and lines and faces on the wall. Look, if you can, for Sharon Miles. Hers is the face on the left, a symmetry of fear, visible only out of the corner of your eye, or in the Twilight Zone.

Introduction to
Our Selena Is Dying

In the second week of January, producer Mark Shelmerdine walked into my office with something that would turn my world upside down for the next three weeks.

It was a simple manila envelope, containing six typewritten pages. At the top of page one appeared the following words:

OUR SELENA IS DYING
by Rod Serling

The document in my hand was an outline for a *previously unproduced* episode of the original *Twilight Zone*, written shortly before the series went off the air on 28 February 1964. Since then, it had languished in filing cabinets and boxes, lost to public sight for twenty-four years. Now it had been located, and the rights obtained, and someone was needed to adapt the story into a full half-hour script.

They picked me.

It was the opportunity of a lifetime.

It was a challenge.

It was unnerving as hell.

Because I knew that the episode would receive considerable attention when it hit the airwaves. The first new Rod Serling *TWILIGHT ZONE* in twenty-four years was N*E*W*S. And sure enough, as soon as word got out, the press descended. The information flashed down news wires, showed up in major newspapers across the United States. Television news crews started showing up. Articles were filed in magazines. *The Voice of America* even came out to my apartment to do an interview about it for broadcast overseas.

If I did it wrong, if what I wrote was perceived as anything less than what Serling might have done with it . . . I'd be hung out to twist slowly, slowly in the wind.

Curiously, though, while public and critical reactions were a concern to me—make that a *substantial* concern—it was not foremost in my thoughts. That place was reserved for the one person whose opinion mattered most to me at that moment.

Carol Serling.

By virtue of an act of creation Rod Serling had committed years before, I had finally been given the opportunity to do what I'd wanted to all along: tell stories. I owed it to him to do the best job I could, as partial payment on a considerable debt. In his absence, that debt was owed to Carol Serling.

Now, I've been writing a long time. As I type these words, I have been a contributing editor with three major national magazines, have story-edited over two hundred episodes of television, and written about one hundred, had twelve produced stage plays, five hundred published articles, twelve produced radio dramas, two novels, a nonfiction book, and this anthology.

In all that time, I've never worked harder on *anything* than I did on "Our Selena is Dying."

The script was completed on 22 February 1988. More than any other episode, I wanted to be on set during the filming of "Our Selena."

Then on 7 March 1988, the Writers Guild of America went on strike. Everybody said it wouldn't last more than a month.

The strike ended 7 August 1988.

And "Our Selena is Dying" was filmed the week of 11 July 1988.

It is one of my deepest regrets that, due to the strike, I was not able to be on set, or anywhere *near* the set, during production. That it was for a worthy and necessary cause is all that sustains me.

That, and one other item, logged in here under the heading of personal validation, which arrived in the form of a letter from Carol Serling, dated 19 September 1988. In part, it read as follows: "Many thanks for sending over the final script of 'Our Selena is Dying.' I got a kick out of reading it, and feel that you certainly were very true to the original story. If you are going to screen it in the next month or so, I'd love to see it."

That night I slept the first good sleep I'd had in what seemed like ages.

Sometimes the gods give you a break . . . and maybe even a little extra.

Consequently, this story is presented as the final offering in this collection, as merited by being one of the most protracted collaborations in television history. From across the years from 1964 to 1989, from manual typewriters to 40-megabyte word processors, from pages to closets to soundstages to phosphor dots and back to pages again . . . "Our Selena is Dying."

"Our Selena is Dying," production #87018, story by Rod Serling, teleplay by J. Michael Straczynski, was directed by Bruce Pittman, and starred Terri Garber (Deborah Brockman), Jennifer Dale (Diane Brockman), Charmion King (Selena Brockman), R. H. Thomson (Dr. Burrell), Paul Bettis (Orville), Patricia Idette (Susan), Aileen Taylor-Smith (Martha Brockman), Jackie McLeod (Nurse #1), Ann Turnbull (Nurse #2), Rob McClure (Doctor), Tim Koetting (Specialist). Produced the week of July 11, 1988, and first broadcast on November 13, 1988.

OUR SELENA IS DYING

(with Rod Serling)

The Brockman mansion was a cheerless, dark, twenty-room brownstone on Beekman Street, the last of its kind. Bordered by wrought iron bars and high hedges, its rooms were an unkempt museum of uncomfortable straight-backed chairs and overstuffed sofas and dark wood, reflecting the somber shadows of the house itself.

Every day, from nine o'clock in the morning, when she was helped into her chair in the high window overlooking Beekman Street, until eight in the evening, when she was escorted out again, Martha Brockman stared out at the street, small tired eyes gazing out of a leathery, ancient face. If she thought, or dreamed, the vacant eyes and the silent mouth offered no clues, only an occasional blink and twitch to verify the fact that she still lived, just a windowpane away from the world outside.

Your attention is drawn to the house on the left: the residence of the Brockman clan. An ancient brownstone, its paneled walls polished by darkness. A lightless, soundless place upon which a greater darkness has fallen.

The object of the death watch: Selena Brockman, Grand Dame of the menagerie, who lies in her bed in an inch-by-inch battle with death, trying somehow to reach a compromise instead of a capitulation.

* * *

(From the story by Rod Serling, as adapted by J. Michael Straczynski.)

It was a dark room, windows shuttered against the grey sky, a subdued collection of antique chairs and cushions dominated by the great four-poster bed in the middle of the room. Selena Brockman, only a handful of years older than her sister Martha, lay without moving, her eyes closed, chest rising and falling in a shallow rhythm punctuated by hesitancy and the occasional ragged shudder. With the passing of each day, Selena was more and more hard-pressed to eke strength out of the frail, wasting seventy-five-year-old body, the used-up lungs, the once regal, impervious spirit that had at last betrayed her.

Diane Brockman stepped into the room, where Dr. Burrell was putting away his stethoscope and replacing old medicines that were no longer effective with new ones that were hardly any better. "And what is your prognosis, Doctor?"

He looked up at her as he continued to pack. Forever miniskirted, even in cold weather, it had occurred to Dr. Burrell that Diane always moved as if keeping time to some exotic music that only she could hear.

The question was asked with false concern, in a voice tinged with quiet amusement at his labors. It could wait.

He touched Selena's hand. It felt like parchment to the touch. Her eyes slitted open, then finally found him. "Two of these every four hours to relieve the pain," he said. "If it gets any worse, call me."

He started to pull away, but she rested a thin, nearly skeletal hand on his arm. "You'll come tomorrow," she said, her voice barely a whisper. There was no pleading in it, only a determined firmness.

"Yes, of course," Burrell said, though he wanted nothing more than to be out of there, away from this decaying place, the close and stifling air. There was something about the Brockman household that had never felt entirely right, or entirely wholesome.

He snapped closed his bag and stepped out of the bedroom, past Diane, who was watching Selena with a faint smile.

There was doubtless an inheritance. There always was, in cases like this. What else could have brought Diane back from another of the European vacations she was known for? In the ten years since she'd first shown up at the mansion, a relative from out of state who arrived shortly after Dr. Burrell's father had retired and left him the family practice, he'd only seen her twice, and never as a patient.

He reached the foot of the long staircase and slipped into his overcoat.

"You didn't answer my question." Diane descended the stairs behind him. "How is dear Aunt Selena?"

He glanced at her over his shoulder. "She is dying, Ms. Brockman. She has been dying for a long time. The only difference now is that death begins to have clearly defined lines and you discover it knows your name. Is that the answer you were looking for?"

She chose not to rise to the bait, only continued to smile. "Just concerned, Doctor." She stopped beside him, near the door. "I was thinking—tomorrow, after your visit, perhaps we can go out for a drink."

He shook his head. "My God," he said, and stepped out onto the porch.

Clean air. He took deep, grateful gulps of it. There was something about that house that beckoned to something worse than death.

She followed after him. "Does this mean you won't be coming by tomorrow?"

"In case your aunt never got around to telling you," he said, "I inherited your family from my father, who got it from his. That carries a certain obligation—a word you may not be familiar with. So yes, I'll be here. The only question is whether Selena will still be here tomorrow."

He stepped off the porch and onto the sidewalk.

"Dr. Burrell."

He turned, looked back at her.

"Selena won't die tonight," she said. "She'll hold on. As long as she has to."

That said, she turned and walked back into the house, moving as always, as though to an unseen audience.

Burrell stuffed his hands in his pockets and walked briskly toward his car. It was cold. It was preferable.

Deborah Brockman pulled the last of her belongings together—those capable of fitting into two flower-print suitcases and the steamer her father had left her—and set them down on the floor beside her as she made a check of stove and heater and lights to make sure nothing had been left on.

A small shiver of excitement ran through her. At the ripe old age of twenty, she was at last going on an adventure. The call had come in the night from Cousin Diane. It had taken them weeks to track her down, Diane had said. The search had been made all the more difficult by the death of her parents five years before, and her decision to take an unlisted phone number. They'd finally had to trace her through the nursing school she'd graduated the year before.

It was an adventure—a journey to the East Coast, the imminent passing of a relative she'd only heard rumors about, and now finally to meet. The conversation had been lightly spattered with suggestions of legacies contingent on loyalties and nursing services provided, but that was secondary to the adventure. And the work. She would earn her keep.

At a knock from the door, she opened it to find Suzy standing outside. She jingled her keys at Deborah. "Your coach awaits, Madam."

"Okay, just let me make one last check." She made a final survey of the one-bedroom apartment that Suzy would be house-sitting for her until her return. Suzy had been house-jumping ever since nursing school, which had consumed nearly all of her savings.

"You sure about all this?" Suzy called to her. "This is a long way to go on the basis of a couple of phone calls."

"She's my aunt. They say she needs me."

"But you've never even met her."

"No, but I've heard about her. My dad used to talk about her in the sort of whispery tone of voice they saved for anything unusual, or exotic, or just plain different."

"She sounds weird."

Deborah came back into the living room. "She's dying."

"Any talk of an inheritance?"

"Some," she said grudgingly. "Dependent on my coming out there and helping out. But I'm just more curious than anything else." She reached down to grab the two suitcases. "Okay, that's it."

Suzy looked at her. "Last chance."

"Suzy, practically my whole life's been spent within walking distance of this place. I think I'm about due for a change, don't you?"

Suzy nodded.

The adventure was finally beginning.

"And this will be your room."

Cousin Diane opened the door to a small room just off the west wing of the house. She stuck her head in. It smelled as if it hadn't been opened in years. But then, the whole house was more than a little musty.

She kept thinking of the House of Usher and, just as frequently, kept putting the thought behind her.

"The kitchen is this way," Diane said, continuing the nickel tour. "You'll have free run of the house. If you need to find anything, just ask."

As they turned the corner, Deborah saw the handyman she'd glimpsed earlier when the cab had dropped her off. He was carrying her suitcases up the steps. He had a soft, round face and long arms, and when he saw them, he put down the bags and tipped his cap at them.

"This is Orville," Diane said, and turned to look directly at Deborah. "He's sort of our combination

handyman and village idiot." She laughed at the
shocked expression Deborah knew must have been on
her face. "Relax. He's quite deaf. Oh, he can lip-read all
right, but all you have to do is look away when you talk
and you can say anything you want."

Diane looked back at Orville. "Isn't that right,
Orville?"

He nodded shyly and glanced away, eyes downcast.

"You can go now, Orville," Diane said, and waited
as he picked up the suitcases and continued down the
hall, looking relieved to be moving on. "He's an orphan.
Aunt Selena picked him up years ago. She's very com-
passionate that way."

Diane said it the way someone else might speak of
acquiring a painting or a vase of no special value. It
occurred to Deborah that the "compassion" Diane
spoke of was probably pretty close to the kind of compassion that had once allowed Chinese immigrants to
come over as cooks for lumber camps.

As they continued down the hall, Deborah noticed
the woman sitting in the upstairs window seat, staring
out at the street. "Who's that?"

Diane glanced back at the woman, and smiled. "My
mother. Martha. She's quite harmless. I don't think she
even knows we're here." The smile broadened. "I'm
told there's a family resemblance."

Diane walked on. Deborah followed, wondering
why Diane seemed to find that idea so amusing.

Diane stopped in front of a door at the end of the
hall, and held a long, carefully manicured finger to her
lips. "Aunt Selena's room," she said, and opened the
door.

Inside, a tall, intense-looking man was administer-
ing an injection to the weathered, shrunken figure
barely visible among the sheets. From Diane's description, she guessed this would be Dr. Burrell. He glanced
up as they entered.

"You'll have just a minute," he said quietly. "I gave
her something to help her sleep."

Deborah approached Selena's bedside and sat

gently on the thick sheets. "Aunt Selena? It's Deborah. Deborah Brockman. You sent for me."

It took a moment, but finally Selena's eyes flickered open, and she reached out, resting a hand atop Deborah's own. It was unnervingly light.

"I'll be helping Diane look after you," she said. "If you need anything, day or night—"

She stopped and winced in pain. Selena's hand had closed tightly on her own, and now was squeezing even tighter. "Aunt Selena?" She tried to pull away, but the grip was surprisingly firm.

And getting firmer.

"Aunt Selena, you're hurting me, please let go."

Selena didn't respond. Deborah would've thought Selena didn't know she was there, except for the vise-like grip that was bruising her hand. With a final tug, she pried her hand free of Selena's. Then, abruptly, Selena's face relaxed, and her head lolled to one side on the high stack of pillows.

"Doctor?" Deborah said, but Burrell was already at her side, checking Selena's pulse.

"She's fine, but asleep," Burrell said. "Come outside."

Nursing her pinched hand, Deborah followed Diane and Dr. Burrell out into the hall, and found she breathed quite a bit easier when the door closed behind them.

"Are you okay?" Burrell asked.

"I think so, yes. It was just a pinch."

"Sorry about that," he said. "It's one of the problems with aging. Sometimes the tactile nerves break down. I don't think she knew how hard she was squeezing."

"It's all right, really."

"I seem to have forgotten my manners," Diane said, without much enthusiasm, Deborah thought. "Deborah Brockman, Dr. Henry Burrell. Witch doctor in training."

He shook her other hand. His hand was large and warm and dry. "I heard you were coming. She could use a good RN. I try, but I can't be here all the time." He suddenly patted his vest pocket. "The thermometer—"

"I'll get it," Diane said, and stepped back into the bedroom.

As soon as she was gone, Burrell started down the hall toward the stairs. Deborah followed him down. "Is she as ill as I've heard?"

"Worse. And yet she hangs on. It's amazing."

"She's a strong woman. I can testify to that much."

They stepped out onto the front porch as Burrell slipped his coat on. "I'm not sure I'd call it strength," he said. "More like a quality of lust, a desperate, unholy clutching of life. It's the kind of thing that transcends science or faith. It's almost as if she were waiting for something." He shrugged within his coat. "Sorry. I didn't mean to be so morbid."

"That's all right. This place could do it to anyone."

He smiled across at her, and she returned it. "For what it's worth, good luck," he said, and opened the door to his car. "I hope you won't need it."

"Wait," she said as he climbed in, "what about your thermometer?"

"Forget it," he called over the engine, and grinned. "I never left it behind in the first place. The only thing that gives me the creeps more than this place is Diane. See you tomorrow."

As he drove away, she waited until he had turned out of sight, then started back toward the house. Even from here, she could see the old woman—Martha, Diane had said—sitting in her catbird seat overlooking the street, gazing steadfastly out at the passing traffic and people more flesh and blood than she.

Deborah drew her sweater closer around her and stepped back inside the old brownstone.

It took her most of the day to decide if it was worth the bother, but finally Deborah sat in the living room and let Burrell inspect her hand by the fading afternoon light that came in through the window. "I feel so silly, bothering you—it's just a spot. I didn't want to mention it in front of Aunt Selena, though."

"No, that's good," he said, turning her hand in his. The spot had appeared overnight, a slightly raised brown blemish in the middle of the back of her hand. "You can never be too careful. In this case, though, it's curious but harmless. It's a liver spot."

"A liver spot?"

"Yes." He closed his medical bag, snapping the locks shut. "It's uncommon in someone as young as you, but it looks completely benign. Probably caused by too much sun."

She turned her hand to examine it. "How could it appear so suddenly?"

"Most likely the skin's been darkening by degrees for some time, and only now became noticeable. Since there's just the one, I recommend a good bleaching creme, two, three times a day. If it doesn't go away in a week or so, we'll take you in for a few tests. And stop hanging out at the beach."

"But I'm from Ohio," Deborah said, and smiled tiredly.

"Doctor?" Diane called from the stairs. "If you're quite finished, your real patient would like to see you."

With a wink and a pat on her hand, Burrell headed up the stairs beside Diane. "Yes, well, if her condition has progressed as I expect, I'm surprised she can still see anyone."

He opened the door.

Inside, Selena Brockman was sitting up in bed, propped up by pillows. The sheets were made neatly around her, and the curtains were thrown back, letting in the afternoon light. She smiled as he entered.

"Good afternoon, Doctor," Selena said. "And isn't it a perfectly splendid day?"

Half an hour later, Burrell began packing up his equipment. Diane hovered by the door, watching, a half smile of amusement on her face.

"Well, Doctor?" Selena asked.

"Pulse is stronger, and the heartbeat seems to have stabilized a little."

"You sound surprised," Selena said.

"Frankly, I am. No offense, but when I walked through that door I expected to find—

"A corpse?"

He winced. "I wouldn't have put it quite so indelicately, but—essentially, yes."

"Perhaps you're a better physician than you give yourself credit for."

He shook his head. "No. I'm good. I'm not that good."

"Aunt Selena has a very powerful will to live, Doctor," Diane said.

"Yes. So it would seem." He turned back to Selena. "But I don't want you overexerting yourself. This could be a temporary remission, and we don't want to cause a relapse."

Selena nodded. "I'll be quite careful, Doctor."

Excusing himself from the room, Burrell returned downstairs, where Orville was waiting with his coat. "Thank you, Orville," Burrell said, and shrugged it on. "See you tomorrow."

When he turned, Orville, who would usually nod and move quickly out of sight whenever he was done, hesitated beside him, and it occurred to Burrell that there was something he wanted very much to communicate. But then he glanced up at the top of the stairs and stepped away, touching his cap in a perfunctory good-bye.

Burrell looked over his shoulder, following Orville's gaze to where Diane stood at the landing above, smiling down at them. "Thank you so much for coming, Doctor," she said, then turned on her heel and walked away.

As she collected the tray and plates of half-eaten food from Aunt Selena's bedroom, Deborah couldn't remember ever feeling more tired. Which didn't make sense. She'd gotten plenty of sleep. If anything, she'd slept in later than usual. But she felt completely drained, exhausted, as though she'd been up all night. She'd had to stop twice on her way up the steps to catch her breath, and she couldn't seem to shake a tightness in her chest.

It's just the strain of the move, all the excitement of the last week, she told herself firmly, picking up the tray. She moved quietly toward the door, hoping not to wake Aunt Selena. But she had gone only a few steps when the weakness returned again, this time settling in her arms. The tray seemed suddenly twice as heavy, and her left hand began to tremble under the load. She fought to make it stop shaking, but it only trembled more, the whole tray vibrating until suddenly a knife and fork slid off and clattered to the floor.

Damn, she thought, and bent to retrieve the silverware, the fatigue easing a little as she knelt on the floor. *Just a moment, that's all, to rest a little.*

"Are you feeling all right, Debbie?"

Deborah glanced up to where Diane stood in the doorway. "I think so. A little tired, that's all. I'll be fine. Probably just need something to eat."

"Why don't you go upstairs and lie down? I'll bring you up something in a little while."

Deborah stood, picking up the tray. "Thanks. I think I'll do that." She moved past Diane to the door, pausing just a moment to look back at Diane, who was standing by Selena's bed, gazing down at her.

Selena opened her eyes, looked up at Diane, and smiled.

At least someone's feeling better, Deborah thought, and continued toward the kitchen.

Burrell awoke with a start. The phone on the nightstand beside him shrieked in the still night. He pulled himself up onto one elbow, cleared his throat, and reached for the phone. "Yeah?"

"Dr. Burrell? It's Debbie Brockman. Can you come here? I know it's late, but—"

He sat up, at immediate attention. This was the call

he'd been expecting anytime now. He'd suspected the remission was only temporary. "Is it Selena?"

"No, it's me, Doctor. Please, hurry," she said, then hung up.

He allowed himself thirty seconds to calm his heart after the sudden awakening, then threw off the covers and tried to remember where he'd put his pants.

Forty-five minutes later, he found the front door of the Brockman house unlocked. He nudged it open, stuck his head inside. "Deborah?"

From somewhere down the hall, toward the living room, he heard her call. "Back here." Her voice was small and unnaturally distant. Moving through the dimly lit hall, he followed her voice to the living room. All the lights were off, and it took him a moment to find Deborah's silhouette against the moonlight bleeding in through the window. She was sitting in a chair, her head down.

"Deborah? What are you doing sitting here in the dark?" he said, and reached for the light switch.

"No," she said, too late, as the lamp beside her glowed to life.

"My God," Burrell whispered, and knelt beside her. Her face was pale, almost frighteningly white and bloodless. Her eyes were shadowed and sunken, the skin drawn tight, her hands trembling, palsied. It was as though all the youth, all the vitality that had been so clearly in evidence when he'd first met her had been flensed from her body.

She looked up at him, and there were tears in her eyes. "Please, help me . . . I don't know what's happening to me."

He took her hand, trying to bury his shock. What on earth could have such a sudden and devastating effect? "It's okay—everything'll be fine."

"But look at me!"

"I know, I know," he said, and reached for the phone. "I'm going to get you to the hospital for some tests. Just try and stay calm."

She nodded silently. She was a strong young

woman. *Stronger than me,* he thought grimly, noticing that his hands were trembling as he dialed.

"Come on, Jack—there's got to be something you can do!"

The specialist Burrell had called out of bed took a sip of badly needed coffee. "Like what? Look, we've run every test we've got. Blood count, cell structure, you name it we've put her through it—and we can't find anything wrong with her."

"You've got eyes. You've seen her. I'd say it's premature aging, wouldn't you?"

"I agree. It's a nice label. But until we know what the cause is, that's *all* it is. Look, I'll arrange for a CAT scan, see what radiology's got. If I hear anything at all, I'll let you know. Now go home and get some sleep."

"Not yet," Burrell said, heading for the door. "I've got one more stop to make."

Diane sighed for the third time as he took her blood pressure. "I'm sure this is quite unnecessary, Doctor."

"I'll decide that for the time being, Diane. Whatever's hit Deborah, I have to know if it's contagious."

"I've never felt better. Neither has Aunt Selena."

"What about your mother?"

"Martha?" Diane smiled. "She never changes. She just sits up there in her catbird seat watching the world go by."

He *hmmmed* a response, watching the blood-pressure meter drop until it hit the right levels. Perfectly normal. He started to unwrap the Velcro material around her arm, then paused at the sight of something further up her arm. He pushed the sleeve up to reveal a burn mark, nearly as wide across as the palm of his hand. It was old, and long ago scarred over.

"Nasty," Burrell said.

She pulled back her arm and pushed the sleeve back down over the scar. "A souvenir of childhood. Now if you don't mind, Doctor, I would like to get back to my life. Trust me, Doctor, we're all fine."

"My niece is correct."

Burrell turned, startled to see Selena out of bed. She sat in a wheelchair at the top of the stairs, her back straight, her gaze imperious and, he thought, almost disdainful. *What the hell is this? She shouldn't be able to move, let alone wheel around like that.*

"Your interest is appreciated," Selena said, "but as you can see, we are quite well."

"Yes, I can. But isn't it a curious coincidence? Deborah's showing signs of premature aging, while you—"

"I said that would be all, Doctor," she said, cutting him off. "In fact, I should think that your services will no longer be required. Your fee will be sent on to your office."

Burrell stiffened. "What about Deborah?"

Diane appeared at his elbow. "We'll see to it she gets all the best care. You needn't concern yourself about it any further."

He looked from one to the other, and from their looks knew that petitioning would be useless. "Fine. But if it's all the same to you, I'll choose what I want to concern myself with, Diane. Good-day."

He stepped back out of the house, slamming the door as he left. It had never before occurred to him how much alike Diane and Selena were, not until tonight, not until he'd seen the way they looked at him. In those eyes he'd seen himself turn from necessary physician to an outcast, henceforth excluded from the tight and jealous orbit that was Selena and Diane, Diane and Selena.

But Deborah was still his concern, and he would do for her whatever he could.

He was nearly to the car when he saw a shape huddling near the fence. He slowed as Orville came out of the shadows, a parcel wrapped in cloth under his arm. "Orville?"

Orville pressed a finger to his lips, looking around nervously. He stepped back again, into a breezeway between two buildings. Burrell hesitated only a moment before following him in.

"What is it, Orville?"

Orville looked around again to make sure they were alone, then unwrapped the parcel to reveal an old book of photographs. He handed it to Burrell. The pages were brittle with age, the photos yellowed and missing in places. Some of them went back as far as the 1900s.

Orville nodded at him to keep looking. "I don't understand," Burrell said.

Then, abruptly, Orville pointed at a particular page, his finger jabbing a photograph in the middle of the page. It was an old black-and-white photo, a shot of a young girl with dark hair, set in ponytails, clutching a woven basket. Her right arm was heavily bandaged above the elbow. Burrell angled the page slightly in order to catch the light and read the faint inscription below it.

July 17, 1940. Our picnic was almost ruined by a fire when a horse kicked over a kerosene lantern. The flames caught hold of the wagon, and the children had to run quickly. Only Martha was injured by the fire. The doctor says she will be all right, but will have to live with the scar for the rest of her life.

Burrell inspected the photo more closely.

The bandage was in the exact same place where Diane's arm was scarred. It, too, had clearly been caused by a burn, and looked about the same size.

How could both mother and daughter have exactly the same scar, in exactly the same place, from exactly the same cause?

He looked up at Orville, who nodded, almost as though reading his thoughts. "Can you get me back in there tonight?"

Orville nodded.

An hour after the medical-records office had closed, Burrell sat in Deborah Brockman's room, in the isolation ward, listening to the machinery beeping and clicking as it monitored her pulse and respiration. For the moment, they only assisted; soon they would be her only support.

Outside, the light was fading. He was distantly aware of the need to go home, change clothes, take a shower. He needed to be clean again.

He sat forward, hands cradling his face. The implications of what he had found in the records were impossible. They defied logic, reality, and even sanity. But the truth—or at least one-half of the *possibility* of truth—was lying in bed in front of him, twenty years old and dying of old age.

The other half was at the Brockman mansion. But that would have to wait until after dark. And then? He felt his stomach lurch with sick despair. So what if he *was* right? What could he do about it?

Or, more precisely, what would they *let* him do about it?

Probably nothing at all, he thought, and let his gaze wander back to Deborah Brockman, her eyes closed, her skin sallow and nearly translucent. Ancient.

God help me, he thought. *God help both of us.*

Burrell found the back door unlocked, as Orville had promised. He nudged it open slowly, looking for any sign of Diane or Selena, but the kitchen was deserted. He stepped through and into the front hall, wincing at every creak in the floorboards. He ascended the stairs cautiously, peeking over the top of the landing. Lights burned behind the closed doors of Diane's and Selena's bedrooms. He moved to where Martha sat in her usual place by the window, her features dull and empty in the light of a storm lamp.

He gently lay a hand on her shoulder, and she seemed to sag under his touch, as though lacking the strength to put up any sort of resistance. He tried to meet her gaze, but it was fixed at a nowhere point beyond the window. Moving the storm lamp closer, he slid her sleeve up until it revealed her upper arm.

There was no scar. Not even a blemish or scratch. He gazed back into her eyes, trying to find some sign of understanding there. "You're not Martha Brock-man at all, are you?" he whispered. "You're Diane Brockman. Her daughter."

He moved the lamp closer, and for a moment he thought he saw a flicker of intelligence behind those tired, vacant eyes, though it might have been only a trick of the light.

"What are you doing here?"

He started at the sound of Diane's voice behind him, almost dropping the storm lamp. Diane was moving toward him, coming fast, switching on lights as she came, her face a mask of rage.

"At first I didn't believe it," Burrell said. "I didn't *want* to believe it."

"What are you talking about?"

"While I was at the hospital I did some checking. According to the last records they had, which would be about twelve years ago, Diane Brockman had green eyes. No noticeable scars. The woman sitting in that chair over there has green eyes. What color are yours? And where did you get that scar? How old are you really . . . *Martha?*"

Diane's eyes widened with rage and something he had never seen there before: panic, and the fear of discovery. "Get out!"

He moved toward her. "Convenient deal, isn't it? Especially with a daughter, or someone like Deborah. Someone with the same name, someone who can legally inherit the house without a lot of questions."

"Get out of here!" She was shrieking at him now. "Get out of this house!"

"Not until I talk to Selena."

He pushed past her.

"No!" she cried, and ran after him.

Barely steps ahead of her, he hit Selena's door and threw it open.

Nothing he had rehearsed in his mind could have possibly prepared him for what he saw.

Selena stood by the mirror and turned as he entered. The lines in her face had been erased, the years smoothed out into a skin that was pink and fresh. Her hair was once more its original jet-black, eyes bright and hard, her posture steady, graceful.

"My God," Burrell said.

"Selena! He knows!"

He advanced toward Selena. "Give them back, Selena. Give Deborah back the years you've stolen. This isn't right!"

"Not right?" Selena said. "What would you know about it? The game is longevity, Doctor. Oh, you play at the game, you with your medicines and your stethoscopes—but we've won. There is only one rule, Doctor, and it has nothing to do with morality, or love. When illness or death encroach, the trade takes place. This is the way it's always been. The way it will always be."

He opened his mouth to respond when pain pinwheeled behind his head. He slumped to his knees, lights strobing behind his eyes as he saw Diane raise the poker she had pulled from the fireplace for a second, crushing blow.

"Mommy?"

Diane stopped in midstroke and turned at the sight of Martha—even knowing their true names, he could think of them no other way—as she stepped into the bedroom, clutching the storm lamp, vacant eyes now replaced by a look of pain, and realization, and memory. "Mommy?"

Diane backed up a step. "Get away from me! *Get away from me!*"

"*Mommy?*"

"NO!" Diane said, and lashed out blindly at the old woman.

The storm lamp fell, crashing against the curtained wall and exploding into flame. The dry, old material blazed as though it had been waiting for the fire all these years. In an instant the room was a swirl of smoke and flame that found Selena's dressing gown and snatched greedily at his own clothes.

He pulled himself toward the bedroom door, the sound of screams and desperate pleas following him out. He put a handkerchief to his face, trying to keep out the hot and bitter smoke that clawed at his lungs, and risked one last look into the bedroom. A tower of fire that must have been Selena writhed in the middle of the room.

And then he glimpsed the sight he knew he would never forget: Martha and Diane, struggling, cut off from the door by a wall of flame, the old woman clutching at her, frightened, holding her fast as the flames encroached despite her frantic screams.

"Mommy . . . *Mommy!*"

He staggered toward the stairs, hoping he would be able to find his way through the thick smoke that curled all around him, half stumbling down the steps to the front door where he rushed out into the cool night, coughing and half blind from smoke, only dimly aware of the sound of shattering glass from somewhere inside the house, and a sudden, high-pitched scream.

Then the world kicked slantwise, and he went away.

He refused to ride to the hospital with the paramedics who revived him. Instead he watched as the Brockman mansion burned to the ground, the fire burning so hot that it was all the fire trucks could do just to contain the inferno.

The sun was already coming up by the time the house was cool enough for the police to go in and search for bodies.

As the stretchers began to emerge, a cab arrived in front of the house, and through still-burning eyes Burrell saw Deborah emerge. She stood straight, and tall, and the lines were gone from her face. As the evil had burned away, so too had its results turned to ashes.

She came to him, and for a moment they clung to one another, each reluctant to speak of what had happened, finally deciding not to. Not here. Not now.

She pulled away, and stood back as he checked the stretchers before they were loaded onto ambulances.

After a few moments, he stepped back to her, wiping the soot from his hands.

"Well?"

He indicated the first stretcher. "Orville. God rest his soul." He pointed to the next two. "Selena. I recognized her bedclothes. And Martha. Maybe, finally, she'll find some peace."

"There's one missing."

Burrell nodded. "Diane. They're still checking. A witness said he saw a screaming woman break through a window and run off, her clothes burning. When he got there, she was gone."

"Do you think she's still—"

"I don't know," Burrell said, aware at last of how tired he was. "And I wish I did."

Nurse Carlson brought the medical reports to room 319, and risked a glance at the bed as she handed the folders to Dr. Leeks. The patient was unconscious, and covered from head to foot in bandages.

"What do you think?" she whispered, even though she knew the woman could not hear them.

The doctor shrugged. "She's old, indigent, with massive burns over most of her body and face—I wouldn't hold out much hope. Best we can do is try to make her last hours as comfortable as we can."

She nodded, and headed out of the room, the doctor following. "Did you notice, though? Her left leg seems to be healing quite fast."

"Yeah," he said, tiredly, "for all the good it'll do her."

She returned to the nurses' station, where Kathy and Lynn were talking. "And it's the strangest thing," Kathy said. "I mean, it doesn't hurt or anything, but just look at it."

She put one foot on a chair and pulled back the skirt to reveal what appeared to be burn scar tissue on her left leg. "I swear I didn't burn it. But there it is. Just found it there this morning when I got up. I've been

wondering if it's psychosomatic. Maybe I've been working the burn ward too long."

Down the hall, the patient in room 319 stirred
slightly.

Jane Doe, age unknown. Sole survivor of a terrible
fire, soon to undergo a miraculous recovery. A living
warning, to those who fail to perceive the distinction,
that there is a difference between the fear of death and
the love of life—especially in the Twilight Zone.

ABOUT THE AUTHOR

At 34, J. MICHAEL STRACZYNSKI has worked in virtually every medium since he started selling his work while still in high school. He has sold over 500 articles and many short stories, his work appearing in *Video Review, Writer's Digest* (where he is a contributing editor), *The Los Angeles Herald Examiner, Amazing Stories, Shadows 6* (anthology), *San Diego Magazine* and others. Previously a staffer with Time, Inc., he was also special correspondent for *The Los Angeles Times,* and a contributing editor with the late, lamented *Twilight Zone Magazine.* He has been a reviewer, essayist, critic, and investigative reporter.

He is the author of four books, including this, his first anthology. His first horror novel, *Demon Night,* appeared in hardcover in 1988. His second, *The Othersyde,* is scheduled for hardcover publication in 1990, with another planned for 1991. His nonfiction text, *The Complete Book of Scriptwriting* has sold over 40,000 copies and is a standard text at half a dozen major universities. He has taught writing at San Diego State University and other colleges.

Author of 12 produced plays and 12 produced radio dramas (some of which he also produced and directed) for, among others, the Mutual Radio Network, since 1987 he has been the host of HOUR 25, a SF/horror/fantasy-themed talk show airing for two hours weekly on KPFK-FM Los Angeles.

In television, Straczynski has story-edited over 200 produced episodes of television, and has written nearly 100, all of them in the area of science fiction/fantasy/horror. His credits include story-editing *The Twilight Zone,* where he was also head writer and, previously, story-editing and writing the syndicated SF series, *Captain Power.* He has worked for ABC, CBS, and cable, most recently adapting "The Strange Case of Dr. Jekyll and Mr. Hyde" for Shelley Duvall's *Nightmare Classics,* airing currently on Showtime. He has finished the screenplay for *The Waiting Darkness* for London Films, and the pilot for a new SF series for Warner Bros., which he will also produce.

In 1988, Straczynski was nominated for a Gemini Award for Best Writing in a Dramatic Series for his work on *Captain Power.* (A Gemini being the equivalent of an Emmy, given by the Canadian Academy of Cinema and Television.) As this book goes to press, he has just been nominated for a Bram Stoker Award by the Horror Writers of America for *Demon Night* as best first novel.

Straczynski lives in Los Angeles with his wife and fellow writer, Kathryn Drennan.

"You unlock this door with the key of imagination.
Beyond it is another dimension—a dimension of sound,
a dimension of sight, a dimension of mind.
You're moving into a land of both shadow and substance,
of things and ideas. You've just crossed over into the
Twilight Zone."

THE TWILIGHT ZONE COMPANION
Second Edition
by
Marc Scott Zicree

Through five years and 156 episodes, *The Twilight Zone*
charted a territory all its own, one filled with magic, horror, and wonder. **The Twilight Zone Companion** is a fascinating show-by-show journey combining synopses of
each episode—including director Rod Serling's memorable opening and closing narratives—with complete listings of cast and credits, incisive commentary, and colorful
behind-the-scenes recollections from the galaxy of creative artists who made the series great.

To celebrate the thirtieth anniversary of the show's debut, here is the Second Edition of **The Twilight Zone
Companion**—with a comprehensive update on the series,
its creator, and its spinoffs, including interviews with the
creative personnel, new photos, and an expanded index!

Buy **The Twilight Zone Companion, Second Edition,** on
sale now wherever Bantam Books are sold.

You are traveling into another dimension...

Stories from
THE TWILIGHT ZONE
by
Rod Serling

A dimension of terror, splendor, and wonder—a shadow land that lies just beyond the limits of the imagination. Your host and guide is one of the world's best-known storytellers—a modern master of fantastic fiction: Rod Serling.

Here are nineteen of Serling's most memorable tales from the legendary series, classic stories such as "The Monsters Are Due on Maple Street," "A Thing About Machines," "The Rip Van Winkle Caper," the timeless Christmas fantasy "Night of the Meek," and many, many more.

Buy **Stories from The Twilight Zone,** now on sale wherever Bantam Books are sold.